Finding Mrs. Winsome

It's About Time Series, Book Three

Courtnee Turner Hoyle

Pale Woods Publishing

Finding Mrs. Winsome
It's About Time
Book 3

Courtnee Turner Hoyle
Published March 27, 2024

This is a work of fiction. Any resemblance to actual persons,
either living or dead, is entirely coincidental. All names, characters,
and events are the product of the author's imagination.
This book may not be reproduced in whole or in part in any manner
whatsoever without written permission, except for a brief
quotation within book reviews or articles.

E-Book ISBN: 979-8-9899846-1-9

Print ISBN: 979-8-9899846-0-2

You may contact the publisher:
Pale Woods Publishing
turnerco6@yahoo.com

To my mama
You didn't know you were Mrs. Winsome.

I wish I had a time machine so I could tell you...

Finding Mrs. Winsome Playlist

1. "Where Are You Going?" by Dave Matthews Band

2. "Satellite" by Dave Matthews Band

3. "We'll Meet Again" by Vera Lynn

4. "Boogie Woogie Bugle Boy" by The Andrews Sisters

5. "White Cliffs of Dover" by Vera Lynn

6. "Run Rabbit Run" Noel Gay and Ralph Butler (performed by Flanagan and Allen)

7. "White Christmas" by Bing Crosby

8. "Lili Marlene" by Lale Andersen

9. "Keep the Home Fires Burning (Till the Boys Get Home)" by The D-Day Darlings

10. "The Space Between" by Dave Matthews Band

11. "Everyday" by Dave Matthews Band

Chapter 1

If a heart could break, hers would be scattered in pieces around her feet.

Celeste stood on the hill in front of the Winsomes' house. The wind picked up her blonde hair, swirling it around her oval face and settling it onto her high cheekbones. She brushed it away with the back of one of her hands.

Police moved in undiscernible patterns. Their blue lights had been on for hours, circling through the air and casting eerie shadows on the unfinished white paneling.

She had tried to stay inside, but somehow the paramedics had nudged her out the door and into the yard. She didn't find solace outside, and she was incapable of escape. The wind blew fiercely against her, and she pulled the blanket more tightly over her child.

Emma slept peacefully against her mother's shoulder, tiny puffs of air releasing with every breath. *What was she going to tell her?*

They had been through so much together, from time jumping shortly after her conception, to returning to tell her father about her, to the kidnapping, and then—

She didn't want to think about it. Even thinking the words might mean it happened.

It was hard to let her thoughts travel back to the scene. All she could remember was the blood and his face. The blood had trickled in dark lines onto the threadbare carpet as David—her wonderful David—stood over his mother with a knife in his hand.

He'd begged, "Help me, *Celeste*."

David had used her name, her *real* name. But as soon as he'd said it, his face dulled, and when his eyes regained focus, his body swayed as he managed his footing.

He'd slipped in his mother's blood, causing him to land with a thud. The noise had startled Ag, and she'd identified the source by running to her mother's room. She'd stood behind Celeste and screamed. The sound had pierced the night, and it didn't stop.

Someone had called emergency services, but Celeste couldn't remember if it was her. She supposed it had to have been her since Ag was still screaming, and David hadn't stopped looking at his bloody hands until the police had kicked in the door.

Celeste had sat on the couch, covering her baby with her body. She'd read about what could happen in high-adrenaline situations, and she hadn't wanted her daughter to be caught in the crossfire.

One officer veered away from his group and approached her. She recognized his athletic build and sporty blond hair.

"Caroline, have they talked to you yet?"

Everyone in the town—except Emma—thought she was Caroline Fletcher, a self-serving woman who bounced back and forth from her abusive ex to half of the other men in town. Lewis Novack was one of her past boyfriends, and he usually treated her with disdain, even though he had a similar reputation.

"No." The shakiness in her voice surprised her.

Lewis put his hands on his hips and stared up at the house. "I didn't think he had it in him."

His casual remark about David inflamed her. "He doesn't."

He looked back at her with raised eyebrows. "Did you do it then? I may not see David Winsome killing his mother, but I could definitely believe he covered it up for you."

Celeste was too tired and upset to argue, but she put power behind her words. "Shut up, Lewis."

He smiled smugly, as if he'd caught her playing her game. "I'll bet that lady over there will tell us." He nodded to the ambulance where they were loading Mrs. Winsome. "If she lives."

"She *will* live," Celeste spat at him.

Lewis was unaffected by the venom in her voice. "You just couldn't wait for her to die, could you? Your little plan with Willie fell through, so you destroyed David's life again. I hope he didn't leave anything valuable around."

That comment sounded more personal, but she was in no mood to entertain him. "What are you talking about?"

He glared at her. "You always take things that don't belong to you. Maybe if you hadn't pawned my dead mother's necklace, I'd be able to forgive you, but I doubt it."

His words struck her like he'd slapped her. It sucked the air out of her next response, so she could only stare at him.

"That's enough," a gruff voice spoke.

Sheriff Connor Murphy regarded them with cold green eyes. "You two have been bickering since you were barely old enough to have jobs."

"She started it," Lewis said.

His joke fell flat.

"I expect more professionalism from you," he said to Lewis. "Mrs. Winsome—a good woman—was stabbed tonight, and you're over here poking at your ex-girlfriend like you're two kids on a playground."

Lewis's head dropped. "I'm sorry, sir."

Sheriff Murphy stared at him as if he were reprimanding a son. "Now, is there anything productive you could do, like classifying evidence or interviewing witnesses that aren't Caroline Fletcher?"

Lewis looked up at his superior before his eyes fell again. "Yes, sir."

"Then you better get to it."

Celeste and the sheriff watched Lewis jog back to the house. Celeste expected Sheriff Murphy to berate her, too, but the baby stirred. Celeste turned Emma's cerulean eyes away from the scene, and Sheriff Murphy stroked her curly blonde hair.

"She's such a pretty baby," the sheriff said. "She has her father's eyes."

The thought of David filled Celeste with restless emotions. He was in the back of a cruiser, the second one from the front. She'd monitored it since the police had led him out in handcuffs, rattling off something that sounded like his Miranda rights.

"I know you've been through a lot," Sheriff Murphy told her, "but don't give up. Don't go back to drugs and leave this little lady all alone."

His speech did not surprise Celeste. Caroline had always embraced drugs for comfort, but Celeste had kept her host clean and sober for almost half of a year.

The sheriff measured her response, and, satisfied, focused his attention on the baby. Emma smiled at him, revealing a tooth that had pushed through her gums.

"What's your name?" He asked the baby, but he expected Celeste to answer.

"Emma. Her name is Emma."

Chapter 2

"You better hope she lives," Detective Roll told him.

David looked up. He'd held his face in his hands so long that a sheen of condensation had gathered on the metal table from his breath.

"Is she going to be okay?"

Detective Roll shrugged. "Maybe I could leave the room and get an update on your mother's condition if you'd tell me what happened."

David had been in the interrogation room for hours, but his story was still the same. "I told you: I fell asleep upstairs, and when I woke up, I was on the floor in front of my mother's bed holding that." He nodded to the bloody knife between them. It was in a plastic bag, but he could still smell the blood. His mother's blood.

Maybe he didn't smell the blood on the knife. Maybe he smelled it on him. He'd washed his hands, but it had saturated his clothes. He'd held pressure over his mother's wound until the EMS arrived, but soon after they'd taken over, a deputy had arrested him, so he hadn't had time to change clothes.

What had happened? He honestly didn't know.

"Look, I could have grabbed a knife away from an attacker."

"Can you describe the attacker?"

It was a fair question, but David didn't have an answer. He put his head back into his hands.

"Your mother had Alzheimer's," the detective noted.

David nodded. Ag had told him about it when they'd filed for custody of Emma. Luckily, the judge hadn't been concerned about Eleanor Winsome's ability to care for the toddler. He only focused on David and Ag.

"That's a hard disease," Detective Roll commented. He'd alternated between sitting and standing. He took the seat in front of David, bringing them to eye level.

The detective was a squat man with average features. The only thing that stood out about him was his attempt to grow a mustache. The hair poked through roughly, with longer patches growing around the sides of his mouth. David could hear him stroking the bristles under his nose.

"I don't know what I'd do if my mother had a diagnosis with a death sentence."

David squeezed his eyes. *Great! Now, the detective was going to relate to him.*

"I mean," Detective Roll went on, "I couldn't watch her decline every day without it breaking my heart. And if I had to see the pain of dealing with her on the faces of my loved ones" —he took a deep breath— "well, I don't know what I'd do." He waited for a beat for effect. "I might put an end to everyone's suffering."

David opened his eyes and looked up.

"Is that what you did, David? Did you try to end her suffering?"

David had been in the same small room for hours. Coffee sat on the table, but he hadn't touched it, and the chair hurt his bones. He understood his situation, and he was aware of how guilty he looked. He wanted to get through the interrogation and either get charged with a crime or go home. He didn't want to say or do anything to incriminate himself, but he felt confined, even though he hadn't seen a jail cell yet. He was tired. He hadn't slept long, and Mindy's pregnancy, his day out with Caroline and Emma, and Emma's injury had completely taxed him before he'd woken up with a knife in his hand.

Even though he knew his actions would reflect poorly on him, David's rage boiled. *How dare that smug detective accuse him of trying to murder his mother!*

Detective Roll was unaware of David's inner struggle. "Well, David," he coerced. "Is that what you did?"

David glared at him. "Go to—"

The door buzzed, and Lewis Novack asked to speak to the detective. He didn't look at David, but David didn't care. They'd fought over Caroline in high school, and he'd dated Hailey before David had allowed himself to have feelings for her.

When the door shut behind the men, David's thoughts went to his mother. *Did Lewis have news about her?*

If he faced facts, his mother was older, and she had suffered a significant injury. He tried to think about the stab wound. *Was it on the left or right side?*

His best guess was that he had stabbed her in the liver or intestines. When he tried to focus on the memory of holding the pressure over her wound, his recollections were fuzzy.

Her chances weren't good either way, but an intestinal injury was more manageable. Doctors could perform surgery, removing the injured part and connecting the undamaged pieces.

If the knife had pierced her liver—

He couldn't think about it. If the knife had ruptured her liver, most likely, his mother was dead.

Sadly, he didn't even know if he had been the one who had stabbed her. He believed he didn't do it, but he had been standing over her with the knife in his hand.

David had only had one sleepwalking experience. He was on a diet to prepare for his marriage to Caroline. He'd wanted to fit into the tuxedo his father had worn when he'd married David's mother. As a healthcare professional, he knew he shouldn't try to lose weight rapidly, but David had been determined to honor his father at the event by wearing the special attire.

He'd eaten only raw vegetables for weeks. He'd eliminated caffeine, so on top of his hunger, David was a bear as his body adjusted to the lack of coffee.

He dreamed of food. He'd have visions of holiday dinners with steaming plates of meat, bread, and sugary sweets. The images were real to him, and he'd wake with a wet pillow, proof of his excessive salivation.

He'd been eating leftover roast when she'd found him. Caroline had been worried when she'd woken up in the middle of the night without him, and she'd discovered him in the kitchen with the refrigerator door open.

After that experience, David was more careful about his diet. He didn't meet his weight loss goal by the wedding, but his mother had surprised him by having the tuxedo altered to fit him.

His mother had been a blessing throughout his life. She'd been a little quirky, and the last few years she'd been cantankerous, but she was the same woman who had climbed the steps on swollen knees to bring him chicken soup when he was sick and had hired a man to play Santa for the children at church every year.

A sound like the buzzing of angry bees interrupted his thoughts. Detective Roll came through the door with a longer face than he'd had before he'd talked to Lewis.

"Detective Novack had an update on your mother."

David's blood turned to ice water in his veins. He couldn't find the words to ask about his mother.

Detective Roll took a seat, and it was agonizing to wait for the man to speak again. Several scenarios ran through David's mind as the detective steepled his fingers on the table, never taking his eyes off David. It was agony to wait the thirty seconds between his first statement and the actual news.

David's jaw clenched. He tried to keep his body calm, but it was a natural reaction.

Detective Roll leaned back in his chair. "You're a lucky man, David Winsome. Your mother's condition was stabilized."

David let out an audible sigh of relief.

Detective Roll held up a finger. "But you aren't out of the woods yet. Without the presence of another suspect, and because of the conditions surrounding the crime, I have no choice but to place you under arrest for the attempted murder of Eleanor Winsome."

Chapter 3

Emma inched across the floor, the cast on her leg prohibiting a wide range of movement. They'd just returned from an orthopedic appointment.

Celeste didn't think she could make it through the appointment, but she knew Emma needed the cast. She couldn't remember half of the visit, but she drove the Winsomes' SUV to Johnson City, and her daughter had a tiny pink cast on her leg when they returned. Celeste stared at her daughter, but her thoughts were in another place.

Emma crawled to the door of her grandmother's bedroom, putting her small hand against it. "Ins?"

Mrs. Winsome had prompted the baby to call her another name, but Emma had insisted on saying a variation of her last name. After the first time she spoke it, the name had stuck.

"She's not here right now," Celeste said, willing the emotion away from her voice.

Celeste couldn't remember a time when Mrs. Winsome's bedroom door had been closed, but Ag had shut it after the emergency medical professionals had carried Mrs. Winsome out on a stretcher. Ag had ridden with her to the hospital, and she'd provided Celeste with updates on her condition.

The last text had been the most comforting. Mrs. Winsome was out of surgery, and the doctors thought it had gone well. The older woman wasn't awake yet, but the doctors thought she'd regain consciousness during the day.

Celeste could smell the grisly scene from her place on the couch. *Did the smell of dried blood really permeate the surrounding air so heavily?*

Even though Emma had slept through most of the night, after a few hours of the altered environment, combined with her broken leg, she allowed Celeste to lift her onto the couch. The new Tele Board was on, and Celeste let Emma hold the remote that analyzed her mood. Within seconds, a rerun of a popular show about a witch popped onto the screen. The selection surprised Celeste. She'd thought her daughter would enjoy a cartoon, but Emma had an "old soul," as Mrs. Winsome liked to say.

Celeste wondered what the Tele Board would put on for her. In her time, Tele Boards were technological dinosaurs. Most everyone was involved in virtual reality. People used it to play games with "aviators" that were considered avatars and they could be characters in their own movies. Only a few older adults still watched Tele Boards.

While she was thinking about the future and her past in it, Celeste's stomach rumbled. She made lunch for Emma and her and tried not to think of the bloody smell in the house.

Soon after lunch, Emma took an early nap, and Celeste thought about calling Ag. She shook her head against the idea, opting not to deal with the woman's emotions on top of her own.

She could have slept with Emma, and she needed the rest, but her eyes kept traveling back to Mrs. Winsome's door. She stared at the unremarkable wood and thought about what was on the other side.

Who would clean it?

In her time, murders and violent crimes were infrequent, as most individuals placed a higher value on human life after the people of the world had experienced the horrors of the Great War. A bloody scene was rare, but after the police investigated the area and collected evidence, a cleaning team arrived to cleanse the scene. It didn't seem like cleaning teams existed yet—unless the family of the victim paid for them.

A tear caressed her cheek. *How could the people of this time expect families to clean the crime scene after someone brutally attacked or killed their loved one? Wasn't that placing an undue burden on their already stressed minds?*

When Ag returned home, she'd have the added responsibility of disinfecting the area. By then, the blood may have permanently soaked into every surface.

And the smell. Celeste couldn't escape it. She could smell it on her when she went into any room of the house, as if the scent of murder had attached itself to her.

She popped off the couch as if her body had decided before her mind had caught up. She grabbed the cleaning supplies.

Celeste stopped in front of the door. She had to prepare herself for the bloody scene. She'd witnessed the product of the crime, but it had been at night. She took a deep breath and opened the door.

Muted light bathed the room. The curtains were closed, so the area wasn't as bright as she'd expected. She stared at the blood on the bed as if she were in a trance. It had stopped dripping from the sheets hours ago, but it had soaked into the carpet, making dark puddles on the brown material.

Celeste steeled herself, attempting to distance herself from any emotion. She started with the bed.

Blood and some other material Celeste didn't want to explore soaked the sheets, so she took them outside and stuffed them into the Winsomes' burn barrel. She set fire to the sheets and went back inside.

Emma was still sleeping, so Celeste scrubbed the mattress with hydrogen peroxide and cleaner. She'd never get rid of the stains, but there was nothing more she could do about it.

She did the same thing to the bloody spots on the carpet. It took the blood and the color from it, but it was clean.

She worked on the splatters on the wall, and she noticed a few stains on the curtains. She took them to the basement to wash, hoping she could salvage them.

The room was brighter when she returned, and the light helped her. She kept finding places where Mrs. Winsome's blood had splattered.

She had just wiped down the baseboards nearest the closet when her eyes landed on a partially open shoe box. She wouldn't have thought a lot about the baby blue box, but it didn't contain shoes.

Before she knew it, Celeste was sitting cross-legged in front of the closet with notebooks spread out in front of her. Letters tied with twine lined the bottom of the box. The postmark on the letters indicated that Mrs. Winsome would have been in her late teens when she started receiving them.

In her time, cursive writing was considered a lost art, but her father had known about the skill, and he had passed it on to her. She could read the words easily and concluded that the sender had mailed them from France to her current residence. Bill Winsome had lovingly signed each letter to Eleanor Martin.

Celeste felt a lump in her throat when she thought of her father-in-law. She'd witnessed his acts of kindness, and he had opened his home to her.

David had adored his father. He'd often called him "Daddy" and taken long walks with him. After one of their walks, David proposed to her.

She put the letters back in the box and stared at the notebooks. Some were old and frayed, while others looked like Mrs. Winsome could have written in them until a few years previously.

Mrs. Winsome had dated the journals, and Celeste arranged them in a stack from the oldest to the newest. She opened the first one and read the words Mrs. Winsome had written when she was still a teenager.

A good school finally accepted me. My parents want me to stay at home and attend to the war efforts, but I can't spend my days sewing and fretting about the fighting that's raging overseas when there's so much to learn!

With most of our boys enlisting the moment they turn eighteen, attendance at the university is down. They accepted me because of it, but I wish my dearest Bill were going there in my place. I'm excited that the doors of education have opened a little wider for the fairer sex—especially in my program of study—but I'd give it up to have him home.

My wonderful man, with his deep blue eyes and soft hands! I wish he could hold me now and tell me about his adventures!

He wants to marry me as soon as we see each other again. I know the reason he's in a hurry. He wants to have the opportunity to father a child, but if marrying me (and what we do on our wedding night) brings him peace and comfort while he's away, I will be his wife.

Look at my fickle emotions! I started this book with the exultation of joy, and then I rescind it when I think of my war-scarred hero.

I'm glad I'm here where the war has yet to touch us with the bloody battles, but the limited rations and grief have taken their toll on my small community. It's better that I go to school and learn about particles and theories than watch my neighbors get thinner and mourn their dead.

My brother is in the war, but he's stationed in a tropical paradise on this country's soil. My family is so lucky that our dear David went into the Navy. He should be safe on a ship in the Pacific until the war is over.

I miss his stories. On stormy nights, I used to climb the stairs (staying off the squeaky third step from the bottom) and sneak into his room. My brother told me stories about the future, where men would travel in time to stop bad things from happening.

David is the reason for my interest in physics, and now I get to attend college with other great minds. I hope my dear brother will be there to see me walk across the stage when I graduate!

Surely, the war will be over by then, and he will be home with us again.

David plans to visit at Christmas. He had the chance to take an earlier leave, but I asked him to come home at Christmas. I couldn't imagine celebrating the holiday without him.

My sweet Bill can't visit until after Christmas. He's stationed in a high-risk area, so it's harder for him to leave. I guess when he sees me, it will be time to tell my mama that I plan to be Mrs. Bill Winsome.

There won't be time for a big wedding, but we'll get married in my family's church. Bill will probably preach there when he comes home for good.

If I am with child after Bill and I marry, I will have to abandon my hopes to obtain a degree. For now, I will attend classes as if continuing until graduation is the only plan.

This morning, I saw a snow-white dove take flight from the back porch. I must have startled her, but I used the sighting as a sign of a future full of promise.

I plan to fill the pages of this book with my hopes and dreams. Like the beautiful dove I saw this morning, I will spread my wings and rise above the carnage of the war and seek education and a happy marriage upon the war's end.

Celeste turned the page, but a knock at the door prevented her from reading further. She jumped at the sound, and Emma let out a cry.

On her way to the door, she picked up her daughter, who was reaching for her. Emma stopped crying when she opened the door. Celeste hadn't thought to check who was on the other side, and it surprised her to see Lewis.

The worst scenarios popped into her mind. *Had Mrs. Winsome succumbed to her injuries? Had the sheriff's department officially charged David?*

Lewis gave nothing away as he stood on the porch, and Celeste's heart fell.

Chapter 4

Lewis was waiting for her to greet him.

"Hey, Lewis. What are you doing here?"

He raised his eyebrows as if the answer were obvious. He pointed a finger toward the backyard.

"Were you going to invite me to your bonfire?"

Celeste's eyes widened. She ran through the house, leaving Lewis standing in front of the door.

The fire wasn't out of control, but it was blazing, and she set Emma down on the back porch before she grabbed the water hose. She sprayed the fire until it was no more, and when she turned around, Lewis was sitting with Emma.

"No chance for a beer and a few marshmallows, huh?"

She rolled her eyes at his joke.

As she trudged away from the burn barrel, Emma played with Lewis's fingers, bending them back until he pulled them away, only to place them back in her small hand for her to do it again. Celeste watched him play with her daughter.

"You're good with children."

A dark cloud settled over his features. "Excuse me if I'm not happy to hear that coming from you."

Celeste crossed her arms. "Can I say anything you won't shoot back at me?"

"I doubt it."

She threw up her hands. "Then why are you still here?"

He looked at Emma and said his goodbyes. Celeste followed him through the house, placing Emma on the living room floor. Lewis stopped on the porch, and Celeste closed the front door so Emma wouldn't hear their conversation. She was shocked when Lewis's eyes showed signs of tears.

"You know what, Caroline?" he started. "You have a lot of nerve."

He pointed back at the house where Emma played. "That little girl is wonderful, and David is so lucky." His voice cracked on the last word. Celeste waited for him to regain his composure.

"Why couldn't you do that for our baby?"

Celeste felt like he'd splashed her with cold water. "We had a baby?"

It had been a question, but he treated it like a statement. "We would have had a baby if you hadn't killed it."

Understanding dawned on her. *Caroline had aborted Lewis's baby.* No wonder he hated her so much.

"I would have paid you to have it," he went on, not hiding his emotions. "I would have paid you to give me the baby after it was born, but you didn't give me the chance."

He wept openly over his lost child. "You told the people at the clinic that it was Willie's baby, and the two of you signed the papers that ended *my* child's life." He jerked a thumb into his chest.

"David may forgive you, but I'm not like him." He scoffed. "If he tried to kill his mother, I'm *definitely* not like him."

"David didn't try to kill his mother." The words were out before she knew she was going to say them.

Lewis didn't dry his face, but a cruel smile played across his lips. "Yeah, he may not have *tried.* The word is that he may have done it."

Celeste didn't respond to his statement. Sure, Ag had given her a positive report that morning, but anything could have happened, and she wouldn't have phoned her brother's ex-wife if she were grieving over her mother.

Lewis enjoyed her uncertainty. "I'll leave you with that. God knows you deserve worse."

Celeste confirmed that Mrs. Winsome was in the same condition as she had been when Ag had last texted her. Ag's response was quick. She related that some church members had brought her some supplies and food.

Celeste was grateful for them. The Winsomes' SUV sat in the driveway, but she didn't know if she could drive it after Lewis's accusal. She couldn't even remember where she'd put the keys, as they weren't in the dish by the door. She had parked her car in Willie's driveway, and she was afraid to go get it.

Her mind raced across the people who might help her. She thought about Kerry Shelton. She'd worked for him at his pawnshop, but she was worried that he thought differently of her since Willie had kidnapped her.

She dialed the number to the shop, and when he answered, his familiar voice brought a smile to her face.

"Hey, Kerry. It's Caroline."

"I know your voice," he said. "Did you choose to leave with the murderer?"

Kerry got to the point. Willie Jones, Caroline's abusive ex-husband, had kidnapped her, but his flee from justice was short-lived when the police found them in a hotel room with two other accomplices. Celeste avoided arrest, as the statement of one of Willie's accomplices, Rowdy, exonerated himself and her. If Celeste had gone against him, Rowdy would have retracted his story, and Celeste would have gone to jail.

"I was kidnapped."

She heard the sigh he breathed into the phone. "I didn't think you'd leave the child."

"Thank you for believing in me."

"If this is about your job, though, I don't think I can stand the reputation that's gonna follow you. I wish you the best, and you were a hard worker, but the news'll have to die down before I can hire you back."

What a sweet man! He had to maintain a business, but he was willing to give her some work after a couple of months. Her heart swelled.

"That's okay. I think Mindy found a job for me."

"Your ex-husband's girlfriend?"

Celeste put her head in her hand. "Yep, that's the one."

"Weird situation."

Celeste laughed dryly. "Yeah. I seem to keep making them for myself."

After a moment, Kerry spoke. "Well, as I see it, you're young, and you get to make a few mistakes. Right now, what you're doin' isn't hurtin' nobody, so you'll learn some life lessons. Just don't hurt that baby in the process."

It was clear Kerry hadn't heard that she was at the Winsomes' house, or that she had rekindled her romance with David before he'd learned about Mindy's pregnancy. She almost longed for the situation he had in his mind, where she was simply trying to get David to acknowledge his daughter.

Kerry continued. "I've made my share of mistakes, but I'm old now. I hope when the Lord reviews my life, I can show him more times that I've helped people than I've hurt them."

His words were wise, and they reminded her of the only man in her time that she'd loved. Kerry may have been Movey's great-great-uncle, but both men seemed to be old souls with sage advice.

The admission of his age made Celeste reconsider her call. She was glad that Kerry didn't think ill of her, but she couldn't ask him to go with her to Willie's trailer and defend her against whatever she faced. Just like Movey, he'd do anything to protect her, and she couldn't put him in that position.

After their call, Celeste made dinner for Emma, but she couldn't eat. She had heard nothing about David. She felt stuck, and Lewis's accusations weighed on her.

If she were honest with herself, the abortion he described was the most upsetting thing she'd heard in a long time. In her time frame, women were overjoyed when they discovered they were carrying a baby. She'd only learned about abortion before her grandfather sent her to pose as Caroline Fletcher. Now she understood the reason.

Celeste had dreamed of carrying a child or raising a war orphan. After a tragedy in her community, she and Zam had applied to raise an eight-year-old girl, but theirs was one of a thousand applications. The little girl ended up with two high-ranking members of the community, and they treated her like a treasure.

Celeste kept staring at her mid-section, wondering how Caroline could be so cruel. *How could she destroy the precious life inside her, especially when Lewis offered to pay for everything and raise the child on his own when the baby was born?* Finally, she decided that Caroline's reasons weren't her own, and she'd have to move past her feelings if she was going to do anything productive.

She needed to pick up her car and throw the things she wanted to keep into the trunk. That only amounted to a couple of bags, as she wanted nothing that had belonged to Caroline or Willie.

She ran through lists of people in her head, but they either didn't like her current host or weren't willing to rush to the aid of a woman who had clung to Willie Jones. There was only one person who came to mind.

Celeste couldn't bring herself to make the call, but she wrote an elaborate text describing her situation. She waited five minutes, and her phone rang.

Chapter 5

Mindy changed the station to pop music. Emma kicked her feet in the back seat while Dalton and Cameron fed her snacks from separate plastic containers. Dalton gave her dry cereal while Cameron shared his orange slices.

"We love Emma," Dalton told Celeste.

She smiled back at him and caught Mindy looking at her. "You won't have to worry about Emma when she's with David and me."

Celeste admired Mindy's positivity. She wondered if David's girlfriend understood he was going to jail for the rest of his life unless an imaginary attacker came forward.

Mindy put her hand over Celeste's and squeezed it. "He'll be back home soon."

Celeste tried on a weak smile. It seemed like it had been the only way she could respond since Mindy picked them up, as anything else she spoke would be a platitude or a lie.

Mindy turned onto the road, and Willie's trailer came into view. The truck had been towed, but her car remained.

"Drive by it slowly," she directed Mindy. "I want to scope it out before we park."

"It's so sweet of you to think of us. The kids and I wouldn't be able to protect ourselves."

Celeste kept her eyes locked on the approaching trailers. It would have been better if she had found someone to watch over the trio of children in the backseat, but she couldn't think of anyone who would help her.

The doors of Willie's trailer were closed, but a few of Emma's toys were on the porch. Randy and Marlene's trailer seemed empty. There were no curtains in the windows, and someone had taken the chicken coop.

Mrs. Floyd was walking her dog, and she eyed the car suspiciously. Celeste had only met the woman once over Halloween, but she had known Randy, Marlene, and Caroline.

Mindy stopped at the edge of the trailer park, and Celeste got out of the car. "This lady knows Caroline." Realizing her mistake, Celeste backtracked, using the proper pronoun in place of her host's name. Mindy stared at her with wide eyes, unaware of her slip.

Mrs. Floyd was a slight woman with a severely straight nose. She looked down it as Celeste approached her.

"Have you come back to clean up your mess?" she asked.

Celeste decided not to answer her question and posed her own. "What happened to Randy and Marlene?"

She glanced toward the trailer. "They're both in jail."

Celeste had thought about that possibility when she'd heard that they had supplied Rowdy with the sleeping pills that had aided in Willie's escape.

"Your nephews are in state custody," she went on, eyeing Celeste. "I guess you couldn't trouble yourself to care for them after all that family has done for you."

"I had no idea," Celeste admitted.

The lady sniffed, and her dog shook on its leash. "I tried to keep the boys with me, but I'm not *family*." She placed extra emphasis on the last word.

"I'm sorry to hear that happened," Celeste offered. She wasn't lying, as she wished no harm to the family, especially Jayden and Jonas.

"I hear your beloved has quit you."

Mrs. Floyd had a unique way of expressing herself. Her speech was haughty, but it carried notes of Southern phrases.

"Yeah." Celeste had heard nothing about Willie Jones, but it did not surprise her he was through with Caroline.

"Are you here to move out of his trailer?"

Celeste nodded. She glanced back at Mindy, hoping that she could leave the conversation peacefully.

"I suppose I could let you inside," Mrs. Floyd relented. "The landlord changed the locks after the investigators damaged the doorknob on one of the doors." She reached into her pocket and pulled out a keychain with two keys on it.

Celeste waved Mindy into the driveway. When Mindy parked, Celeste opened the door.

"I'll just be a minute," she whispered. "Lock the doors until I get back, and if anyone else comes near the car, blow the horn and leave with the children."

Mindy nodded solemnly.

Mrs. Floyd unlocked the door, but she didn't leave. Her dog ran down the hallway sniffing, its owner unwilling to restrain it. "The landlord taxed me with a responsibility. Your lot rent has been paid until the end of the month, but the state hasn't issued another check. The investigation violates your lot rental agreement, so you can get your items, and Willie may arrange to move his trailer, but you can't live here anymore."

Mrs. Floyd regurgitated what the landlord had told her, so Celeste didn't take it personally. She ran through the house, grabbing anything that she had purchased or had been given to Emma. She pulled up the loose boards in Willie and Caroline's bedroom and took Caroline's latest ultrasound pictures. It seemed unfair to leave them in the tired trailer.

Mrs. Floyd walked through the rooms, observing Celeste as she stuffed personal items into large garbage bags. It horrified Celeste when Mrs. Floyd's dog peed in the hallway. Mrs. Floyd pretended she didn't notice the trail of urine, but she stepped over it when she followed Celeste to the kitchen.

The electric company had turned the power off, so Celeste left the refrigerator door closed. She took the other food, but it only amounted to one shopping bag.

In the living room, Mrs. Floyd picked up a photo frame Celeste had tossed behind the television. "Aren't you going to take this?"

A glance told Celeste that it was a picture of Willie and Caroline. "No."

The older lady nodded, throwing the picture back where she found it. The noise startled her small dog, and she picked it up.

"Snuggles and I are glad to hear it." She comforted her dog, bringing it close to her face. Snuggles squirmed, hoping to be released.

Celeste carried her bags to her car. When she returned for the last one, Mrs. Floyd stopped her.

"Are you going to leave all your clothes?" She pointed to the bedroom.

Celeste had kept her clothes hanging in the laundry area, and it had never crossed her mind to take Caroline's clothes. She decided her actions seemed strange.

"They remind me of my old life."

The lady nodded, and for the first time that day, she seemed to sympathize with her. "You could donate them. If the landlord takes possession of the trailer, he will sell everything in it. He may keep the trailer, but he favors your husband enough to give him the proceeds of the sale."

Celeste said nothing when Mrs. Floyd called Willie her husband. She went to work gathering Caroline's clothes, and she took them to Mindy's car, stuffing them into the floorboard of the passenger side.

Celeste thanked Mrs. Floyd, and she didn't cast a backward glance. Mindy rolled down her window when she approached her car.

"Do you mind following me into town?" Celeste asked. "I don't feel comfortable transferring Emma's car seat here."

A weight seemed to lift off her slowly as she drove away. The only thing that bothered her was that Jayden and Jonas were in foster care. She tried to brush off the feeling unsuccessfully.

"I'll figure that out tomorrow," she promised herself, but she doubted she could do anything about it.

Celeste pulled into the parking lot at CHIPS and noticed another car parked next to Stella's. She hoped it wasn't Shelly's car, as the woman held a grudge against Caroline.

Mindy pulled into the parking space beside her. Celeste transferred Emma's car seat.

"Could I ask you for one more favor?"

Mindy raised her eyebrows.

"Could you take the clothes I left in your car to the back door? They take donations there."

Mindy shook her shimmering blonde head. "I can't carry them." She put her hand over her stomach to emphasize the growing life inside her.

Celeste wasn't willing to compromise the health of David and Mindy's baby, so she thanked Mindy for her kindness and waved at the boys in the backseat.

Celeste pulled the bags out of Mindy's passenger floorboard. It surprised her when David's girlfriend didn't leave as she walked to the donation door.

The buzzer sounded when she pressed the button, and she waited for an uncomfortable stretch of time. Emma laid her head on her mother's shoulder and shivered.

"Are you cold?" she asked the child.

"No," Emma said as the door opened.

The smile Shelly had been wearing slipped off her face. She looked down at the bags at Celeste's feet. "We don't need anything from you."

"I wanted to give something back to the organization and the people who have been so kind to me," Celeste tried.

Shelly rolled her eyes. "You couldn't possibly have anything in those bags that's worth anything."

"Shelly!" a voice admonished.

Mindy had gotten out of the car. Her boys ran circles around her. "That's not a very Christian response."

Shelly's voice softened. "Mindy, you're a sweet girl, but you don't know what Caroline's capable of."

Mindy smiled. "I think as David Winsome's fiancé, I know a lot about Caroline's past. I also know about the way she's behaved for the last few months."

Celeste should have shown gratitude to Mindy for coming to her defense, but she was stuck on the reference Mindy had made to herself. *Had David proposed to her again?*

"She left with her abuser," Shelly said, crossing her arms. "She probably promised some sort of deal with the police or they wouldn't have let her go."

Mindy put a hand on Shelly's shoulder. "Caroline was kidnapped. She didn't commit a crime."

Shelly scoffed.

Celeste didn't like to be talked about like she was somewhere else. She cleared her throat, preparing to say that she'd drop off the clothes with another charity.

Shelly let out a sigh. "Fine. I'll take the clothes," she told Mindy. "But I'm doing it for *you*. That woman still isn't allowed in the store."

"I think that's a mistake," Mindy said.

Shelly held up a hand. "Not everyone is a saint like you."

Mindy blushed. "You're a good person, Shelly. I hope one day you can see that there's beauty in everyone."

Shelly forced a laugh before she picked up the bags. "You'll see her true colors one day. Someone that cruel doesn't change overnight, and if they do, it doesn't last."

"We'll see," Mindy whispered as the door closed.

Chapter 6

Celeste stopped at the hospital. The receptionist glanced at a list and waved Celeste on, calling out Mrs. Winsome's room number as she walked away.

Celeste knocked softly and ducked into the room. Emma slept on her shoulder.

Ag rose and ushered her out. Celeste cast a look over her shoulder when Ag gently pushed her out the door. The women stood in the hall, Ag with her arms crossed over her chest and Celeste trying to balance Emma.

Ag stroked Emma's back. "I don't want her to see Mama like that."

Celeste hadn't considered Mrs. Winsome's condition when she'd brought her daughter. "She's sleeping, though."

Ag looked up, and creases lined her eyes. "Mama wouldn't want it either."

Celeste nodded. Ag was right.

"I'm sorry. I just thought about the way we all rallied around you when you had your aneurysm."

Ag's eyebrows went up. "Who told you about my aneurysm?"

Celeste felt the color drain from her face. "I heard a rumor about it, and I prayed for you."

Ag ran a hand through her mousy brown hair. It was limp and oily, so it stayed in place, revealing more of her veiny forehead.

"That's what Mama needs now. She needs everyone to pray for her."

It was the worst possible time for her to ask, but she had to be sure she could stay at the Winsomes' home. Ag stared at her for a long moment before she answered.

"Will we still have our TeleBoard when we get back?"

Even though Celeste knew Ag directed her accusation at Caroline, it stung her. "Never mind. I'll go stay at a—"

Ag's eyebrows came together. "Why can't you stay at Willie's trailer?"

"We were evicted," Celeste admitted.

Ag let out a sigh that seemed to come from the depths of her soul. "I can imagine why." She massaged her nose with her thumb and forefinger. "You can stay at the house—"

Celeste interrupted her.

"I don't want to stay there anymore. I'll—"

"You'll what? Take that child somewhere dirty or unsafe because I wounded your pride?"

Several nurses raised their heads at Ag's elevated voice. Celeste smiled at them, but the nurses stared at them warily.

Ag noticed the nurses' attention. "You'd be kicked out if they knew who you were."

Celeste didn't have to ask for the reason. The police had recently rescued her from the man who had killed five healthcare professionals in that hospital. As his ex-wife and rumored accomplice, the workers wouldn't want her there.

Celeste looked at the floor. "I didn't kill their friends."

Ag turned her attention back to Celeste. "You may not have pulled the trigger, but you signed their death certificates when you called Willie Jones to get you."

Tears rolled off Celeste's cheeks. Just as she was about to turn away, Ag put a hand on her arm.

"I'm sorry." She pulled her hand away. "That wasn't very Christian of me."

Celeste noted the brown half-moon circles under Ag's eyes. "That's okay."

"No, it's not. You came by to check on my mother and me, and I've taken out my frustrations on you. Mother would be furious with me." She pulled her arms around herself more tightly. "At least she would have been—"

"Don't talk that way," Celeste said, embracing her with one arm. "Mrs. Winsome will be fine, and she'll be back to giving us down the road in no time."

"You don't understand," Ag cried. "She wasn't like that before—"

"The wreck," Celeste finished. Her grandfather had caused her to miss the horrific accident that claimed Bill Winsome and severely wounded his wife. Her grandfather could have stopped it from happening, but he pulled her back, causing Caroline to leave David just before the hardest event in his life.

"And now, I don't even know if she'll wake up." Ag buried her face in Celeste's hair and cried.

Ag spent the next few minutes sobbing. Celeste was glad to be there for her friend, but she was anxious about the nurses. When she chanced a glance in their direction, they weren't looking at Ag and her. Shouting in the hospital was alarming, but grief was commonplace.

Ag withdrew, drying her eyes. "Do you still have your key to the house?"

Celeste nodded. Ag had given her a key when she was watching Emma so that Celeste could attend CNA classes.

"I'm not going to use it, though."

Ag held up her hand. "I don't have the energy to argue with you, Caroline. During the times you want to rise above your circumstances, you get mad at the people who are wary of you. But you made the choices that shaped their opinions of you, and you're going to have to live with that."

Celeste pushed back her tears with every fiber of her being. She wanted to scream, "I'm not Caroline!" but that admission wouldn't help her situation.

Ag put her hand on the knob. "I don't want to remind you, but my brother and I still have custody of Emma. If you try to stay somewhere else, I'll have Lewis Novack find the two of you and bring Emma to me."

The burdens of her host weighed on her, and she could hardly breathe. She wished she could go back to the time before her grandfather had jerked her out of David's bed. Back then, the Winsomes had believed she was capable of change.

Ag waited for a response, and Celeste nodded. She turned on her heels. Ag called to her once, but Celeste kept walking.

Emma continued her nap in the car, and Celeste drove to the river. No cars were in sight when she parked and fell on her knees beside the car.

She wept. She cried over her lost love for David, the extinguished acceptance of his family, and her situation. She cursed Willie's name and that of everyone who had encouraged Caroline to believe that he was worthy of her time and attention. Then she cursed her grandfather's name.

Because of Dr. Alexander Maze, she couldn't go back and live in her house, and she was bound to Zam by union. In the current time, everyone hated her. She didn't have legal custody of her daughter, and she couldn't tell anyone the truth without getting locked away in a padded cell.

Her grandfather had taken almost everything away from her. Celeste didn't have love or support, but most of all, she didn't have a home.

Chapter 7

Celeste pulled into the police station as Sheriff Murphy was walking out. She couldn't believe her luck. Emma had napped so long that she'd be awake until the early morning hours, but it was best for her to stay asleep while Celeste carried on adult conversations.

She got out of the car, but she didn't move from it. Sheriff Murphy joined her.

"Is the little lady sleeping?" he asked, peeking through the window at Emma.

"We moved out of Willie's trailer today, so she's a little tired."

He raised his salt-and-pepper eyebrows. "Do you have a place?"

"Ag wants me to stay at their house until she comes home with her mom."

"How is Mrs. Winsome?"

Celeste glanced away. When she looked back at him, he was staring at her intently.

"She hasn't woken up yet, but her surgery went well."

"That's good," he said. "That's really good. Sometimes, the mind needs to rest so the body can heal."

She stood uncomfortably with the man she had thought of as a father figure. Now that all her memories had returned, she recalled their closeness when Sheriff Murphy had believed Caroline Fletcher had made a drastic change. Of course, Caroline had ruined all of that when Dr. Maze pulled her out of Caroline's body for the first time.

"I came by for a reason." She let her statement dangle in the air.

"I imagine you did." He ran his thumb and forefinger over his full mustache. "David has been officially charged."

Celeste felt like someone had punched her in the stomach. "Does he have bail?"

Sheriff Murphy's forehead crinkled. "Not the kind of bail you'd be able to raise. He was charged with attempted murder."

"But there is a bail?"

There was no mirth in his green eyes as he surveyed her. "Whatever money you have or you can get should be used on that baby." He jerked his thumb in the direction Emma was sleeping. "If you thought a little more about your responsibilities and a little less about men, then you'd be livin' a much different life."

As far as Caroline went, Celeste agreed with him. *But was she the same as her host?*

"Is he okay?"

The sheriff looked at the long brick building where David was held. "Yes. He's doing about as well as he can with a bunch of criminals trying him."

Celeste's hands flew to her hips. "What does that mean?"

Sheriff Murphy was undeterred by her response. "It means that those boys will poke at him until he fights them or says something they respect. They team up on the ones that do crimes against women and children." He huffed. "You'd think the drunk driver who crashed into the seniors' home and the boy who gave his friend so much meth that he overdosed would give a little grace to a man who may or may not have tried to kill his mother."

Celeste's anxiety had been on a roller coaster since Sheriff Murphy had told her David had been charged. "You only have two other prisoners?"

He forced a chuckle. "I've never seen that number since I've worked here." He glanced back at the building. "I think David makes eight right now."

"He's in a cell with seven criminals?" Celeste felt like her view was tilting.

"David is in a cell with the two men I told you about. They're the ones who have done the worst crimes in our county right now."

The sheriff's patience with her was waning, so she took a proactive approach. "What can I do to help him?"

"I imagine you know the drill by now." He pointed to a box next to the visitation building. "Commissary money is dropped off there. We don't give them credit for checks or large bills until they clear the bank."

Celeste remembered Randy and Marlene discussing Willie's commissary money, and she thought she understood the process. The thought of her neighbors brought another problem to her mind.

"How are Jayden and Jonas?"

She was relieved when Sheriff Murphy's mouth moved up in the corners. "They're with a good family in Johnson City. They had to switch schools, but with all the publicity around their parents, it was for the better."

"I'm glad they're okay." She could feel emotion move up from her chest to her face, and she tried to control it. "They don't deserve to be punished for everything that happened."

Sheriff Murphy noticed her reaction and patted her arm. "I went by there a couple of days ago. The boys were throwing a frisbee with a dog, and there's a little girl in the home that the younger one watches over."

Celeste smiled sadly. "That's Jonas. He was the same way with Emma."

The sheriff moved a dial on the radio attached to his belt. "That's one less thing you'll have to worry about. The foster parents are the type that will adopt them and take care of them if both their parents stay in jail, and Randy and Marlene are looking at some serious time."

Celeste hoped to change the subject before he asked her if she knew about the sleeping pills they gave to Rowdy. She nodded to the visitation building. "Will David have a set time for visitation?"

Voices squawked out of the radio, and Sheriff Murphy jerked to attention. "You'll have to call the station about it." He held up his hand as he jogged to his cruiser. "Take care of the little lady."

Celeste glanced back at Emma, who was still sleeping soundly. She'd kept the motor running, so the car was warm when she climbed inside. She rummaged through the bags and found a twenty-dollar bill. She drove in front of the visitation building and dropped the money off for David before she drove away.

She went back to the Winsomes' house, but she only brought in two bags of the items she had taken from Willie's trailer. She was transient in more than one way, and the feeling left her heart burdened.

She prepared a small dinner, but Emma seemed disinterested in the vegetables that she usually loved. Despite her lengthy nap, the toddler fell asleep at her usual bedtime.

Celeste wondered if she needed the extra rest because of her broken leg. She supposed it was possible, but it seemed more likely that she was getting sick. Celeste had kept a blanket over her daughter's head when the police had been cataloging Mrs. Winsome's stabbing, but the cold and wind could have caused her to catch a cold.

Emma lay peacefully on the couch while Celeste cleaned the house and showered. As she wondered what to do with the rest of her evening, a thought came to her mind.

After her disagreement with Ag, Celeste felt a little less guilty about reading Mrs. Winsome's diaries. This time, she selected one of the newer ones, turning to a time when David was a little older than Emma.

I never thought God would grant me another child. It had been so long since the cries of a baby had filled the house. The missed chances were hard to bear, and every single one of them made it a little harder to keep trying.

My sweet boy turned two today! He has his father's eyes and my quick wit. My brother, his namesake, would have doted on him non-stop as he played with his toy ships.

His father calls him "Davey", but I say his name fully. It's a strong name, like his uncle, who was named after a good king in the Bible.

I got a phone call today.

I was running around the kitchen, getting David's cake ready, when the phone rang. I thought it was someone asking about the party, so I hurried to get it. I could hear the strange breathing as soon as I picked up the receiver.

"You better watch yourself," the man said.

It sounded like he was talking through a tunnel or on one of those handmade phones my brother and I used to use. I didn't want to keep listening, but I couldn't stop myself.

"Do you know how easy it would be to ruin your life?"

That's when I knew who had called me. In the moments of my greatest blessings, he always found a way to hurt me. I don't know how he located me, or how he was communicating with me, but he did and he was.

I hung up the phone. I must have slammed it several times against the cradle before my dearest Bill ran to my rescue. I cried in his arms, and he held me. That man is a saint, and I hope he never learns about what I've done. He'd never forgive me.

Chapter 8

Emma cried out in her sleep, and Celeste rushed to wrap her in her arms. As she lay with her child, she thought about what she'd read.

Bill Winsome had called David by a special nickname, and even as a grown man, David had called his father "Daddy." The two men had shared a special bond.

David's dad had insisted that she call him by his first name, and he had embraced her immediately. His speech had drawn her and the way he communicated his love for God so easily. Jesus was the subject of almost every conversation, and his blue eyes had sparkled when he'd baptized her in the Nolichucky River.

His hair was as white as snow—even though he sometimes added silver hair color to it—and it made it easy for her to pick him out in a crowd. And a crowd always gathered around Bill Winsome. He was so loving and charismatic that people gathered around him.

He was a little taller than David, but only by a few inches. The war had taken one of his legs up to the knee, but Celeste had never met a man who had walked taller.

Bill had accepted her into his home, and he had quieted the rumors about her with his unending faith. After her baptism, more people in the town supported her, and she started a small business out of the Winsomes' home. She fixed clocks, computers, and radios, waiting for the day when she'd be able to put her real skills to use.

It had been a monumental affair when Bill had officiated the marriage between David and her. She closed her eyes and pictured the ceremony. The First Baptist Church was decorated in navy blue and silver, and David had worn his father's tuxedo. He'd scared her with the crash diet he had tried to fit into it, but his mother had paid for the adjustments days before their nuptials.

Why couldn't she go back to that day? She wished Sheriff Murphy could walk her down the aisle again and place her hand in David's loving palm.

She closed her eyes and wished for her dreams to take her back to a time her grandfather wouldn't let her go to again.

"When is David Winsome's visitation?" she asked the dispatcher who answered her call.

Emma still wasn't awake, and she'd taken the opportunity to dial the sheriff's department. She hoped she hadn't missed his first scheduled time.

"It's at ten o'clock this morning," the lady responded after a few moments.

Celeste asked about the proper procedure and learned it wasn't complicated. She ran through her morning routine, trying to give herself as much time as possible.

Just after eight-thirty, she dressed Emma as the toddler's eyes lolled with sleep. She'd grown out of another outfit, but Mrs. Winsome had bought a couple of dresses in larger sizes, so Celeste put one on her.

On the way into town, Celeste wondered if it was a good idea to take Emma with her. David was her father, but it might be an upsetting memory when Emma was older, and Celeste doubted David wanted her to see him in his current accommodations.

Mindy was at work, and Kerry operated a pawnshop, so she doubted they could help. She dialed Mindy first, and to her surprise, Mindy was at home.

"I had a bad day yesterday," Mindy explained when Celeste asked why she wasn't at work. "We lost someone, and it bothered me." She took a shuddering breath. "I know they're with Jesus now, but it broke my heart."

Mindy jumped at the chance to watch Emma, but Celeste was forced to explain why she needed her to keep her toddler. Celeste thought about lying, but her ethics won over.

"I'm going to David's visitation."

"Oh! I didn't know he'd have one so soon. I'll meet you there in ten minutes."

Celeste's heart sank. She'd wanted to talk to David alone, but she'd have to share him with Mindy. At least she wouldn't have to be in the same room while they expressed their devotion to each other.

Mindy was there before her, parked in a spot nearest the visitation booths. She brought the boys to the car, and they sat on either side of Emma. She hardly moved in her sleep, and they curled up against her car seat and closed their eyes.

"Don't they have school today?" Celeste asked.

"No. It's a snow day."

Celeste looked at a fourth of an inch of snow on the ground. She'd walked through a much heavier accumulation for her studies, but that was in a different time.

There was an awkward moment where the women tried to decide who would see David first. Mindy tried to be the bigger person.

"It was your idea. Why don't you go first?"

"But you're with him," Celeste countered. "You should see him first." She looked at Mindy's thin stomach. "And you'll need to give him any updates about the baby."

Mindy gave her a forced smile. "If you're sure, I'll go first. I'll stay in for thirty minutes, and you can have the rest of the hour."

Celeste sat in her car while Mindy talked to the man she loved. The seconds felt like they were eating into her skin and igniting her nerves until they were on fire.

Mindy didn't come out in thirty minutes, and Celeste was ready to stomp her frustrations on the pavement when five more minutes went by. *Did she expect Celeste to knock on the door when it was her turn?*

Five more minutes passed. Celeste had her hand on the door handle when Mindy emerged.

Celeste wanted to make a passive-aggressive comment about how long she'd been waiting, but Mindy sobbed at the door. Keeping one eye on the children in the car, Celeste approached her.

"The door will lock us out if I close it," she said through her tears. "I don't want you to miss out on your part of the visit."

Celeste's heart softened, but she didn't console Mindy. The woman patted her arm as she left.

The door closed behind her, and she took a seat on the folding metal chair. A receiver was hanging from the wall, and she picked it up. David's image was on an old television screen behind a sheet of plexiglass.

After Mindy had left in tears, Celeste tried to start her visit with humor. "This isn't what I thought it'd be like when I came here to visit you."

He looked up at her. "You're beautiful."

His comment made her lose her breath. "Th-Thank you."

"You sent the twenty dollars, didn't you?"

"Yeah." She shifted uncomfortably in her seat.

He moved the receiver from one ear to the other. "Then, it should be me thanking you."

"Will they let me bring you anything else?"

He stretched in his seat. He was wearing a white shirt and a pair of matching thermal pants. Flip-flops brought the only color to his outfit.

He chuckled. "Even if you could have smuggled some home-cooked food through before Willie's little stunt, they would have found a nail file." He winked at her.

She didn't understand the reference, as she'd grown up during a different time. "I think I have another twenty in the car—"

He stopped her. "I don't want you to send me any more money. One guy in my cell is leaving to go to prison, and he gave me the clothes and shoes I have on." He leaned back to give her a better look at his ensemble, and she feigned impression. "He's even going to teach me how to play poker to make money." He leaned forward. "So, I want you to spend your money on Emma."

"But I'm staying at your house."

"Then use it to help Ag and my mama," he replied simply. "If Mama makes it." He choked back a sob.

"She'll make it," Celeste said confidently. She twisted the cord connected to the receiver. "You talk like you're going to be there a while."

He held his hands up. "I've been charged with attempted murder. That usually carries a pretty lengthy sentence."

Hearing him say the words made it real to her. She moved as close to the screen as possible.

"I love you, David."

He touched the bottom of the screen on his end, where Celeste imagined he could see her face. "I love you, too."

She could have pressed him for more, bringing up Emma and Mindy, but she let it go. It was enough for her to hear him say the words she needed to hear.

She cleared her throat. "We need to work on your defense."

He raised his eyebrows. "What defense? I was holding the knife over my mother's bleeding body. I think the prosecution has this one in the bag."

"I was thinking about the windows in the basement."

David put his head in his hand. "Here we go."

Celeste was stung. "What do you mean?"

He lifted his head, shaking it. "I mean, do you think the judge is going to believe a thief slid into the 8X10 windows in the basement and stabbed my eighty-year-old mama?"

Celeste balanced the receiver on her shoulder and crossed her arms over her chest. "Why not?"

"Well, for one, no one had the motive to attack her."

She put the receiver back in her hand, wishing she could throw it at the plexiglass in her frustration. "I'm just trying to help, David."

He sighed and scrubbed his cheek with his free hand. He'd abandoned shaving, and he already had a good start to a full beard.

"I know. I'm sorry."

The door behind him buzzed, and two feet with shiny black shoes entered the screen. David looked back and nodded.

"My time is up. Tell Mindy I'll see her next week."

He hung up the receiver and left her sitting there looking after him.

<h1 style="text-align:center">Chapter 9</h1>

Mindy's eyes were dry when Celeste got back to the car. She had gotten Emma out of her car seat, and the baby was playing with her keys.

"Did you have a good visit?" Mindy asked.

Celeste tried to smile, but it fell flat. "It was short."

"I'm sorry," Mindy said, getting out of the car. "I lost track of time, and we were both crying so hard."

"It's okay," Celeste told her, even though it was far from fine.

Mindy pushed her into a one-armed hug. When Celeste counted to three, she tried to pull away, but Mindy held her firmly. "I know you miss him, too."

Celeste tried to keep her face blank when Mindy released her. "I love him."

Mindy nodded. "He's easy to love, but he and I are together. We agreed you shouldn't come back to visit him."

Her statement let everything fall into place. Celeste understood the reason for David's abruptness. He had told Mindy he didn't care for Caroline, and they'd decided she was no longer needed.

Her heart burned in her chest, but she tried to keep her emotions in check. "I need to put Emma in her seat."

Mindy handed Emma over, but it seemed to take more effort. "She's getting big."

Celeste had to admit that Emma seemed to weigh more. She babbled happily as she strapped her into her restraints.

When she closed Emma's door, Mindy was watching her sons climb into her car. "You can visit him if you want to."

The statement was so contradictory that Celeste responded before she could catch herself. "But I thought you two had decided against me."

Mindy shifted her feet. "It was more David than me. I don't see you as a threat, but he wants you to stay away from him."

But he wants me to live in his house, she thought.

"I can talk to him, though," Mindy said.

"That's not necessary." Celeste opened her door before Mindy pulled her into another uncomfortable embrace. "I don't mind staying away from him."

Emma didn't fall asleep until late that night, and the strain of holding her emotions back took its toll on Celeste. She wanted to cry herself to sleep, but by the time Emma dozed on the couch, she felt almost numb.

What kind of game was David playing? He told her he loved her, but then he asked Mindy to keep her away. Mindy didn't think Celeste was a threat, and she had the right to feel that way since David had no trouble leaving his visit with Celeste without a backward glance.

But why did he tell her he loved her?

Maybe he thought he was supposed to return the endearment, as Celeste was the mother of his child. Something about that didn't feel right.

Celeste wasn't really Emma's mother, or, at least, she wasn't her full mother. Emma shared some of Caroline's DNA, and it was easier to see the woman's nose on Emma's face.

Celeste decided she couldn't cry, so she found herself in Mrs. Winsome's room leafing through her notebooks. She went back to the oldest diary and scanned pages about Mrs. Winsome's acclimation to college and how the boys teased her. Finally, she landed on an entry that piqued her interest.

I don't love him anymore. I can't.

It's not my fault. He went to the war and left me behind.

I can't bear to lose anyone else to this God-forsaken war, so I'll just cut him out of my life. Maybe he won't even notice.

We got the telegraph today. The government sent a telegram to our house instead of coming to the door.

I'd been traveling back and forth between the university and my home, and after December seventh, I stayed at home. Most of my professors understood, as our entire nation was grieving.

I think we already knew our dearest David was gone. Somehow, we all felt the light leave our home when we heard the radio reports.

We thought he was safe from the fighting. *How didn't our country know the Japanese had planes flying across the Pacific until they attacked us?*

My father wasn't at home when the telegram was delivered, and I came downstairs to my mother, trembling with a piece of paper in her hands. I'd been sleeping in David's bed, hoping he'd wake me up and tell me one of his stories. Now he'll never come home.

He was only twenty-one years old. *How was that enough time?*

David left so many people behind who adored him, and I was one of them. He was my big brother, my protector, and the war took him away.

Bill wrote me a letter. I ripped it up. A piece of paper can't be arms that hold me or fingers intertwined with mine.

So, I understand loss, and I hate it. I never thought I could hate anything as much as the devil, but it's a close second.

It's best to end things with Bill now. There are plenty of young women in our hometown who write to men who are stationed overseas, so he won't lose anything. Maybe he'll find a nice young girl to marry if he makes it out of the war alive. Death has touched me, so if I stay with him, Bill will probably die, too.

We were supposed to get married when he came home, but I sent a letter today ending any hope he had of marrying me. I'll stay Eleanor Martin—at least until the end of the war.

I think I'll sleep in my brother's bed again tonight. Too soon, his scent will be gone, and I'll have to truly face my grief. For tonight, I'll let my heart believe he is on a ship in the Pacific, and we'll see him soon. My father may wake me up with the shower's groaning pipes in the morning, but I can sleep on the pillow that once held my brother's head and maybe the Lord will send him to me in a dream.

Celeste had tears in her eyes when she finished reading the entry. She stayed motionless, allowing herself to absorb some of Mrs. Winsome's pain.

She had ended her relationship with Bill Winsome, but they'd gotten back together. *It must have worked out, right?* She wondered if Bill had made a grand display when he'd rushed back into her arms.

Something else struck Celeste in the entry. She always thought the house had belonged to Bill, but it seemed the groaning pipes, creaking step, and the description of the location of her brother's room suggested that Mrs. Winsome had inherited the house from *her* family.

Against her better judgment, she read through a few more entries.

Danny Brown is a hoot. He makes all the girls laugh. He says he has a condition that kept him out of the war, but I think his father paid for his doctor to cite asthma on his records. My lab partner, Steve Wilson, truly suffers from the ailment, and there are times I wonder how he drowns in a sea of air.

I waited to go out with Danny until after I knew Bill had gotten my letter. It was only fair.

Danny's a sweet guy, but I don't plan to get serious with him. We hold hands, but I don't let him kiss me.

He's part of my physics group. Linda, Steve, and Liz round out our band of misfits. Al joins us every now and again, but no one really cares for his company. Each one of us is gifted, and we hate the war.

We talk about everything but the war and fireside chats. We have our own corner of the county's library, and we stay until they kick us out. After that, we drift over to Danny's house.

I never thought I'd do it, but I drink wine. When I do, Liz Monticello drives me to her apartment, and I stay on her couch.

Danny tries to kiss me more when I've been drinking, but I never let alcohol confuse my feelings. I won't let myself become one of those girls who needs a shotgun wedding.

Mr. Hart caught me dozing during class, and he pulled me aside to talk about it. Gossiping women comprise most of the classroom, now that the men are at war, so I can't imagine what they're telling each other.

I told my professor that the wine made it easier to deal with my brother's death. He lost his father in the First World War, so I thought he'd be sympathetic, but he was angry with me. He told me I was the brightest person at the school, but alcohol was dimming my light. I don't think I'm going to drink anymore.

Bill paid me a visit a couple of days ago. He was on leave, but he had to return soon.

I sat on the porch with him, and I wanted to rush into his arms, but I confirmed it was over. He told me Becky Wright had been sending letters to him, and his family wanted him to marry her. It makes sense, as she lives next to his family's home. He talked to me as a courtesy to see if I still had feelings for him.

I assured him I was fine, and Danny and I were doing well. Of course, Bill has no idea that Danny is just a friend who fancies himself as my boyfriend.

I let my sweet Bill go. I watched him walk down the dirt driveway, and I wanted to run after him, but I didn't move.

My mother and father went to his wedding today. They said it was a small ceremony and reception in the church's pavilion.

So, Bill is a married man now, and Becky Winsome can bear his loss. He goes back to the war in two days, and I'm sure he won't come back. I have a bad feeling.

I wish the war wouldn't have happened. I wish I could go up to my brother's room and tell him that Bill Winsome had asked for my hand in marriage. And I wish I could have been Becky today, surrounded by the people who love her as she joined her life to a wonderful man.

Bill was my first love, and he will always hold a piece of my heart. Maybe now that he's married, I can put my feelings for him to rest.

The truth is: I love him. I will always love him, but maybe his death will hurt a little less now that we are estranged. I just hope enough time goes by to keep me from feeling too much pain. Because he's going to die. They all do.

Celeste couldn't read more. She put the book down and quietly left Mrs. Winsome's room.

She hadn't known Bill had been married before Mrs. Winsome. *What had happened to Becky?*

She typed a quick search for Becky Winsome, but it yielded no results. It wasn't a surprise as most of the people in her age group didn't have social media profiles. It was a long shot. Becky had either died or remarried, so Celeste probably wouldn't find her on the web-based engines of her current time frame.

In her time, it was much easier to look up anyone who had lived in the last several centuries. Piles of data had been amassed, and it made it unchallenging for Alexander Maze to locate the perfect hosts for Celeste.

Full of unanswered questions, Celeste lay next to her daughter. She fell asleep in a house full of history, and she had hardly touched the first layer of it.

Chapter 10

The phone vibrated against the arm of the couch. It shocked Celeste out of a dream she couldn't remember.

"Do you know how to get in touch with Ag?" Mindy asked.

Celeste sat up and rubbed her eyes. "Why?"

Mindy let out an irritated sigh. "I need to get a lawyer for David, but they want to be paid before they'll take a case, so I need access to his bank account."

Celeste's head cleared a little. "You want Ag to get money out for you?"

"She can pay the lawyer if she wants to. I just need to make sure someone pays her."

Celeste rushed out of the room so she wouldn't disturb Emma. She settled in the kitchen and cupped her hand over her mouth and the phone's receiver.

"Who did you find?"

Mindy waited a moment before she responded. "I have a friend from college, Rayna Baird. She just passed the bar exam last year, but she's really good."

Celeste wasn't usually skeptical of associations, but she got a bad feeling. "How much does she want?"

Mindy told her a number and Celeste's heart dropped.

"There's no way David can afford that!" She shook her head, even though Mindy couldn't see her.

"I thought he still had the money from his dad's life insurance policy," Mindy commented. "Well, whatever he had left after you took half of his share in the divorce."

"What?" Celeste massaged her temples.

"The word around town was that you gave the money you got in the divorce to Willie to buy that trailer beside the one his brother lived in, and then you guys—" Mindy was too polite to relay the rest of the rumor.

"They used it for drugs."

"I'm sorry to hear that," Mindy acknowledged, even though Celeste had only guessed.

A thought struck Celeste. "Mrs. Floyd said it was Willie's trailer."

Mindy was patient with her. "I heard you bought the trailer and put it in Willie's name, so he'd stay with you."

Celeste mumbled something unintelligible.

"What was that?"

"Nothing," Celeste said. She gave Ag's number to Mindy.

After her call, Celeste prepared breakfast for Emma. Emma stumbled into the kitchen and latched onto her mother's leg.

Celeste lifted her, making a greater effort than usual. Emma ate, and Celeste bathed her to get the yogurt out of her beautiful blonde locks. It hit her when she was combing her hair.

Emma had always had long hair. She'd been born with blonde hair, and by six months old, Zam had told Celeste that she'd had her first haircut. But her hair was really long! It was almost down the length of her back.

Emma's hair wasn't the only big change. Celeste had to put her in another one of the larger-sized dresses Mrs. Winsome had purchased for her, and her shoes didn't fit.

Celeste tried to find another pair, but there were no other shoes in the house for a growing toddler.

Celeste checked the size of the dress, and it had been made for a three-year-old toddler. *Was Emma really old enough to wear that size?*

By Celeste's calculation, Emma should have been nearing sixteen months old, but her size and speech were way beyond a small toddler. She put her child on the floor and watched her stack blocks and wind her fingers through the loops of a colorful toy. Her motor skills were well-developed, and she concentrated intensely on anything Celeste put in front of her.

Celeste tried to consider the trauma her mind had gone through when she'd switched bodies with her hosts. There was a period of acclimation, and she'd eased into their physique. But Emma was a different story.

Emma had traveled through time in her own body. *What stress had that caused her?*

Celeste stared at her daughter, willing her revelation to go away. She wanted to be wrong, but she knew her thoughts had led to the only reasonable conclusion.

Emma was growing at twice her normal rate.

Chapter 11

Celeste dropped off the letter at the post office before she took Emma to find another pair of shoes. She felt strange addressing a letter to her grandfather in her current time frame, but she hoped he received it. She guessed the day and time of his present time and wrote on the envelope that he shouldn't open the letter until that time. She hoped it would work.

When they began their missions, she'd asked her grandfather how she'd be able to communicate with him if she was in the past. He'd mentioned that she could mail him a letter and he wouldn't open it until the appointed time on the envelope. The next day, he'd seemed contemplative as he'd looked through his mail, so she assumed the trick had worked. She wondered how the postal service had located his unclaimed mail and then decided she didn't care.

Caroline was banned from the local thrift store, so Celeste took Emma to a discount store to buy shoes, socks, and clothes. She had a limited amount of funds, but she took most of her money with her. The rest of her meager funds were in the bank, but she couldn't access them.

When Willie had kidnapped her, the investigators assigned to his case froze her bank account. It was still inaccessible, so she had to buy their necessities with the cash she had hidden for reserve money.

She picked up a few cheap meals, including some freezer fries for her and yogurt melts and broccoli for Emma, and headed to the infant section. It was a sad moment when she realized that her child no longer fit into the tiny sleepers and onesies.

In the toddler area, Emma shuffled through pantsuits and sleepers, keeping the changing seasons in mind. Soon, the trees and flowers would bloom and the weather would warm.

The thought of the dogwood trees blooming reminded her of the previous year in her current time. She had been Hailey Hall, and she had been completely unaware she was from the future or that Emma existed.

She and Braeden had parted under less than agreeable terms, but she wanted to tell him about the baby she saw in the nursery. Based on the description of the baby, she was certain that he was Braeden's son, but she doubted he would believe her. She was lost in thoughts about the best way to approach him when a voice sounded from behind her.

"May I help you?"

Celeste had wondered about residual memories. Her hosts left something behind, as she knew how to operate most of their current devices, like TeleBoards and microwaves, but she had never experienced something that stemmed beyond casual knowledge. That all changed when she turned around and saw Maria.

Caroline had met Maria in the battered women's home four years ago. The woman looked the same, with flawless mocha skin and dark eyes, but her eyes had lost some of their brightness. Her face was thinner, too. When Caroline had interacted with her, Maria had been eight months pregnant.

Caroline and Maria had shared their laughter and tears in the short days they had in the home. The "house mom" assigned them to clean together, and they were "buddies" during the outings to farmer's markets or hiking trails.

Maria had endured her boyfriend's beatings until she'd gotten pregnant. She left him and ran to her sister's house, but after several months, he found her and threatened her sister's family. After an unlucky experience at a gas station, Maria had been forced to quit her job and seek shelter in the battered women's home.

She showed off the ultrasound pictures of her baby and was delighted that she was having a girl. She had discussed possible names with Caroline, and Emma had been one of them.

Celeste tried to block the memories of Willie rushing into the house with three men. One fell on his knees, pleading with his wife to return home, but the other two were more forceful, grabbing their significant others and dragging them to the door. Lucy was one woman who had resisted, and her boyfriend had been relentless. His punches started at her head and traveled down her body. The other women tried to pull him off her, and they succeeded, but then he kicked Maria, and she stopped fighting. Her injuries caused her to lose her baby.

Celeste hadn't remembered the woman when Shelly had talked about her, but now that she saw her face, she knew it was her. Celeste didn't know if it was the trauma of the event or Caroline's guilt that had left the woman's image imprinted on Caroline's residual memories, but she hoped it was the latter. Caroline should have gone to jail for opening the door for the abusive men.

The memories hit her in a rush, and tears stung Celeste's eyes. "Maria," she whispered.

Her name tag on her vest confirmed it, but the woman nodded. "Caroline."

Celeste took a deep breath. "I'm sorry for what I did to you."

It took a lot for Celeste to apologize for another woman's actions, but it needed to be done. Caroline wouldn't have asked for forgiveness, but Celeste was ready to right her wrongs.

Maria glanced at Emma and smiled, but her face hardened when she met Celeste's eyes. "I don't forgive you. I can never forgive you for what you took from me."

"I understand," Celeste squeaked out. "I can't take back what I did, but I can tell you I know I was wrong and I regret it. It's one of the worst mistakes of my life."

Maria sucked in a breath through her nose and looked away. When she turned back to Celeste, her eyes were glassy.

"Why do you deserve a little girl when you killed mine?"

Celeste didn't know how to respond, so she remained silent.

"I don't know who I hate more: you or him."

Maria meant her ex-boyfriend. He had been the one who had murdered her baby, but Caroline was the reason he knew where to find her. Celeste thought her feelings were justifiable.

"I'm trying to do better," Celeste told her. "It doesn't make up for the harm I've caused, but maybe it will keep me from making more bad decisions."

"You ran away with him and left your little girl behind," Maria accused. She started trembling and tears coursed down her cheeks. "I don't know why you have her back, but nothing bad ever seems to happen to you, so—"

"Maria?"

Another employee with bright red hair and meaty arms approached them. She pulled Maria into an embrace.

"It's her," Maria cried.

The woman seemed to be well-acquainted with Maria's past. She glared at Celeste.

"I think it's time for you to pay for your items and leave." For Emma's benefit, she kept her voice calm and even, but she was firm.

Celeste nodded and turned out of the section. She stopped to look at the shoes and speedily selected the first pair that fit Emma's growing feet.

She almost ran to the register, and it seemed the lady positioned there recognized Caroline, as she didn't greet her or wish her well after she'd completed the transaction. Bad news traveled fast.

Celeste was glad when she made it to her car without another confrontation, but she didn't feel safe until she was inside the Winsomes' home. She laid a tired Emma on the couch and closed Mrs. Winsome's bedroom door.

She felt unworthy to sit on the bed, so she cried silently on the floor, wishing she could be anyone but Caroline in a world that existed before her time.

Chapter 12

Mr. Hart gave me a letter from the defense
department. He had recommended me for a program
at Oak Ridge, and I jumped at the opportunity.
I'd heard Albert Einstein had recommended a
project there, and I hoped to run into him.
Also, I need to get away. Everything in my house
reminds me of my dearest brother, and my mother
walks with a cloud of misery over her head.
It will be nice to leave town, too, as there
are rumors that the new Mrs. Bill Winsome is
expecting their first child.

When I arrived at Oak Ridge, my dreams of
late-night chats with Albert Einstein dimin-
ished. He was a pacifist, so everyone I talked
to said that he wasn't directly involved with
the work.

I felt like I was entering a prison or
concentration camp with armed guards and barbed
wire around the perimeter. I kept my head down
and moved quickly when I got out of the car that
delivered me to the Secret City.

They placed my team in living quarters with
our lab at the center. It's a truly magnificent
lab! There are machines in it I never thought

existed, and I can't wait to learn how to use them.

My room is simple. It has a bed and a dresser with a vanity. I put everything I'd brought from home away in under ten minutes. My coat, jackets, and dresses fit nicely in the closet, and I hid my picture of Bill at the bottom of my undergarment drawer. I put a family picture and David's Navy photograph on my bedside table.

I forgot to mention the best part! All my study friends from the university are in my group. We aren't part of the big project that's the focus of the new city, but we're responsible for researching the science behind a concept that the German dictator is pursuing, too. We'll receive university credit while we're here, and Danny, Liz, Steve, Al, Linda, and I will work together. I couldn't have planned it better.

Danny took it as a sign we should get married. I tried to tell him I wasn't interested in marriage, but he kept pushing the idea. Finally, I told him I'd consider it after graduation. My lie will buy some time to find an easy way to break it off. I hope it doesn't destroy our working relationship, as I'll need to pick his brain before I propose my theories.

Liz flew into our project, and when we were officially briefed on it, my legs almost gave out from beneath me. It's so secret that I can't write about it. My discretion is for my safety and for any other person who may read my journal later.

I'm in charge of managing the theory behind the machine. Al is my partner, and we never seem to agree. We believe in two different sides of string theory, and he isn't keen on Einstein's new work. I, however, think Einstein is revolutionary and will change the world for the better.

I hope Albert Einstein will visit Oak Ridge, but even if he supervises the daily application of the project he suggested, I doubt I will see him. I'm lucky I know about the letter he wrote to our prestigious president, as I'm only aware of Albert Einstein's proposal due to a slip.

Linda misses her home, but she is a genius with electronics. Even the new devices give her little problems. I'm amazed by her ability to adjust controls on any machine and have it obey her.

She has a listener's heart, and she misses her family. She keeps a silver hairbrush by her bed that was passed down from her grandmother. Sometimes, she lets me brush her long, dark hair with it.

Danny is a whiz on computers. They're new to me and everyone else in the world, but he took to their systems like he was born while typing on a computer.

Danny is fetching—in his own way. All the girls have brown eyes, but Steve has some kind of strange lenes in his eyes (maybe they help him see better), and Danny's green eyes could almost swallow me. I haven't studied Al's eyes, but I don't think they're brown.

Right now, Danny's hair is a little too long, but our supervisor will change it. Mr. Greene promised we would all keep a clean-cut appearance while we're here.

Al works with me, and I find him intolerable! He completely embraces the war now, and he often refers to our soldiers as "cannon fodder." Steve shoved him across the room the first time he said it, but Linda reminded him that Al's words were only his way of dealing with the strange situations the war created.

I don't know why Steve is here. He walks around with his hands in his pockets, looking at our work and smiling, but he doesn't do much for our team besides bringing our meals and cracking jokes.

As I mentioned, I can't write about the reason I'm here, but I don't think the project is possible. What the German tyrant is trying to do, and what the supervisors have told us to do, isn't impossible, but I don't think it's probable with our materials and technology.

I'll be happy to live in the Secret City for as long as they want to keep me here, though. Other than the people dressed in uniforms, I don't have a constant reminder of my dearest brother. Right now, that's all I need.

Celeste felt sorry for Mrs. Winsome. She didn't know anything about her project, but based on her history lessons, she could only assume that nothing came out of it.

Bill's first wife and baby must have died in childbirth, as it explained why she hadn't heard them mentioned when she was married to David. She read another entry from deeper inside the book.

I had an idea, and Danny ran it through the system. Linda thinks it will work, but Liz is skeptical. If I'm right, my name will be in the history books beside Albert Einstein's. I might even invite him over for tea, but I'm getting ahead of myself. First, my idea has to work.

Al has proposed at least ten different ways it could go wrong. I don't mind his input, but that haughty voice he uses makes me want to punch him in the mouth.

Now, I'm starting to talk like Steve. Violence is not the answer, but that man drives me crazy!

Al once told me he was starved in a closet for days at a time. While that shows he had a difficult childhood, it doesn't account for the way he struts through the lab like a peacock with all his feathers on display. He could demonstrate a little humility, especially when I'm smarter than him.

Steve is gone for long periods of time. It makes Linda nervous because they're going steady, and he won't talk about what he's been doing when he gets back.

I wouldn't stand for it. If I thought my beaux was seeing another woman, I'd stand up to him and find out the truth, but Linda is worried that she'll be an old maid.

I hope I am an old maid. I can't stand the idea of waiting around for a man who may or may not be there when I need him.

David would have been a good husband. He and Patty were high school sweethearts, but he didn't marry her before he left for his tour of duty.

I haven't seen her since David's funeral, and I wish I felt bad about it. I should comfort her, but I can't think about her without envisioning my brother's life if he had married her and stayed in Unicoi County. I could have been an aunt, and he would have told his stories to my children.

I could have filled these pages with my hopes and dreams before my dearest brother was killed, but now I only want to exist. I suppose I'd like to help end the dictator's tyrannical rule in his country, but it wouldn't bring David back.

I know I've loved two men in my life, and they're both gone. One of them I pushed away with both hands, but Bill is doing fine without me. I miss my brother with every beat of my heart, though, and I doubt I'll ever get over his loss.

As a Christian, I should be celebrating that he's with our Heavenly Father, but I want him here with me. For all I care, God could take me, and I could see my brother again.

If the forces find out about the Secret City, we will all be destroyed, but I doubt they are looking anywhere in Eastern Tennessee. But if they drop a bomb over our heads, I'll only be sad for the other people in and around the facility.

I'll be glad to be dead. I know my brother will be there waiting for me.

Chapter 13

Celeste called Mindy about the job opening she'd mentioned when Emma had broken her leg. Mindy gave her an email and directed her to send her resume to it.

Celeste had written a resume when she was in Hailey Hall's body, but she had trouble writing another one. She couldn't list her actual skills, as everyone thought she was Caroline, and she wasn't sure if Caroline could do anything.

A quick search on David's laptop revealed Caroline had graduated from high school, but no colleges were mentioned. She looked back several years on social media, but all she could find was a vague post about working as a cashier. She didn't even know a store to put down.

Her completed resume looked incomplete. She added some of her skills that weren't earned with her degrees and hoped it would be enough to be considered for the job. She sent her resume with a pleasant email, but she doubted she'd hear anything.

Ag called her as Emma was lying down for a nap. Celeste grabbed the phone before it could disturb her cranky toddler.

"Hey, Ag. How's your mother?"

A silence followed that worried Celeste. "Ag? What's happened?"

It must have been the rising panic in her voice that caused Ag to answer quickly.

"Mama's okay. She's not the reason I'm calling you."

Celeste waited for Ag to get through the heavy emotion in her voice. "It's David. They've charged him."

Celeste cringed. Not only had she known David had been charged, but she'd neglected to tell Ag about David's visitation. She decided the best way to go forward was to be honest, and as expected, Ag didn't take it well.

"Did you ever think to tell me?" she yelled over the receiver. "I'm his next of kin!"

"I don't have an excuse," Celeste told her. "I'm sorry."

"If I weren't in a hospital lobby, I'd tell you exactly where you could stick your 'sorry'." She took several audible breaths. "But I've been in the hospital for a long time, and washing off in the staff's shower and drinking day-old coffee may put me a little more on edge than usual."

"I was in the wrong," Celeste told her. "To be honest, all I could think about was getting to see him."

"What did he say?" Ag asked.

"He thinks he's going to prison for a long time."

Ag didn't speak for a moment. When she did, she sounded grave. "He's probably right."

Ag and David had inherited their mother's pessimism. Maybe it was more practical than negative, but Celeste wasn't willing to accept it.

"I've got to get back to Mama, so I'm gonna need you to do a favor for me."

"What?" Celeste was eager to help, as anything she did helped justify her presence in the Winsomes' home.

"I need you to call Mindy. Tell her she is not visiting my brother this Saturday."

Celeste's body tensed with the thought of telling Mindy that she wasn't allowed to see her boyfriend. "Since the two of you had him all to yourselves during the last visit," Ag went on, "I'll take your part of her visit and her part, too." She clicked her tongue like she had just remembered something. "And let her know I will be handling my brother's finances and his attorney."

Celeste decided she needed to respond, so she said, "Okay."

"You asked about Mama," Ag said. "She's stabilized, but that's all."

"I hope she improves," Celeste offered.

"I'll call you later," Ag clipped. "Thank you for bringing the flowers."

She ended the call before Celeste could utter another word.

While Emma was still napping, Celeste moved onto the front porch. The air held a subtle chill, but birds were singing.

She dialed Mindy and repeated Ag's message to her. She waited for her to erupt.

"Is this a way for you to keep me from seeing David?" Mindy asked.

"No." Celeste expected her reply. "You can drive down on Saturday morning and watch Ag go into the visitation building."

"I don't need to do that," Mindy said. "It hurts me that Ag wants to take away my visit with David just because you forgot to tell her about it."

Celeste was stung and emotionally exhausted. She hardly recognized the words as they tumbled out of her mouth.

"Well, I guess Ag and David will decide whether you get to see him," she said, coming as close to Mindy's words as possible. "Oh, and your college friend is off the case. Ag is going to handle her brother's money and defense."

"I see." Mindy's voice had an edge to it, but she didn't follow up on it.

They spoke strained farewells, and Celeste ended the call. She walked inside, running straight up the steps and into David's room.

Surrounded by his smell, she cried into his pillow, pausing only to grab mouthfuls of air between sobs.

How could she have had everything she wanted and lost it so quickly?

She wished Mindy wasn't pregnant, but that wasn't the only thing that kept David from her. He was in jail, and he'd committed a crime with his hands that she was certain her grandfather had planted into his mind.

She hated her grandfather for it. He had seen her happiness on his Predictor, and he'd jerked her out of it. *Why? Why couldn't he have left her in the best place for her?*

She was his investment. In reality, Celeste doubted her grandfather had ever thought of her as a granddaughter. When she was young, she'd been an experiment. He'd schooled her and written about her progress. As an adult, though, he'd used her, and once he'd deemed she was valuable, he thought of her as an asset.

Did she have a safe place? She remembered feeling safe with her father, but Celeste no longer felt like their apartment was her home after he died. Bill and David had fully embraced her when she arrived at their home, but no one really wanted her at the Winsome house now. David asked her to stay there, as it was a convenient place for Emma to remain under the watchful eyes of his family. If Celeste wasn't Emma's mother, she'd have nowhere to go.

Celeste wished she had a haven. Much like Mrs. Winsome when her brother was killed, Celeste wanted to get away from anything that reminded her of the Winsomes. She waited until Emma opened her eyes and she left.

Emma brushed her doll's hair as Celeste drove. She turned away from Erwin, not caring that the man she loved and his family were in the opposite direction.

Celeste wanted to get away from her problems, but she moved into a new set of troubles. She had seen Braeden's baby in the future, and she had to find a way to tell him. By the time the dogwood trees that lined Braeden's mother's street came into view, Celeste had lost her resolve. She was ready to turn around when she noticed a woman sitting on her front porch.

When Celeste had been in Hailey's body, she had called her Aunt Lynn, but Caroline wouldn't know the woman. She pulled Emma out of her car seat, fastening a coat around her as she walked to the porch.

Aunt Lynn watched them with a benign smile. Celeste remembered her agreeableness, and she would have treated her as an approaching guest, but something was missing in her dark eyes.

"Hello," Celeste called to her from the porch steps. Aunt Lynn had a blanket draped across her legs, and she seemed unaffected by the chilly afternoon. She bid Celeste to sit next to her on a metal glider. Celeste took the seat she offered her, wincing as the cold metal seemed to go through her thin jeans.

"Are you Mrs.—"

"Call me Lynn," the woman said with a smile.

"Lynn, I'm looking for Braeden Hall—"

"Braeden!" she said. "He's such a sweet boy. He helps me in the kitchen when Hailey and Robert play their little war games."

Her statement threw off Celeste. Lynn had been nostalgic for the times when Hailey, Braeden, and her nephew, Robert, were young, but she'd never referred to their childhood antics in the present tense.

"Could you tell me where Braeden lives?" she tried.

"Why, he lives two houses down with his parents." She nodded toward the property where Celeste had stayed for several months when she'd thought she was Hailey Hall.

It hit Celeste that Trish was experiencing a cognitive decline. "Okay. Thank you."

"Why are you looking for Braeden?" she asked, reaching out to stroke Emma's cheek. "This one is too little for a play date with a boy his age."

Celeste reached for an answer, unwilling to upset the lady's delicate grasp of time. "I found one of his jackets, and I'm going to return it to him."

Lynn seemed pensive. "That's so unlike him. He never loses anything."

Celeste panicked. She thought about clarifying her explanation until the lines smoothed on Lynn's face and she patted Celeste's hand. "There's a first time for everything, isn't there?"

Now that Celeste had inhabited several bodies in her lifetime, she couldn't agree more.

She glanced at the time. Forgetting she was mostly a stranger to Lynn, she spoke with the knowledge she'd gained from her time as Hailey.

"I guess we'd better go. It's almost time for you to make dinner for your husband."

There was a trace of cognition in her brown eyes. "Dan will be alright. I'll just whip up some shepherd's pie."

She said her goodbyes, thanking Lynn for her information about Braeden. Before she left, Lynn grabbed her hand.

"The people from the future will be here soon."

Celeste drew her face into a somber expression and nodded. Even though Celeste had tried to go along with Lynn's hallucination, the lady guessed she was putting her on and her posture fell.

Celeste walked Emma to her car as the toddler bounced her doll up her mother's arm. Celeste didn't expect Lynn to follow her.

After she buckled Emma into her car seat, she turned around and almost ran into Lynn.

She had draped a blanket around her shoulders, and her expression was clear. "Tell him Dan and I know what he's done, and he won't get away with it."

Chapter 14

Celeste pulled into the driveway at the top of the hill. From that angle, she hoped to see Braeden's vehicle without him locking onto the car that he believed had belonged to his sister. It was almost six o'clock, and if his mother expected him for dinner that evening, he would be arriving soon.

Celeste tried to organize her thoughts about her experience with Lynn. Lynn hadn't had the same mental edge she'd had when Hailey had visited her the previous year, but she'd spoken with undeniable clarity. Celeste got the feeling Lynn knew Celeste wasn't from her time frame. On the other hand, though, the woman's brain was rapidly deteriorating, so she could have made a vague reference to a show she'd watched.

Braeden's car turned onto the road, and Celeste slouched in her seat. He got out of the car alone.

Celeste wondered if Macey was still in the hospital, but she decided that Braeden's wife was probably at home, avoiding the dinners with her abrasive mother-in-law.

Celeste played "I Spy" with Emma while they waited. A child under two shouldn't have recognized the colors Celeste called out, but her heart almost stopped when Emma picked out letters, too.

She stared into her child's deep blue eyes. "You know more than you let on."

It was a statement, not a question, and Emma smiled with jagged teeth.

Celeste was ready to have a deeper moment with her daughter, but Braeden came out of his mother's house balancing a paper plate of food in his hand. Celeste rushed to put Emma back into her car seat and drove after Braeden.

She tried to drive a respectable distance behind him, but Braeden wound down so many streets she couldn't mask her intentions and continued to follow him. Finally, he stopped at a modest ranch-style home in the middle of an open subdivision. Another car was parked in the carport, but it looked like it hadn't been moved for a while. Stacked boxes sat behind it.

Celeste gathered her courage and stepped out of her car before he could go inside. He almost dropped the plate of food when he saw her.

"How did you—" he started before he sneered. "You're done! I'll ruin you, and you'll never be able to crawl out of the hole I bury you in."

Macey opened the door, and she stood there with great effort, swaying. Braeden put the food on the hood of his car and ran to help his wife.

Once Braeden was holding her up, Macey asked Celeste, "Who are you?" She turned to face Braeden. "Are you sleeping with her?"

Braeden and Celeste answered her at the same time. Macey appeared skeptical. "But you've been at your office late, and—"

"I know where your baby is," Celeste blurted.

Macey's attention turned to her before she started slapping Braeden's arm. "You *are* sleeping with her! She took our baby!"

"No," Celeste said, moving from the street into their yard. She stressed her hands in a downward gesture, hoping Macey would lower her voice. "I know who took him, though."

"Why haven't you called the police?" She repeated her question to Braeden.

"She's just looking for money, Mace."

Macey pointed to Celeste's car. "But she's driving Hailey's car. How do you know her?" She crossed her arms and the action almost threw her off balance. Braeden reached for her, but Macey batted his hand away.

Braeden sighed. "Fine. She approached me after Hailey's funeral. She tried to come on to me, but I pushed her away. That was when I learned she was pregnant."

Macey jerked her thumb at the Volkswagon on the curb. "That girl is too old—"

"She was pregnant with another one," Braeden interrupted. "A couple of months later, she offered me her baby to replace the one we lost."

Macey's fists flew to her sides. "I didn't lose him! If anyone lost him, it was the nurses at the hospital!"

Braeden raised his hands in submission. "I know, sweetheart. You were fighting for your life, and I should have followed him to the nursery."

Macey's posture softened. "You didn't know what would happen."

He approached her and Macey allowed him to hold her.

"I was afraid I was going to lose you."

When he spoke, it was sincere, but Macey pulled away. "It's okay."

Celeste felt uncomfortable, but she had come to Braeden's house with a purpose, and she intended to fulfill it. "I really know where he is. He has one green eye and one blue eye, and his skin is the same color as Macey's."

Macey and Braeden glanced at each other. Macey took the lead. "Then why didn't you go to the police?" She took a shaky step to the stairs that emptied into the yard. "Better yet, why don't you take me to my son?"

"I wish it were that easy," Celeste said. She stood her ground, even though Macey's face contorted with rage. "He's in a facility overseen by Dr. Alexander Maze."

The color drained from Braeden's face. He stared at Celeste in shock.

Macey had stumbled to Celeste, and she saw the visible marks she'd gotten in the wreck. Black stitches rested against her neck and collarbone, and weakness wasn't the only reason for her unsteady steps. She'd had an injury to her hip, and she cupped the area when she walked.

Celeste had little time to react when Macey grabbed her wrist with surprising strength. "You will take me to the doctor who has Gable."

Celeste sucked in a breath. She'd been ready to defend herself, but the child's name was too much for her to process. Macey took the opportunity to throw Celeste onto the ground. She hardly felt the woman's slaps and punches. She instinctively covered her face, but she cried out in pain when Macey's fist connected with her ribs.

The hit was enough to bring her back to the moment, and she slung Macey off her. She stood up, breathing heavily.

Braeden rushed to his wife. She was surprised that he wasn't screaming at her.

She walked back to her car, but before she got inside, Braeden called after her. She looked up, narrowing her eyes at him.

"I'll be in touch."

Emma didn't seem affected by the display. "Mommy, okay?" she asked.

"I'm fine," Celeste assured her. "It was a big misunderstanding."

She realized too late that her daughter might not understand her word choice, but a quick look in the mirror confirmed Emma wasn't confused. She brushed her doll's hair again.

Celeste settled into her thoughts. As she drove, she thought about her father. He'd been the most influential person in her life, and she missed him. She knew he could solve all her problems with a passive approach.

He was passive to a fault. It made him easy for her grandfather to control, but he used to provide the most eloquent solutions to her problems.

Braeden may have been surprised by the mention of her grandfather, but Celeste had been shocked when Macey had said her baby's name.

The name itself was a strong enough coincidence, as she'd only met one other person with the name *Gable*, but there was something more. A memory sparked, and she recalled a time when they had passed a football in their front yard.

Her father had blinked after he'd caught a strong pass, and his contact had flipped out. After an unsuccessful crawl across the ground in search of it, he ran into the house to find another one.

He only wore the contact outside their home, as he didn't need it to see clearly. He only wore it to make both of his eyes the same color.

Her father had one green eye and one blue eye, and his name was Gable.

Chapter 15

Celeste had thoughts in the back of her mind as she treated her bruises and a scratch that resulted from her scuffle with Macey. Emma seemed puzzled by her changed appearance, but she stroked her face as she fell asleep.

Celeste experienced far from a restful night.

None of the timelines matched her hypothesis. Her father had lived in *her* timeline, and he was dead. *Even though there was a baby that matched his name and eye condition, didn't her father belong to her grandfather and grandmother?*

She thought about the space in the foyer where her grandmother's picture had once hung. Movey Shelton's father had painted it, and his business relationship with her grandfather had allowed her to get to know Movey better.

She had seen a portrait of her father, grandfather, and grandmother when he was a teenager, and he hadn't covered the colors in his eyes. Heterochromia was passed down the genetic line, but her grandparents didn't have it. *Was he somehow adopted?*

No, Celeste thought. Her eyes were only one color, and he had definitely been her father. Furthermore, the timeline would have been too confusing for the baby in her grandfather's nursery to be her father.

It seemed too much to wrap her head around, and she finally decided it was a coincidence.

She couldn't sleep, so she wandered back to Mrs. Winsome's room. She picked up the oldest journal and read through a few mundane entries until she came to one that held her interest.

I don't know how much longer I can stay with Danny. On Saturdays, the facility has movies on a projector and on Sundays, a chaplain holds a small church service. Other than the drills, it's the only time my group leaves our living quarters and lab.
Danny thinks of the movie and church service as a date, and he embarrasses me by telling everyone that I'm his girl. To my surprise, it irritates Al.
Al finds little ways to mention Danny's possessiveness as we work together. I steer him away from the topic, but he's right. Danny's presumptions are becoming too much for me.
I'm finding it hard to come up with a reason to break up with Danny. He never asked me to go steady with him, so why should I have to come up with a scripted breakup?

Celeste read the next page, already knowing what would be on it. Mrs. Winsome had never been good at holding in her feelings.

I did it. I should feel elated, but I don't. In fact, I feel like a terrible person.
Danny cleared the lab last night. We ate our dinners in relative silence, so that should have given me a clue about his intentions. He was sweaty and nervous, but instead of making the obvious conclusion, I asked him if he was sick.
He led me around to the other side of the lab, and our friends had decorated it with flowers and a homemade congratulatory sign.

I thought I had been promoted. Even as I wrote the last sentence, I was shaking my head. Yes, I have a revolutionary idea, but we're still a week away from actually testing my work.

Danny's hand was trembling, but he held onto mine as he got down on one knee. I felt the gentle tug as he moved to the floor, and it got my attention.

"I want you to be my wife," he said.

I had a hard enough time trying to understand what he was doing, but once I did, his proposal irked me. He hadn't asked me to be his wife. He had simply told me what he wanted. I saw my opportunity, and I took it.

"What's that supposed to mean?" I asked him with the hand he wasn't holding on my hip. "You 'want' me to be your wife?"

The poor boy fumbled for an answer. "I-I'm sorry. I don't know how to say it. I've never watched romance movies."

I didn't soften, though I wish I had. "You don't have to watch romantic movies to know you're supposed to *ask* the woman to marry you."

He was still on the ground, holding my hand hostage. "Isn't that what I did?"

I jerked my hand away. "No, you did not, and even if you had, the answer is 'no'."

It took him a moment, but he got up and dusted the imaginary dirt off the knee of his pants. "It's been a year. I thought you'd be happy."

Had we been going out for a year? I decided it didn't matter.

"How would you know? We don't have a date to go by because you never asked me to go steady with you."

Some mirth lit up his face. "Is that what this is about? Eleanor, you know I've called you my girl since our first date, and that's why I asked you to marry me today. It's been one year since our first date."

I'd been glad to have the moral high ground, but his recollection of our date and the proposal itself was diminishing my argument. I had to think of something fast. I fumbled through my mind and spoke before I thought of the repercussions.

"I love someone else."

It was the truth because Bill will always be in my heart, but I wish I would have told a lie. I watched Danny's spirit crumble.

"Y-You what?"

I had said it, so I stuck to it. "I love someone else."

He ran a hand through his hair, which had gotten a little long, and I thought I noticed tears in his eyes. "How?"

He'd choked out the word, and it was the first time I felt truly guilty for what I was doing. I steeled my nerve.

"You never asked me to go steady with you, so I had no reason to think you were serious."

It was a terrible excuse, and we both knew it.

"I thought you were a little distant." He cracked a smile. "You're the first girl I couldn't talk into making out with me. But I thought it was because your brother had—"

"Don't bring up David!" I shouted.

At the sound of my raised voice, Linda came out. Steve followed her, putting a hand on her shoulder.

Danny didn't seem to notice our audience. "Can we talk about it? I'm willing to do anything to make it right."

I remember crossing my arms, but I'm not clear about what I said. I think I told Danny I would never marry him. It was his reaction that haunts me.

I've never been a bully, but I feel like a villain. I watched him walk away with a hanging head and a broken heart. Linda stared at him with concern and then shook her head at me. She and Steve condemned me with their eyes, and I deserved it.

When I realized Danny had feelings for me, I'd stayed with him because I didn't want to hurt him. I realize now that I was being selfish. I should have been up front with him about my feelings as soon as I realized he thought highly of me. In waiting to tell him, I didn't just break his heart. I damaged his soul.

Celeste couldn't help but wonder if David had done the same with her. *Though their reunion had been short-lived, had he only toyed with her emotions because he woke up with her in his bed?*

Maybe his mother had counseled him to break up with women cleanly, as he did it quickly as conditions changed. He'd broken off things with her when she was Hailey after Braeden had announced her engagement in the Winsomes' living room, and he told her about his plan to go back to Mindy immediately after he found out she was pregnant.

No. It didn't feel right. David was driven by duty, and it came from his father. David broke up with Hailey because he didn't want to covet another man's fiancée, and he broke up with her again as he wanted to be present for Mindy during her pregnancy.

Celeste wished he could have been with her while she was pregnant with Emma. Zam had been great, but she didn't love him. She wanted so badly to share that experience with David, but Mindy would get that pleasure, and she'd keep him for the rest of her life.

Celeste laughed at herself. Actually, Mindy wouldn't have a man by her side as she went through her pregnancy. She would deliver the baby without David's help, as he would be in jail, and according to the sentencing she'd looked up, he'd stay incarcerated until the baby was an adult.

Celeste flipped to the next page, deciding it would be the last entry she read that night. She was glad she hadn't closed the book.

Al has been as happy as a little bird for weeks. Our small group is strained, and Danny works mostly by himself at night, but Al seems to think it's a much better arrangement.

Danny found a girl in food service, and he sits with her on Saturdays and Sundays. He made a display of kissing her just outside the doors to the chapel, and I could hear her giggling all the way down the hall.

Just like Bill's wife, she's blonde, and it seems they both get the same shade from the drugstore.

My mother wrote to me, and even though she sent it over a month ago, I just got the letter. She spoke of the war effort and her volunteer work, but I skimmed over it. I'm involved in a project with the defense department, but I don't want to hear about the war.

She wrote about community projects and church luncheons, and she mentioned seeing Becky Winsome with her baby girl. It's hard to think about Bill with another woman, but he has a family now.

My mama said Becky talks about the way he acted with the baby when he could take leave. Bill was lucky. Most men won't get to meet their children until the end of the war, but he got to hold her and dance around with her.

It was hard for me to think about. It could have been me in Becky's place. Bill and I could have a darling daughter.

My mama was disappointed in the way I treated Bill, so she filled up a page about his family. She talked about how happy his parents were to welcome the new baby and how Dot, Becky's sister, helps her with late-night feedings and diaper changes. My mama wrote Dot may end up an old maid unless the Bailey boy marries her, so her sister's children may be the only ones she will hold.

I understood her meaning. My mother wishes I would have kept Bill, but she wants me to focus on marriage. I'm her only hope for grandchildren.

Even the people who were hungry for war are tired of it. Rations have dwindled, and some families are starving, even with plentiful livestock and vegetable gardens.

I keep wondering if they will reveal the weapon soon. I know that's what they're developing. The same loose-lipped member of the personnel who revealed Einstein's letter to the president let it slip.

Our brave Commander-in-Chief's health is failing. He doesn't try to walk anymore, and I've seen a picture of him in a wheelchair. War carries a price, and as the man who makes the decisions that affect us all, the heavy burden has weighed on his health.

I agree with the mumblers. The war has gone on too long, and it has taken many lives.

Linda told me that her father had lost a younger brother, her uncle, last week to the war, and he isn't taking it well. It's difficult for her mother. She has to keep up with the housework and make sure the crops are maintained.

There was a break on the page. Jagged print replaced Mrs. Winsome's curly script.

I got another letter from my father, and he dated it a few days after the one my mother wrote. Bill's troop was attacked, and his leg was blown off. He's in a hospital in Switzerland.

I should say he *was* there.

For years, Switzerland was impartial in the war. The horrible dictator must have gotten tired of their neutrality, and he struck them. The hospital was bombed, along with other important sites.

Bill couldn't move from his bed, so he died in the attack.

Chapter 16

The next page went into her grief for Bill. Her superior didn't release Mrs. Winsome from her project so she could attend Bill's funeral, so she mourned him in her room.

She kept flipping pages, but Bill was still dead. She viewed dates long after the war's end, but Mrs. Winsome still wrote about him in the past tense.

Celeste tried to understand what she was reading. *Could Bill have been in the rubble and mistakenly identified as someone else?* It didn't seem so, as Mrs. Winsome wrote that his friends and neighbors had been able to "look upon him" at his viewing while she had to remain in the Secret City.

Was there another Bill Winsome?

That possibility seemed unlikely. A quick check of the census in the area at the time confirmed it. He and his father were the only William "Bill" Winsomes.

Celeste checked her memory. She had met David's father. They had broken bread at the kitchen table, and he had officiated her marriage to David.

Another possibility entered her mind. *Had her grandfather erased him somehow? Was David a different person who belonged to another father?*

She bolted up the stairs and into David's room. Two pictures stood proudly on his dresser, and relief washed over her when she recognized the man with his hand on David's shoulder.

"Thank God," she said aloud.

She held the picture against her chest and sat on David's bed. It creaked under her weight.

"What is going on?"

Bill Winsome had been alive, but he had died in Mrs. Winsome's journal. Unless the time hops had frazzled her brain and affected her experiences, Bill hadn't died.

Maybe someone who looked a lot like him had been found, and it had taken years to discover it. By then, Becky may have moved to another state with a new husband, and that would explain why he had eventually married Mrs. Winsome.

What about his daughter, though? Bill never would have abandoned a child.

Perhaps the girl had developed a bond with her stepfather, and he didn't want to ruin it. It seemed like the only rational explanation.

Satisfied with her thoughts and where they landed, Celeste placed the picture back on the dresser and crept down the stairs.

When she joined Emma on the couch, the sleepy toddler woke up long enough to extend the blanket to her mother. Celeste stroked her daughter's hair until she fell asleep again.

She tried to forget about what she'd read and reaffirmed her theory in her head. Bill was alive after the attack. They buried a man who looked like him.

It had to be true, but it still wasn't right. Bill's leg had been missing. *Had the other man's leg been missing, too?*

What about the attack on Switzerland? She'd never read about that in any of her history books. Maybe it was military information that was considered classified information.

But that didn't make sense either. It had been Mrs. Winsome's father who had told her about Bill's death, and he had been a civilian.

Someone had to be messing with the timeline. *But to what end?*

There were simply too many unanswerable questions, and it was pushing on Celeste's brain. She took deep breaths, concentrating on the darkness behind her eyes, and hoped she was wrong.

Chapter 17

Celeste and Emma were eating breakfast when Ag breezed through the back door. Her appearance startled them, and they both cried out.

Ag embraced Emma, assuring her she wasn't an intruder. "I guess you guys are a little isolated up here."

Celeste pointed toward the nearest neighbor. "I can hear his lawn mower, but I don't know how your mother could have heard his television."

Ag smiled sadly. "She had the ears of a bat."

Celeste's breath caught in her throat. "Is she—"

Ag shook her head. "No, Mama is doing the same. She hasn't woken up, but I think she knows I'm there."

Celeste waited until her breathing returned to normal before she spoke. "I cleaned her room."

Ag nodded. "I'm sorry you had to do it. The sheriff mentioned a cleaning service, but I completely forgot about calling them."

"I didn't mind," Celeste cut in quickly. "It made me feel useful."

Ag motioned for Celeste to step into the living room with her. "I'm sorry about the way I behaved on the phone. I'm glad you got to see my brother. Did he look okay?"

"As well as can be expected."

"That's a diplomatic answer."

Celeste shrugged. "He's convinced himself that his life is over. He's cutting ties and getting ready to spend his life in prison."

Ag turned her face, but Celeste saw a tear run off her nose. "It's hard. I love him, but he tried to kill Mama."

Celeste embraced her, but Ag stayed rigid in her arms. "I think if you search your heart, you'll know he didn't do it."

Ag shrugged her off. "Face facts, Caroline. He was caught with the knife he used to stab our mother with in his hand. He did it."

"Maybe there was an intruder."

Ag shook her, surprising them both. "There was no intruder. I don't know if he did it to get more money for himself and Mindy or if he was only sleepwalking, but he did it."

She let go of Celeste and wiped her eyes resolutely. "I need to grab a few things, then I'll be on my way." She turned on her heel and marched into Mrs. Winsome's room.

Celeste was at the kitchen table when she came out. "I see you found Mama's stories."

Celeste's eyebrows went up.

Ag pointed to Mrs. Winsome's room. "Her notebooks. They were full of stories she wrote."

"She dated them like journals."

Ag laughed dryly. "Yeah. Mama wrote those while she waited for Daddy to come home from the war. She made up stories to keep her mind occupied after I fell asleep at night."

Celeste's blood ran cold. "They were all made up?"

Ag lifted a suitcase she'd packed before heading into her room. "Definitely. You didn't think my mama was part of the Manhattan Project, did you?"

Celeste shook her head, and Ag went into her room. Actually, Celeste had known Mrs. Winsome hadn't been part of the major project in the Secret City, as her work had stated she handled one of the smaller projects.

Ag stopped on her way out the door. "You can go with me to see David on Saturday."

"Are you sure Mindy won't mind?" she asked.

Ag smiled. "I think she'll mind a lot, but I don't care. My brother loves you."

Celeste thought she was finished, and she turned her head to hide her blush.

"Keep reading Mama's writings if you want," Ag called. "You'll really like the part where Steve time travels."

Celeste could hardly breathe. *Did she hear Ag correctly? Did Steve actually time travel?*

"No," Celeste said, causing Emma to jump in the otherwise quiet room.

She stopped short of Mrs. Winsome's door. "She said they were just stories."

Saying the words out loud seemed to confirm them.

"Mommy?"

Celeste picked up her daughter, marveling at her heaviness. "You're getting bigger, aren't you?"

Emma nodded emphatically. "I'm so big."

Celeste was used to Emma's speech patterns, but she recognized the developmental leap. Emma should not have been able to talk to her that easily until she was over two, but she was still a few months away from her second birthday.

Guessing from her height, speech, and developing fine motor skills, Emma was almost two and a half years old. She wished she could shrug it off, but her growth was becoming noticeable. At her current growth rate, Emma would be five years old by the end of the year.

"I love you," she told her child.

"Love, too, Mommy."

Emma ran off to play with blocks, and Celeste took a moment to weed through her email. A response from the hospital surprised her.

Fiona Sanders from the human resources department had requested an interview with her. The available days and times were listed. Celeste wanted to choose the one for the next day, but she didn't have anyone she knew who could watch Emma.

An hour later, Mindy called. "Did Fiona call you yet?"

"She emailed me."

"When are you going to go for your interview?" Mindy seemed more excited than Celeste.

"I was going to take the time for tomorrow, but I don't have anyone to watch Emma."

"I'll do it," Mindy volunteered.

Celeste knew it was a good idea. She could trust Mindy, and Emma knew her, but she didn't want David's girlfriend to watch her daughter.

She closed her eyes. She was going to have to accept Mindy's involvement. David was going to be in jail for a long time, and Mindy was having Emma's brother or sister. They were going to have to rely on each other.

"Okay. Don't you have to work, though?"

"I do," Mindy said. "But I'll take my lunch at whatever time your interview is scheduled."

"Are you sure? I think the earliest time is after one."

"I'll be fine," Mindy assured her. "We always have snacks at the nurses' desk, and everyone is really understanding."

Celeste responded to the message and requested a two o'clock meeting. It surprised her when she received an email within the hour confirming her interview.

Celeste was restless that night, and even though she tried to sleep, she lay awake well after midnight. She dipped into more of Mrs. Winsome's words to take her mind off her job interview.

That man is infuriating! I think God Almighty placed here him to test my patience.

Al won't listen to me. He questions everything I say, even though I'm right, and he won't wash beakers.

Who is he? Does he think he's some sort of prince? Well, his only kingdom is in his head and the dignitary is a fool.

I know exactly what I'm doing, but he creeps into my conversations with Liz and Linda, and he contradicts me. Sometimes, they seem like they understand his concerns, but other times, I

think he's just picking on me because he doesn't
see me as his equal.

In other news, Steve finally revealed his
purpose, and we were all stunned. I tried not
to worry about his life or health, but Linda was
in tears. She doesn't want him to leave her for
any length of time. They aren't married, but
Steve and Linda have been living like a married
couple for almost a year. I say nothing when I
see him leave her room, as I know he's given her
a ring, but I hope they're careful. Her father
is the type who will demand a shotgun wedding.

Linda told me Steve had revealed a big confidence. I don't know how he could have a bigger
secret than his role in our mission, but he is
secretive. No matter how hard I tried, Linda
was tight-lipped about it.

Danny shocked us by coming out of his room
during the day. He listened to me explain my
idea, and he started typing a program on his
computer. It took several weeks to design the
program, but he thinks we're ready to move
forward.

Al is completely against it. I don't think he
believed in the assignment's validity, but now
that Steve has a clearly defined mission, Al has
been more vocal about his feelings. We haven't
gotten through a meal in the last week without
him listing all the ways we'll fail.

Liz and I were yelling, and Steve stopped us.
He didn't exactly come to Al's defense, but he
made us stop arguing. I wish he would have left
it alone. If Liz and I don't get the last word,
Al goes around for days with his beak higher in
the air.

We're set to proceed next month, and none of
Al's concerns will stop us.

He tried to talk to a superior officer about it, but they laughed at him. Everyone else wants our team to succeed, as our success would end the war—or maybe erase it from our history.

Chapter 18

Celeste wrung her hands as she waited for Fiona Sanders. The woman had taken a late lunch, but her secretary directed her to her office to wait.

Celeste had left Emma with Mindy in the emergency room. They planned to go to the cafeteria, as Emma had said she wanted fries.

"I'm sorry to keep you waiting." The lady joined her, wearing a smart pastel green suit that stressed her flaming red hair.

"That's okay, Mrs. Sanders."

She sat in her chair, smiling at Celeste with bright red lips. "Call me Fiona."

Fiona stared at her laptop screen, scrolling with her trackpad. "It doesn't look like you have a lot of experience."

"I don't," Celeste admitted.

Fiona looked up at her. "There are many people here who remember what Willie Jones did."

Celeste cringed involuntarily. "He was a horrible human being."

Fiona's eyebrows went up when she used the past tense verb. "Did he die?"

"No, but he's dead to me."

Fiona nodded. "Well, Caroline, what can you offer Oak Health?"

She raised an eyebrow. "I thought this was Unicoi County Hospital."

Fiona laughed. "Yes, Honey. But Oak Heath Care owns the hospital."

Celeste acknowledged her explanation and went into a prepared speech about values and principles that aligned with the company's mission statement. It sounded scripted but not robotic.

Fiona held a pen in her hand, occasionally clicking it. "That all sounds good."

Fiona clicked a few more places on her computer. "I see you've listed Ag Winsome and Kerry Shelton as references. They're both good people."

Celeste watched Fiona survey her screen until she thought she was going to burst. It could have been minutes or seconds, but her nerves were putting her on edge.

"Can you start on Monday?"

Celeste almost lost her breath. "Monday?"

She thought she'd have to go through a two-part interview like she did when she was Hailey, but the custodial positions may have had a different process. Finding childcare for Emma would be a challenge, but she could work on it after she knew her schedule.

"I can start on Monday."

Fiona smiled at her. "Good. You'll need to come in a little early so Mindy can show you the rounds."

Celeste leaned forward. "Mindy knows about custodial work."

Fiona laughed, and the sound was almost a melody. "Nurses wear many hats, but she won't be showing you the custodial closet."

Fiona noticed her bewilderment. "What job did you think you were applying for?"

Celeste thought back to the form she filled out online. "I completed the application for the custodial position. Mindy told me about it."

Fiona nodded. "We have a custodial position available, but I thought with your new accreditation you'd want the nurse position."

Celeste treaded carefully. When Hailey had been her host, Celeste had completed the requirements, but as far as she knew, everyone thought Caroline had dropped out after her battle with the flu.

"You have my records?"

Fiona turned her laptop in her direction. A certificate with Caroline's name was on the screen. A quick scan made Celeste's heart drop.

"LPN?"

Fiona smiled in response, as she hadn't seen Celeste's reaction as a question. "You put in the work, so why shouldn't you have the rewards?"

Celeste wasn't familiar with everything in her current time period, but she was certain that it took more than a couple of months of classes to make a person an LPN. She stayed quiet, wondering if her grandfather had interfered somehow.

Fiona brought out a stack of papers and went over each one, having Celeste sign in the appropriate places. When they finished the obligatory procedures, Fiona asked if she had questions.

"What is my schedule?"

Fiona sighed, and it was the first time she lost her positivity. "Since you live with the Winsomes, I won't dance around the subject." She leaned forward in her chair, but she didn't lower her voice. "Since David's arrest, we've had to do some major reshuffling. Mindy told me you'd need to rely on each other for childcare, and it seems easiest to keep her on the day shift and move you to the night shift on the same days she works."

The first thought that entered her mind was Mindy thought they needed each other for childcare. After a few seconds, she dismissed her qualms, as Mindy had been right to assume it.

Her next thought concerned sleep. *How was she going to sleep enough to keep going* and *still spend time with Emma?*

Fiona rose from her seat, signaling an end to their meeting. "Welcome to the team, Caroline."

On the way back to the ER, Celeste thought about the mysterious certification. *There were ways for Dr. Maze to plant certain documents, but why would he help her?* The only answer was that he wanted her at the ER for a reason.

Mindy handed over Emma as soon as Celeste entered the nurse's station. "How did it go?" Her smile showed that she already knew about the outcome.

"I have a job as a nurse."

Mindy clapped her hands. "That's great! I have to admit, though, that Fiona told me about it before you came in today. I knew the job was already yours, but she swore me to secrecy." She mimicked zipping her lips.

"I'm supposed to have you show me the rounds on Monday."

Mindy said something to another nurse and returned her attention to Celeste. "Yes! You'll need to run through the day with me, so you'll be able to assist the nurses on the night shift."

Celeste cocked her head. "But if we're both working, who will watch our children? Ag can't—"

"Oh! I'd never dream of asking Ag. I have a sweet lady who watches my boys when they get out of school. I'm sure she'll look after Emma for a day."

Celeste adjusted Emma's weight on her hip. "I'm not sure I feel comfortable with that. Emma doesn't know her—"

"She can meet her today," Mindy suggested. "And it's only one day." She leaned in and whispered. "To tell the truth, she's very expensive. It'll be a huge relief not to have the expense."

David's girlfriend could wipe away Celeste's concerns in a moment. Her easy-going character made it feel like they had known each other for years.

Mindy had helped her with the job, and she seemed to have an answer for all of Celeste's immediate problems. "Okay. I'll meet her."

Mindy patted her arm. "Great! "If you'll come back here at seven, you can follow me to her house."

Celeste agreed, and she and Emma left. As they walked out the doors, her experience felt bittersweet. It appeared everything was working out, but she knew her grandfather was always watching his Predictor, and he'd be ready to upend her new life at any moment.

Chapter 19

Doris was Mindy's babysitter. Celeste recognized her, and she knew Caroline, but she was good with Emma, so Celeste decided Doris's opinions of Caroline didn't matter.

She talked to Emma about her changing schedule, and since she was only going to be staying with Doris for a day, Celeste focused on Mindy. She hoped it would be an easy transition for her daughter.

"Do you like Mindy?"

Her toddler stacked yellow blocks. She stopped and nodded without looking at her mother.

"Would you be okay if she watched you while Mommy went to work?"

Emma grabbed one of the red blocks, but it didn't join the yellow ones. She dropped it and brought her hands to her eyes.

"No, Mommy. No work."

Celeste stroked her daughter's hair. "I know. Change is hard, and I don't want to be away from you either, but I have to work to make a better life for us."

Emma buried her head in Celeste's hair. She held her baby for the rest of the evening, and it was almost a relief when Emma closed her eyes for the night.

Celeste crept into Mrs. Winsome's room, carefully inching the door over the carpet. It rubbed, making an odd static sound.

I'm tired. Actually, I think I might be hungover.

I have had nothing to drink in ages, but we gave Steve a big send-off, so we drank a bottle of liquor Danny bought from someone who smuggled it into the facility. It tasted like liquid fire, and it burned my belly, but I had more than my fair share.

Linda doesn't handle alcohol well. She was already upset about Steve's trip, but she drank several shots before Steve stopped her. She called him another name, and he decided it was time for her to go to bed.

Linda resisted, so he held her hand as she swayed in her seat and carried her to her room when she passed out on his shoulder.

When he returned to our little party, Liz turned on the radio, and we took turns dancing with the men. It was a little awkward to dance with Danny, but he smiled at me as if we were old friends. It could have been the alcohol, but I think he's forgiven me.

After the merriment, we each told Steve how much we cared for him. Even Al teared up a little. Al is closer to Danny than he is to any other member of our group.

Steve shared why the project was so important to him. His father was in the First World War, and he died. His death was painful. The enemy had tortured him until it was clear he would not reveal pertinent information.

After his father died, his mother met another soldier. She let the soldier abuse him and his little brother. Steve said he wanted to put an end to those situations before they happened.

Liz revealed she is a Jew. She and her family are terrified of the dictator and his massacre of their people. She wants to end their suffering and keep him from taking over our country.

I had missed her religious affiliation. She didn't look like the people who I identified as Jews. She has dark hair and brown eyes, but her nose seems Scotch-Irish. I'm embarrassed by my stereotypical thoughts.

Everyone was already well aware of Danny's and my reasons for moving full speed on the project. We shared it again, but our speeches were brief.

Al's reason was shocking. His father abused him. He drank heavily and beat him unmercifully. He spent days locked in a closet with a water bowl and a bucket. They rarely fed him, and when he was, it was comprised of the remnants of their meals.

Somehow, someone reported his parents, and his aunt received custody of him. As badly as his parents treated him, she treated him that much better. She hugged him often and baked cookies with him. She took him to school every day and climbed trees with him.

When he graduated high school, she went to Germany to visit her dying cousin. She was caught in a political scuffle, and she died. There was more to the story, but he couldn't speak it. It hurt him worse to talk about someone he loved than it did to discuss the abuse he had suffered from his parents.

We stayed silent for a few moments after he spoke. In part, it was to understand the severity of his story, but it was also to allow him time to collect himself.

"She was the most important person in my life," he told us. "I want to kill the people who ended her life over something so trivial."

Steve teared up and patted him on the back, but Al jumped away from his touch. He ran to his room.

I don't know what compelled me to follow him, but I rushed to his room. I didn't knock, and when I closed the door, we stared at each other.

I don't like Al. I think he is an insufferable human being, but he was in pain. He'd laid his soul bare for us, and his eyes were cloudy with tears.

I intended to hug him. I held my hands out, and after a brief internal struggle, Al met me for an embrace. When I moved, he didn't let go.

I imagined his pain was too intense. He didn't want me to see him crying. I gently rocked him until I thought his emotion had passed.

I was wrong about going to his room. He leaned back to look at me, and I saw what he was feeling before he smashed his lips onto mine.

I bolted out of his room, holding my mouth. I rejoined our group, and they smiled at my flushed face.

"I guess I know who you love," Danny remarked with a smirk.

Before I could object, Al stormed out of his room and attacked Danny. The men swung wildly, damaging some of the equipment.

Today, I skipped church service and slept. I think our project will be delayed a couple of days as they fix the damaged equipment, but we will send Steve on his way by the end of the week.

If he can change the past, I hope he erases what happened in Al's room. It could have been worse, but Al's different from Danny. If Al thinks we're together, nothing short of death will keep him from exerting his hold on me.

Chapter 20

Ag allowed her to visit David first, and she stayed in the car with Emma. Celeste felt guilty for leaving Mindy out, especially when she had been so kind to her, but seeing David wiped the guilt from her mind.

His face was thin and drawn, and some of his skin sagged around his midsection. She could see his form well through his shirt, as it was too tight. His arms had more definition, and he'd grown a short beard that he'd shaped around his cheeks.

He didn't seem disappointed to see her, but his lips formed a thin line. He picked up his receiver and spoke briskly.

"You know Mindy's a pushover. You shouldn't have asked her to see me again."

Celeste tried to keep her tone even. "Ag invited me, and Mindy isn't here."

She was glad he wasn't upset. He seemed to relax a little, throwing his elbow onto the back of the chair.

Celeste talked about Emma and her fast growth. Of course, David had no idea just how fast Emma was growing, but Celeste needed to fill the awkward silence with words.

"How are you?" he asked.

"I'm okay," Celeste replied with a smile.

"I hate when you do that."

It threw Celeste off. "Do what?"

She couldn't be certain, as the screen was black-and-white, but it seemed like he rolled his eyes. "You give me a half-hearted smile when everything's falling apart."

So, he paid attention to her actions that closely? She hadn't felt that he truly cared since they were married, even though he seemed to like her.

He mistook her silence for denial. "Tell my baby I love her."

She reeled him back to the statement about her tight smiles. "How do you know when I'm masking my feelings?"

He blew out a puff of air and crossed his arms. "I was married to you, so I picked up on a few things."

"Like what?" Her voice softened.

He leaned forward, fixing her with his eyes. "I know you love mornings, but you get anxious at night."

Celeste colored. "What?"

He threw up a hand. "You're bright and cheerful in the morning, but when it gets dark, you seem edgy. It's almost like you don't expect to live until the next day."

She hadn't expected the revelation. David didn't know the real reason she was afraid of falling asleep, and he'd be upset if she mentioned her role in the future again. She wished she could say, *I was scared my grandfather would jump me back to the future while I slept and I wouldn't be able to tell you goodbye.* Instead, she said, "Everything was perfect. I didn't want it to end."

For a moment, David seemed overcome with emotion. He opened his mouth to speak, but he closed it sharply before sharpening his tongue. "But *you* ended it. I was happy with you and excited about our baby, and you took it all away."

Celeste couldn't think of the right thing to say. She couldn't tell him that her grandfather had pulled her back, and she'd waited for the chance to go back in time and find him. She couldn't tell him how she'd fought to bring him back into his body when Zam had used him as a host. She couldn't tell him that all she wanted was to go back to the time when he loved her with his whole heart.

Ag knocked on the door, signaling her turn. Celeste looked at the door behind her and back at the screen, where David was staring at her with a hard expression.

"I don't want you to come back here, Caroline. Stay away from me, and don't waste any more of my time with your lies."

Celeste bolted out of the room, leaving the phone dangling from its cord. She took Emma from Ag without looking at her, and Ag entered the room as Celeste held the door.

Pretending to be happy for her daughter was difficult. Emma tried to get her attention, but Celeste had to look away whenever tears threatened to fall.

"Daddy in there?" Emma pointed to the visitation building.

"No. He's actually in there." She pointed to the jail. "But we can see him on a screen in that building." She pointed to where Ag was leaving.

Emma allowed herself to be buckled without a struggle. Ag waited for her to shut the door before she spoke.

"He ran me off early."

"Why?"

Ag crossed her arms over her middle. "I guess he didn't want to see me get emotional."

"Did you talk to him about a lawyer?"

Ag pulled out a stack of papers from a bag slung over her shoulder. "Yeah. He's gonna go with the lawyer we've always used, Roger Benton."

"Is he good?"

Ag shrugged. "He's as good as anyone else around here."

"I hope it's enough to help him."

Ag let out a long breath. "We don't see eye-to-eye on that."

Celeste's eyebrows went up.

"I want him to serve his time," Ag said. "I'll help him because he's my brother and Mama and Daddy would want me to do it, but I don't want him to walk away Scott-free."

Celeste chose not to argue with Ag. Deep in her heart, Celeste knew her grandfather had orchestrated Mrs. Winsome's attempted murder. David was the tool he used to carry out the heinous act.

She changed the subject. "He doesn't want me to come back."

"That's no surprise."

Celeste backed away after Ag's flippant reply. "I'm not the enemy, you know." She reached for her door handle, but Ag's hand on her other arm stopped her.

"Of course you're not." She rubbed a space between her eyes. "I'm exhausted, and life in prison has David rattled. You're the closest person to us, so you catch all the flack. I'm sorry."

Celeste looked through the window at Emma, who was dancing her doll across her legs. She was oblivious to the tension outside the car, and Celeste envied her ignorance of it.

"I love him," she told Ag. "I love all of you." She turned, wiping away a rogue tear. "I can't even be mad at Mindy. She's too nice."

The women shared a chuckle.

Ag withdrew her hand, but she tilted her head to study Celeste. "We love you, too."

Tears rolled freely down Celeste's face as she shook her head. "No, you don't. David never wants to see me again. Most times, your mother hardly tolerated me, and you barely liked me. You all think I'm something that I'm not."

Ag narrowed her eyes. "What's that, Caroline? What haven't we seen?"

Celeste looked up at her, ready to reveal everything. *What was the worst that could happen now that David didn't want to see her anymore?*

As she opened her mouth, Emma cried out. Both women directed their attention to the backseat. Once their eyes were on her, Emma gave them a mischievous smile and repeated the sound.

"I know your baby has brought light into the family," Ag said, playing with Emma through the window.

"She's a star." Celeste opened the door, giving Ag access to the backseat.

After Ag's long goodbye with Emma, Celeste drove back to the Winsomes' home. Knowing that they thought poorly of her, and hearing David dismiss her, was too much for Celeste.

It was almost impossible to get through the day. She had to walk away from Emma several times, stealing away into the bathroom or the basement to cry for a minute before she faced her responsibilities.

After Emma fell asleep, Celeste went upstairs and slid into David's bed. His sheets were losing his smell, but the room was still familiar. They'd consummated their marriage, laid their souls almost bare, and conceived Emma in the same bed.

When she was numb from expending her emotions, she went back downstairs. She thought about climbing onto the couch with Emma, but she wasn't ready to sleep. Instead, she pushed open Mrs. Winsome's bedroom door and sat in front of her journals. She picked up the one she'd been reading and skipped ahead to the part she expected.

It was a success! I can't stand the secrecy any longer, and now that it's done, I want someone to know about it. Even if that person reads this journal decades in the future when the technology is commonplace.

My theory sent a man into the past! Yes! I, a small-town girl from Northeast Tennessee, could change history!

Yes, I borrowed one of Albert Einstein's equations, but the math is mine. Linda and Liz helped me set up the equipment we needed and Danny designed a computer program for it, but it was born from my brain.

Al only contributed to the negativity. He tried to prove me wrong mathematically, and when that didn't work, he tried several times to derail our experiments.

I don't want my journal to fall into the wrong hands, so I won't place the formulas in this book, but the Department of Defense has a copy of my notes, and they're really proud of me.

After it worked, our brave president called me. Well, I waited in a room for his call, but he spoke to me. I was so flustered that

I didn't remember most of our conversation. I hope I didn't make a fool out of myself.

We sent Steve to a point in history where he can make a difference. He was scared. I could see the fear in his eyes when he looked wildly from Linda to me as we prepared the equipment. He had walked to the chair bravely, and that is how he will be remembered if we aren't able to bring him back.

I gave him a plan to stop us and save himself if everything went wrong. I told him to intercept us at the college on the morning before we leave for the Secret City. If he tells us it doesn't work, then I will never put my theory to the test, and the timeline should reset at that moment.

It's been almost a week since we sent Steve into the unknown, and I was feeling positive, as we were still in the lab with no memory of an older Steve stopping us before we started our adventure. Now, though, I'm worried.

As the days went by, I made comments about the project. Al has been irritable with me, but I decided he was only jealous of my success. However, something he said made me question my hubris.

We were in the lab. Linda was staring longingly at the chair while everyone shared doughnuts and coffee.

Al kicked the chair where Steve had been when we last saw him. "Nothing's changed."

"Give it time," I responded.

"I miss him," Linda said. "I wish there was a way we could know he was okay."

My heart went out to her, and I shared what I had told Steve to do if we were unsuccessful. Linda seemed hopeful until Al spoke.

"What if he died?" he asked in that irritating voice that made me want to claw his eyes out. "He couldn't meet us before we left if he died in the time jump or while he was in the past."

Linda ran to her room, and Liz went after her. Danny glared at him and marched out of our area, leaving me to deal with the pessimist.

"You can't think of it that way," I told him. "Envision our success—"

He laughed outright. "I believe in concrete facts. You've given me no reason to think Steve has completed his mission."

"His mission will be complete when he's back in that chair and debriefed by the defense department."

"That's cute," he said. I wasn't really familiar with the phrase. "You think that his mission will be over if we can bring him back?"

"When—" I emphasized, but he took a step toward me, raising his hand and cutting me off.

"If, Eleanor, *if."*

I crossed my arms and glared at him. "I *will* bring my friend home."

He shrugged his shoulders. "I hope you do. I'd hate to think we'd wasted our time on a fruitless project."

Have I mentioned how angry Al makes me? By that point, my blood was boiling.

He went on. "But have you thought about what will happen if you are successful?"

That gave me pause. I had a feeling I knew where he was going.

He smiled smugly. "Let's say Steve comes back in one piece and is full of life. What then? Maybe he didn't stop the war, but what can he stop?"

I watched him as he paced the length of the lab. He turned on his heel and settled in front of me, putting his hands on my elbows.

"What will you do if your friend, Steve, becomes part of a government program? What if he never has a real life with Linda because he's time-hopping through the past at the will of our Commander-in-Chief?"

I hadn't thought of the long-range effects of my project. I looked at my feet, lowering my guard.

Al lifted my chin. "I'll help you with the burden. I'll share the blame if you'll agree to be by my side." His face was inches from mine, and I turned my head.

Al's grip on my elbows tightened. "You and I are made for each other."

"You aren't made for anyone!" I spat back.

My remark made him smile. "Neither are you, and that's why we should get married."

"I'll never marry you." I tried to break away, but he was too strong.

He pressed his lips to my mouth. I opened it to cry out, but he stuck his tongue inside, muffling my attempts.

The nearest part of Al to me was his ribs, so I grabbed at them and pulled. My nails connected with the flesh through his shirt and I yanked unmercifully. He pushed me away and slapped me.

His actions horrified him, and he apologized, but I turned away, yelling for help. Liz and Linda ran out of Linda's room and flew to my aid. Al tried to tell them I'd slipped on the floor, but his attitude before they'd left us allowed me to tell them a story they believed.

Liz advanced on him, and he backed away from her fiery temper. She pointed her finger in his face.

"You won't work here anymore after I get done with you."

She raised her hand as if to slap him, and Al winced. I felt a stab of pity for him because he reacted because of his years of abuse, but Liz laughed.

"Are you afraid of a woman? Is that why you keep assaulting our poor Eleanor?"

He seemed genuinely bewildered, and I hated him for it. "Assaulted? I don't want to hurt her. I want to marry her."

Liz looked back at me, and I shook my head. I wanted no part of Al in my life.

"I don't think she wants to marry you," Liz said. She grabbed him by his arm and led him to his room.

Al went with her easily. I'd felt his strength. If he hadn't wanted to move, he would have remained in place.

Linda and Liz fussed over me, and when Danny didn't return, we all slept in Liz's room. I felt safer with my friends piled in the bed with me at odd angles, even though Linda kicked my head once in her sleep.

We went to our superior the following morning. He listened to our concerns gravely. They packed up Al's room by that afternoon.

Sadly, it wasn't enough to get him kicked out of the facility. They moved him to a different department, and he scowls at me during Sunday morning chapel services.

Last night, I was asleep, and I felt a hand on my shoulder. I turned over, ready to attack the intruder, but Danny put a finger to his lips.

Once it was clear I would not scream for help, he sat on the bed. "I despise him."

I knew who he meant without asking. "He's had a hard life, but it's no excuse for the way he behaves."

Danny grunted, and I thought I could smell liquor on his breath. Maybe his girlfriend in food service had snuck some to him. They kept some bottles for cooking.

He grabbed my hand, and I tensed. He released it quickly and scooted down my bed. "I'm not like that monster."

"I know," I told him. "But I don't want you to think—"

"I don't think anything like that," he assured me. "I'm only angry and drunk. I wish I wouldn't have stayed away that night. If I would've seen him with his hands on you, I would have—"

"Liz did a good job of running him off."

He nodded. "Maybe. I shouldn't have left you defenseless. It won't happen again."

"Everything's fine now. Al is gone, and I'm doing fine."

"You wore a bruise on your cheek for a week."

"I covered it up," I said before I thought about it. "Linda gave me some of her makeup, and—"

"It should never have happened."

At that moment, Danny seemed more like a big brother to me, and my heart warmed. "I'm okay."

Danny walked to the door, but before he closed it behind him, he whispered, "You may be okay, but I promise you, if he touches you again, I'll kill him."

Chapter 21

Celeste carried Emma as Mindy briefed her on her responsibilities. There were only two patients in the ER, and they only needed Celeste in two rooms.

She met a middle-aged man and noted the placement of his arm.

"It's broken," he told her through the haze of pain medicine.

Mindy advised her to assist during the application of the splint, and Celeste was thankful that her responsibilities seemed similar to what was expected of her as an LPN.

Was she supposed to have done everything she did without a more advanced certification? No. However, the hospital was always under-staffed, and it had been easier to follow the directions of doctors and senior nurses while she helped than to worsen the situation by acting uncooperative.

The man interrupted them. "I didn't know this was where all the pretty women were or I'd of broken my arm sooner." He chuckled at his joke.

The women stared at him blankly. Mindy smiled wanly, volunteering to speak on their behalf.

"I think your pain medicine is finally working, Mr. Hendrix."

"Kurt," he cut in.

"Kurt," Mindy corrected. "Caroline and I have to make our rounds, and she'll check on you soon."

Kurt stared at them with an open mouth as they left.

An IV and tachometer beeped beside the other patient. She was sleeping, even though the monitor showed the pulse and blood pressure of a more active person.

"She'll be transferred," Mindy informed her, taking the woman's temperature with a device that never touched her. "The Heart Hospital in Johnson City will give her the best help."

Mindy stared at the older woman as if she were looking fondly at a family member. "I wish we had more to help her here."

Celeste thought about the advanced techniques in her time and repressed a sigh. Since Slover's disease, the rate of individuals with heart disease was down, but genetic defects were still possible. Future doctors could correct heart murmurs within hours, and artificial hearts gave people decades more of life.

Mindy tugged her arm, and they went back to the nurse's desk. Amber playfully punched Scott, and he pretended her aggression was too much for him.

"What's this?" Amber asked, pointing to Celeste.

Scott ducked out. Celeste didn't watch him as he walked around, but she was almost certain he went into an empty room.

Celeste had expected some backlash from Amber, as she was David's best friend, but she thought she could get away from most of it since she and Amber worked different shifts. She stared at the woman, unwilling to incite her anger.

Amber's blonde hair was shorter, placing it just past her shoulders. Bumps of bunched hair around her ears showed she had just taken down a ponytail she'd put up when her hair had been wet.

She put a hand on her round hip. "Why didn't you tell me about this?"

Mindy searched for an explanation, and based on Amber's reaction, Celeste understood why Mindy had kept her in the dark. Even though it put her life in a whirlwind, Mindy's baby was precious, and Mindy's stress needed to stay low.

"Mindy is pregnant, and she didn't want to field your comments about me."

Amber didn't look at her, and she continued to address Mindy. "I don't know how you could allow this to happen. You know what she did to David, right?"

Emma let out a cry, and Amber's face softened. She smiled and talked to Emma without looking at Celeste.

Emma went to Mindy easily, but it puzzled her when Mindy walked away from her mother. She looked over Mindy's shoulder as Celeste blew kisses at her.

Amber left with Mindy and Emma, presumably to talk to her about Celeste's position at the hospital. She didn't say her name, but Celeste thought she caught a side-eyed glance from the woman.

Celeste welcomed her coworkers, introducing herself by her first name. Travis and Fran didn't seem to recognize her, but Grady, a dark-haired, middle-aged man with a pointed nose, knew her right away. Thankfully, he had the good grace not to say anything to the other nurses.

Dr. Goodman asked for an update as Scott slinked out of the room where he'd been hiding. He asked for the nurse who was most familiar with Mr. Hendrix and Celeste volunteered the information.

The name of Celeste's host was stamped beneath her picture, and the doctor referred to her by name. "Caroline, have you assisted with a splint before?"

She nodded. When she had been Hailey, she had helped with a variety of emergent and non-emergent procedures.

Grady rolled his eyes. "Unless she's put a cast on Willie Jones, then she hasn't done it. She is an experienced liar, though."

The silence was so loud Celeste thought she could hear it. She was glad when the doctor spoke.

"This is a place of business. I shouldn't have to remind you to conduct yourself professionally." To Celeste's horror, he looked from her to Grady, including her in his chastisement. "If you and Caroline have a history, that needs to stay outside the walls of the hospital."

No one contradicted him. Celeste bit the inside of her lip.

He glanced at Travis. "You can help me with the cast." He turned on his heel, and Travis went to the supply closet.

Fran excused herself and went to the bathroom. She scurried away, holding her stomach.

"You've been here less than five minutes, and you've turned everything upside down," Grady commented. He smiled without warmth. "As usual."

Exhausted from dealing with people who didn't like her, she crossed her arms and looked him in the eyes. "So, what's your problem with me?"

Grady surprised her by grabbing her arm. When she cried out, he loosened his grip.

"*You* are the problem!" He pushed his face within inches of hers, and with his next words, he pressed his nose against hers.

"We were together!" he whispered, spit flying from his mouth.

Celeste tried not to gag from the smell of his breath. From the scent, she could tell he'd eaten red meat shortly before she met him.

He searched her eyes with his dark brown ones. "You're still mine, aren't you?"

Celeste panicked. She pushed him away, and he fell into a chair.

"What's going on here?" Fran barked.

Grady assumed innocence. He held his hands up as if Celeste caused the outburst.

It didn't fool Fran. "Will you help me in room five?" she asked Celeste.

Celeste was relieved to follow Fran to the older lady's room. The woman was still asleep, but before they checked her vitals, Fran put her hand on Celeste's shoulder.

"I know we don't know each other well, but I'd request to be on any other shift than the one with Grady on it."

She looked up at her stern green eyes. "I don't really have a choice."

Fran shook her head. "There's always a choice. Grady is going to harass you until you go."

"Why me?" Celeste asked, even though she was sure the reason had something to do with Caroline.

To her surprise, Fran shrugged. "It could be anything, but he's going to say it has to do with Willie Jones." She let out a sigh. "I try to give everyone a chance, so I won't judge you based on your husband, but if you cross a line with me..." She let Celeste fill in the silence.

The lady on the bed moved and lifted her gnarled hand. "Water."

Celeste hurried to fill a cup for her, and she drank it too eagerly. She coughed up some of the liquid, and Celeste dabbed it off her face and clothes with a nearby towel.

The emergency room was silent for most of the night. In a way, it was fortuitous, as Celeste worried about performing an LPN's duties, but there was a downside, too. Grady had plenty of time to make her uncomfortable.

That night, Fran didn't leave her alone with him, but at some point, she'd have to work alongside Grady. Even though the other nurses didn't seem to know that Grady and Caroline had some type of past relationship, it was obvious they did, and if Caroline had been afraid of him, Celeste was terrified of the man.

<h1>Chapter 22</h1>

A steady stream of days followed, and Celeste grew more accustomed to an LPN's duties. She changed bandages, collected urine, and prepared rooms. She wasn't under-prepared for her role, and she was always glad to help any coworker who wasn't Grady.

Her shifts were long and tiring, and it was difficult to stay awake until Emma fell asleep on the nights she was off. Mindy liked to sleep late, and it had shifted Emma's schedule, making her alert until midnight. Celeste couldn't begrudge her the rest, as Mindy was carrying life and it made her sleep more important.

Emma seemed to be happy with Mindy. She had potty-trained her, and Celeste was thankful for it, as she hadn't thought about that next step.

Mrs. Winsome was still in intensive care. Celeste asked Ag if she needed anything from the Winsomes' home, and she had her bring fresh sets of clothes and launder her used ones. It embarrassed her to ask her brother's ex-wife to wash her clothes, but Celeste tried to treat it casually.

The first time Celeste brought items to Ag, she tried to walk into the room, but Ag met her at the door. She saw the flowers in the room, daisies and carnations that Ag had kept fresh-looking and beautiful. As her mother wasn't awake, the moments she spent caring for the flowers distracted her.

Ag had texted her about a book while she'd been eating with Emma the previous night. Celeste held the book, *Little Women*, in her hand as she waited for the last seconds of her shift to end.

"I loved that book," Fran commented, admiring the hardback cover. "It brings back so many memories of my childhood."

Celeste raised her eyebrows. Fran had admitted that she'd never been north of the Mason-Dixon line.

"I had four sisters," she explained. "We made up fun games and explored the woods together."

"That's sweet," Celeste said.

Fran stared forlornly at her car keys. "Two of them are gone now, and the youngest is sick all the time."

Celeste tried to think of something consolatory. "I'm sorry."

Fran flipped her car keys into her hand and patted her arm. "That's the price you pay when you get to be my age. You may live longer, but you have to watch the people who knew you die."

She left while Celeste was logging out of the computer-based time clock. She smelled Grady before she saw him, his musky scent announcing his presence.

"He killed one of her sisters."

Celeste rounded on him. "What?"

Grady's eyes narrowed. "Your knight-in-shining armor, Willie Jones, shot her in the head."

Celeste lost her fiery spirit. Grady had a way of dragging her down as he spoke about the pain her host had cost the people in Erwin.

When she'd found out Caroline had called Willie to pick her up at the hospital, Celeste had made it her responsibility to learn the names of each of Willie's victims on that bloody day. Based on Fran's features, she thought she knew which one had been her sister.

Grady inched closer to her, and she was stuck between the desk and him. He brought his face within inches of hers and she turned her head.

"Stop."

"Why?" he whispered like he was speaking to a lover. "We used to have so much fun."

Celeste had never been with Grady, but Caroline had been with a lot of the men in the county. "That's over."

He ran his finger down her cheek. "I don't think it is."

He walked away, leaving her shivering.

Celeste was still unnerved when she approached Mrs. Winsome's door. She walked inside after a brief knock, and Ag jumped out of her chair.

"Hey."

Celeste returned her greeting, crossing the short distance to place the book in her hand. Ag took it automatically.

Other than a thin paleness that sagged the skin around her eyes and neck and made her veins more visible, Ag looked the same. Her eyes were dull, almost like she'd cried until the pain became part of her.

Celeste looked over at Mrs. Winsome, and Ag followed her gaze. "She moved her fingers yesterday."

Celeste nodded. "That's good."

The lady on the bed looked like anything but good. Ag seemed to have washed her hair with dry shampoo, making it less oily, but the brown-silver curls fell limply around a wan face. Mrs. Winsome's eyes were closed, and her lips caved into her mouth in the absence of her dentures. Her body was thin, seeming to have too much skin around it, but as she watched, Ag covered Mrs. Winsome to her shoulders with a white sheet.

"You don't want anyone to see her, do you?"

Ag sighed, looking at her mother's frail form. "No. She was a proud lady, and she wouldn't want anyone to see her this way." She turned around and opened the blinds wider, exposing the setting sun. "The preacher comes by every Friday to pray for her—for our family—but I won't let any of the parishioners see her."

Celeste hung on one word Ag had said. "You said 'was'. I thought the doctors were hopeful?"

Ag laughed drily. "What do you tell the woman who's been at her mother's side for a month?"

Celeste thought about the doctors at the hospital, and something didn't seem right. She'd heard none of them give out false hope.

"They're *not* hopeful, are they?"

Ag squeezed her eyes tightly together like she was trying to defend herself from Celeste's words. "No," she squeaked out. "They expect her to die any day."

Chapter 23

Change is inevitable. It happens to us and all around us. Sometimes, it brings new life and order in a chaotic world, but other times, change pushes people to their limits and bears them down until they cry out. Celeste thought about it as she dished out soup beans for Emma and her.

For once, Emma seemed tired at her usual bedtime. Celeste took advantage of her daughter's exhaustion to creep into Mrs. Winsome's room.

It seemed fitting to read her books, as she had discovered that Mrs. Winsome would likely die. It meant a murder charge for the man she loved, and Celeste wasn't ready to think about it, so she immersed herself in the time before he was born.

Linda cries for Steve. She thinks we don't hear her, but the sounds of her pain travel outside her door when the lab is silent. I'd wager Danny hears it the most, as he has transitioned back to his late-night schedule.

We're set to bring Steve back tomorrow. If everything goes well, he will be eating supper with us and revealing the secrets he's uncovered.

Since the war efforts remain the same, I doubt we've altered anything. However, with Steve placed in an opportune time and location, we may understand our next move.

Linda isn't hopeful about her lover's return. She claims she doesn't "feel" like it will work. As a scientist who plans to be accepted into the community now that I've made a revolutionary discovery, I can't put stock in her feelings. I hope she's wrong and Steve reappears with news to share.

Celeste was far from finished, but Emma cried out. She almost fell asleep as she coerced her toddler back into her dreams, but she jerked herself awake, eager to read about Steve's return.

I am a failure. I'll be a laughingstock if anyone ever learns about my mistake.

Al tried to warn me that people could travel through time and never return, but I wouldn't listen to him. I thought my math was flawless.

We prepared everything to bring Steve back. Danny sweated over his fourth cup of coffee, and Liz secured the equipment. She tried, but Linda was of no use to the team.

We counted down the moments to the exact second we'd sent Steve into the past. Danny pushed the button, and we stared at the chair Steve had occupied a month ago to the day.

Nothing happened. Danny checked his program, and Liz looked over the equipment, but it was useless. We couldn't bring Steve back.

Linda was inconsolable. Liz ran after her, but Linda locked herself in her room, wailing. I didn't approach her door, as I felt ultimately responsible for the team's inability to return Steve to her.

The supervisor came into our lab with a smile that quickly vanished. He said he was going to

put our project in a "File thirteen", and we'd
have to sign papers that promised we wouldn't
speak about it again.

I didn't know how the government planned to
erase Steve from Linda's mind, as he had been
her first love. As for me, I'd always remember
my friend and my theory that had taken him from
us.

Many dark pages followed Mrs. Winsome's defeat. She spiraled
into a deep depression that sank her team.

Two days after Steve didn't return, Linda received a letter about
her father. She abandoned the Secret City to return home and help
nurse her father after his heart attack.

Al seemed to move up, going as high as possible in the system
without a military background. It upset Mrs. Winsome, but she
had fallen so deep into her depression that Al's advancement only
earned a brief mention.

Celeste had to admit that Mrs. Winsome's detailed description of
her sadness was pointed and heartfelt. Celeste wondered what pain
she had drawn on to help her write them.

Celeste was almost finished reading for the night when she
skimmed across a sentence that made her turn back to the beginning of the entry. She was glad she did.

I have my own apartment. Liz rented the one
across the hall and she shares it with a
roommate. I don't have that option, as I only
have one bedroom.

I went to the church picnic with Mama, and I
saw Becky Winsome. A widow can't be in tears
all the time, but everything seemed to spur an
emotional outburst. She'd always been a little
excitable, but I was surprised when I offered
my condolences to her, and she put her baby in
my arms. She ran away before I could react.

Her sister, Dot, went after her, and her mother was in a social circle, so I didn't want to interrupt her. That left me caring for her daughter.

I thought the child would cry out, but she looked up at me and cooed. I lifted her in my arms and she put her head against my shoulder. I took her to my mama, and she talked to her as if she had belonged to Bill and me instead of Bill and Becky.

"What's her name?" I asked.

My mama put her finger to her chin. "I don't know. Maybe Danielle." She shook her head. "That's just awful of me. I should remember her name. After all, they presented her in church."

I stared into her brown eyes and saw very little of Becky. Sure, she had her chin, but other than that, she was the spitting image of Bill Winsome.

Just as I was getting used to caring for her, Dot pulled her away. I was alarmed when she jerked the baby by the arm, but I let her go to her aunt.

"Get away from her," Dot spat.

My mama was shocked and moved away to discuss her feelings with Dot's mother. She glanced over at me as she talked, her mouth pressed into a thin line.

After the church social, my mama informed me that Dot had heard that Bill had been to see me before he married her sister. She claimed I had bewitched him, and he didn't go into his marriage purely.

I laughed. "Well, I'm still innocent, so if Bill wasn't, then it's not my fault."

My mother closed her posture. She hated to talk about anything of a sexual nature. "Men do things when they're away from home, and certain women take advantage of their lust and naivety."

"That still doesn't sound like Bill," I told her. I was convinced Dot had been jealous of him and she looked for a way to soil his good reputation.

Linda never visited with us, but Danny, Liz, and I met every Friday night at the library. It had been a ritual when we were in class, and now that we were no longer students at the university, we felt comfortable in the rows of books.

Most of the time, we read silently, but other times, we left and drank at a local bar until one of us couldn't stand. My failure had awakened my taste for wine, and seldom did I pass through a day without drinking it.

One Friday night, after Danny had gone home with a woman who had attached herself to him, I felt like someone was following me. I'd heard that the government monitored you after you were ejected from one of their programs, and I wondered if our weekly visits to the library had spurred an investigation.

Regardless of the reason, I was a small woman who was unaccompanied on the dark streets, so I quickened my pace. I practically ran to my door when it came into view, noticing that Liz's light was already out.

I slid the lock into place, hoping it guarded against whoever was on the other side. Just when I had mustered the nerve to scream for help, I heard my name.

I inched toward the door, trying not to breathe. I could hear feet shuffling on the other side.

"Eleanor, open the door! Hurry!" The words were whispered shrilly.

Something about the tone of the voice guided my actions before my brain caught up with my movements. Before I knew it, I was face to face with the man who had been following me. He brushed past me, almost knocking me over in his eagerness to get inside.

He paced as I watched him, noticing the length of his hair and the deep circles around his eyes. His erratic behavior should have frightened me, but a sense of relief washed over me.

"We have to get back to the lab," Steve said. "I know how to end the war, but I have to go back in time again to do it."

Chapter 24

Celeste thought about Mrs. Winsome's book all day. She was productive, dusting, sweeping, and mopping, but her thoughts seesawed between caring for Emma and the last thing she'd read in Mrs. Winsome's book.

How did Steve come back? Did someone else bring him into the future?

She had mentioned that Al had moved up in rank, but the projects were kept so private that no one knew the duties or directives outside their labs. Especially in Mrs. Winsome's case, as they had kept her team in the dark about Steve's mission until he came forward about it.

Emma demanded her attention, and Celeste didn't mind giving it to her. They took advantage of the late spring weather to visit a park in the middle of town. After school was dismissed, young children with helmets and kneepads on scooters were replaced with wiry teens with reckless tricks and secretive meetings at the far corner of the fence.

After the smell of a certain plant reached her nose, Celeste decided it was best to take Emma back to the Winsome's house. She couldn't call it their home, and she doubted it would be more than a landing place between where they were now and where she intended to go.

Based on her pay schedule and their current expenses, Celeste believed she could rent an apartment within the next month. The rentals in Unicoi County were snatched up quickly, but she hoped the summer season would bring a listing for a small house or quiet apartment.

She'd left her phone behind, and it was ringing when she opened the door. Placing Emma carefully on the floor, she ran for it before it stopped ringing.

"Mama's coming home," Ag told her.

Celeste paced between the kitchen and living room. "I can put a set of fresh sheets on her bed."

"Her insurance is providing us with one of those beds—" She paused as she searched for the right word. "Ah, never mind. It doesn't matter what type of bed it is."

Celeste tried to evaluate Ag's tone. She was tired, but there was something else in her voice. *Was it resignation?*

"What is her outlook?" Celeste chanced.

"Not great," Ag answered, a crack in her voice.

Celeste had hit on the source of Ag's pain. She tried to think of something to say, but all she could get out were ways she could be helpful.

"I'll get the living room ready."

She assumed Ag wanted Mrs. Winsome downstairs in her favorite spot. She could hear the television, and maybe familiar sights and smells would encourage her to remain conscious longer.

"You'll need to take over Mama's room for a while."

"I couldn't do that," Celeste said. "I'll make a place for Emma and me in the spare room upstairs. I have enough money for a bed, and—"

Ag's extended sigh stopped her. "Don't be ridiculous. I have enough to worry about without you adding to it. Emma's leg isn't fully healed, so she doesn't need to be upstairs without a baby gate. You don't need to buy a bed when we already have one. I realize the mattress was probably—"

"I saved the mattress," Celeste cut in. "I had to take the plastic off and throw it away, but it's still useable."

"You can thank Mama's incompetent bladder for the mattress liner."

The conversation was clipped, and Celeste was thankful when it was over. She made sandwiches for dinner and planned a vegetarian chili for the following night. It was her last day off before her four-day shifts resumed.

Mindy! What was she going to do about watching the boys while Mrs. Winsome was home?

She quickly dialed Mindy, and she answered on the second ring.

"Mrs. Winsome is coming home tomorrow," she informed her.

"That's wonderful!"

Celeste moved into Ag's room so she could speak privately. "Her health doesn't look great, and Ag might need my help."

"I understand," she said. "You can't watch the boys when you're needed at home. I'll ask Doris to look after them."

"Do you think she'll let me pay her to watch Emma?"

"Don't be silly," Mindy responded cheerfully. "I'll look after Emma. You can't afford the extra expense."

Her kindness overwhelmed Celeste. In her time, most everyone worked together, but in her present time, people with that mindset were few and far between.

"I truly appreciate you, Mindy."

"It's my pleasure to help you. David and I were just talking about how I'll need to pass along information about Emma, and there's no better way to do it than by relating my first-hand experiences with her."

Celeste was still grateful, but Mindy's cheerful attitude and the mention of David were wearing on her. She thought of another question.

"You've been a nurse for a while. Do you think Mrs. Winsome will be okay?"

Mindy took a moment to answer, and when she did, the mirth had left her voice. "I snuck a peek at her chart," she confided. "From what I can tell, it's not a hospice situation, but the outlook isn't good."

Celeste nodded, even though Mindy couldn't see her. "Okay. What do I need to do?"

"Make her as comfortable as possible, and if she wakes up, keep her talking. It doesn't matter if it's about the shape of the moon or her favorite soap opera characters."

Celeste took her words to heart. Ag had chronicled little interaction between her mother and her while she had been in the hospital, but Celeste hoped to change it.

Celeste hadn't intended on reading any more of Mrs. Winsome's book when she started preparing the room for Emma and her, but there she was, sitting cross-legged on the floor with a notebook in her lap.

```
    Steve and I talked for hours. It wasn't until
the sun came up we realized it was time to take
action.
    He told me about his trip to the past, and based
on his location when he jumped, I had miscal-
culated the spin of the earth. Fortunately, he
didn't end up inside a building or a mountain,
but he was knee-deep in a free-flowing stream.
    We discussed the political temperature, and
the papers we gave him put him in a notable
position. He played his part well, but it wasn't
enough. Amazingly, though, he gathered intel
that could change the course of the war if he
went back again.
    "I tried to get back into our lab," he said.
"The guards didn't believe me. They threatened
to kill me both times I went up to the gate, even
when I told them the name of the supervisor."
    "I'm surprised they didn't kill you."
    "Me too."
    We talked about Linda, Liz, and Danny. None
of us had the clearance to return to the Secret
City.
    "Where are your notebooks?" he asked.
```

"The defense department took them. I suppose they're keeping them wherever they put our equipment."

He paced my living room, which was so small he took three steps, turned around, and took three steps more. "Do you think you could repeat the math?"

I tapped my temple. "It's all up here."

We collected everyone else except Linda. We were with Steve as he climbed the steps to his girlfriend's family home.

It was a fine reunion when Steve held out his arms to her. She'd been in her father's house for weeks, and his health was declining. She ran into her lover's arms, holding him tightly even when he tried to look at her face.

When we approached her about our idea, she balked. She wanted to be with Steve, and she condemned him for his recklessness. After a lover's spat that we witnessed, she ran inside, slamming the door behind her.

Liz was uncertain if she could duplicate Linda's applications, but she had most of the work completed within a couple of weeks. We were relieved another member of our team could do Linda's work.

We didn't have the government's inexhaustible funds, but Steve had invested money into certain stocks and bonds while he lived in the past. It earned him tremendous gains, so we had the money to rebuild the machine.

Several months passed, but before we knew it, it was time to send Steve back into the past. Unfortunately, that was when Al showed up.

Chapter 25

Mrs. Winsome was easily transitioned from the hospital to a hospital bed in the living room. The television played continuously, even at night.

Emma had no trouble sleeping in her grandmother's bed, and she was resting through a late nap when Celeste handed her off to Mindy before she went to work. When Celeste returned with her and lay her on the bed, the birds were chirping, and Emma was still asleep. Her eyes popped open the moment Celeste lay next to her.

She wrapped her limbs around her mother, barring her escape. "You're mine."

Celeste chuckled at her words and kissed her nose. "And you're mine."

At Emma's suggestion, they got up and ate cereal. Ag joined them and noted Celeste's tired eyes.

"When do you sleep?"

Celeste glanced away, wishing she wasn't the topic of the conversation. "I rest until Emma wakes up and I nap when she does."

Ag counted hours on her fingers. "That's no more than three or four hours after the nights you work, and from the looks of it, you missed any opportunity to sleep this morning."

Celeste shrugged. "I needed a job, and the schedule worked out for Mindy and me."

"That Mindy..." Ag shook her head.

"I'm not watching the boys now," Celeste defended. "Mindy made other arrangements when she heard Mrs. Winsome was coming home."

Ag grabbed her mug of coffee, almost slamming it down after she sipped it. "Is she watching Emma for you?"

Celeste nodded.

"Well, she's not anymore." She pulled out Celeste's chair and indicated she should get up. "Go rest for a couple of hours. I'll look after Emma until you're ready to get up, and I'll watch her at night. I'll keep her awake as long as possible so you can sleep through the morning."

Celeste was full of questions. "What about Mrs. Winsome? Won't staying up late hurt Emma's schedule?"

Ag edged her out of the room. "My mother hardly moves. It'll be a good distraction to watch Emma instead of waiting for my mother's hand to twitch or for her to wake up and yell at me randomly."

"Are you sure?" Celeste looked back at Emma. She waved at her mother and dipped her spoon back into her cereal.

Ag pushed her in the direction of her makeshift room. "Completely."

Celeste typed out a message to Mindy. She wanted to give her as much notice as possible, and she wasn't sure when Mindy would have a break to look at her phone.

Celeste slept peacefully, and it surprised her the sun heated the room when she woke. A glance at her phone told her she'd slept for almost six hours.

She emerged from the room, feeling more refreshed than usual after a night at work. Emma was in Ag's lap, counting with her.

"Did you teach this baby to count to twenty?" Ag asked her.

Celeste nodded. Most children in her time could count that high by two years old.

"Listen to this."

Ag counted to fifty while she looked at Emma. The toddler watched her lips move and concentrated on the words. Afterward, Emma repeated the numbers.

Celeste congratulated her daughter, but Ag seemed bewildered. She stood, conferring with Celeste out of Emma's earshot.

"I'm sure everyone in our family would think Emma was a genius, even if she stuffed blocks up her nose, but don't you think she's exceptional? At church, there are kids entering kindergarten who can't count to fifty."

Celeste shrugged. "She just repeated what she heard you say. She's not ready for college yet."

Ag let the matter drop, but at dinner, when Emma could count to fifty without hearing the numbers first, Celeste had to concede the point. She had wanted to keep her family off her grandfather's Predictor, but with Emma's increasing awareness and intelligence, Celeste was convinced her daughter had spiked his data.

She received a letter on her way into the hospital.

The sun still lit the sky, but an eerie feeling came over her. She quickened her pace to the doors of the hospital, but a hand grabbed her arm before she reached their safety. The empty parking lot absorbed her cry.

"Fran?"

Fran stared at her with a different expression. Clearly, she was not herself.

"It's Talon."

Celeste remembered her childhood friend who had taken classes with her in higher learning. "Are you in the time-jump program now?"

"Most of the nurses are," he responded. "This is my first jump."

Celeste remembered her first time jump. She had been so disconcerted that she'd taken a week to recover after only a ten-minute experience.

During her trial run, she spent ten minutes inside Caroline's body, eating, drinking, and trying to go to the bathroom. Thankfully, Willie was not with her.

Talon pushed a piece of paper against her chest. "I wrote his message on this." He made a face that looked strange on Fran's features, but she thought it might have been pity. "It's hard to read, but I think I got it all down."

Then he was gone. Fran blinked several times and stared at Celeste.

"What were you saying?"

Her grandfather had counseled Celeste on the right way to handle a similar situation. She held Fran's hand and spoke sweetly to her as they entered the hospital.

"You said you thought you might be getting a headache."

Fran's fingers went to her temple. "It must have passed, but there's still a dull ache."

Celeste patted her arm knowingly. "My head felt the same after I experienced a cluster headache."

"I haven't had one since I started blood pressure medicine," Fran commented. "It's so weird."

Mindy led Celeste over to a quiet area beyond the nurse's station. "Why is Ag keeping Emma?"

Celeste smiled awkwardly. "She thought it might give me more time to sleep."

Mindy rolled it around in her mind. "She may be right, but it places a burden on her." She forced a frown. "It has to be hard for her to care for her mother and a baby."

Celeste held her hands up. "I tried to talk her out of it, but she insisted."

Mindy stared up at her with soft blue eyes. "Are you sure it's not a little selfish?"

At first, Celeste thought she was talking about Ag, but when she realized Mindy meant her, she almost exploded. She reminded herself that Mindy was carrying a life, and some holistic doctors in her time believed that the baby exerted its control over its mother through hormones. Celeste disagreed with the notion, but it was unlike Mindy to say anything unkind, so she treated it like a rhetorical question.

"No. Not at all. Ag wouldn't have made the offer unless she was ready for the additional responsibility."

"She may not be aware of how much work goes into taking care of a child," Mindy suggested.

Celeste defended Ag. "She's kept Emma when she was younger, and everything went well. I trust Ag with her."

"But not with me."

Mindy had finally revealed the reason for her questioning, and Celeste had missed it.

"Are you upset with me for allowing Ag to watch Emma?" A note of anger rose in her voice, and she promised herself she would deal kindlier with Mindy.

Mindy looked away, blinking rapidly. Celeste condemned herself for her insensitive statement.

"I love that little girl," she said, her voice cracking.

Like any mother, Celeste could understand the attachment to Emma. She was sweet and helpful, and she hardly ever cried.

Celeste put her hand on Mindy's elbow. "Of course you do."

Mindy continued to cry. "I'll never see her anymore, and David won't know anything about his daughter."

Celeste jerked her hand away. Mindy was too consumed with her own reaction to note the difference.

Celeste wanted to talk to her about David. She wanted to tell Mindy she wouldn't be David's girlfriend if she hadn't been pregnant. David would be with Emma and Celeste. She wanted to remind her that Ag could relate her experiences with Emma to her brother, or she could write him a letter. Emma belonged to Celeste and David, and Mindy had no right to assume a role that hadn't been given to her.

Within a second, though, her perspective changed.

Mindy was pregnant, and her child belonged to David and her. Celeste wanted to have access to the child to keep Emma involved with the baby. The only difference was that she wouldn't report back to David. *But it wasn't Mindy's fault that David had asked her to keep him informed about Emma, was it?*

"Hey," Celeste said, and when Mindy responded to her softer tone, she went on. "What if I bring her over on one of my days off? We could make it a weekly thing?"

Mindy smiled, and her tears glistened on her lashes. "Really?"

Celeste nodded.

Mindy hugged her several times before she left, and Celeste pushed the paper Talon had given her into her pocket. Grady watched them out of the corner of his eye.

Celeste made her rounds, checking on three occupied rooms and readying another room. It was almost midnight before she was alone at the nurse's station, and she read the paper.

It had once been a gas receipt, and its edges crumpled. She smoothed it out, and Talon's jagged script spread out over the length of the paper.

Celeste remembered how hard it had been to ground herself inside another person's body. She hadn't even registered pain right away, but some of the smaller aches and pains in a person's body became excruciating for her. Caroline had a cavity when she'd entered her body. Caroline had dealt with the pain from the point it started, but Celeste felt the full effect as soon as she hopped into her host.

She read the words slowly, and even though it angered her, she read the paper again.

CELESTE, DO NOT CONTACT ME AGAIN. EMMA WAS BORN IN THIS TIME, AND THE JUMP SHIFTED HER DEVELOPMENT. SINCE SHE JUMPED INTO THE PAST, HER AGE WILL ACCELERATE BY HALF EVERY THREE MONTHS. YOU CAN EXPECT HER DEATH WITHIN A THIRD OF THE AVERAGE LIFESPAN OF YOUR CURRENT TIME. ENJOY YOUR DAUGHTER AND LIVE WITH YOUR DECISION. I HOPE DAVID WINSOME WAS WORTH IT. I SINCERELY DOUBT IT.

Chapter 26

David watched the poker game, but no matter how many pointers Ace gave him, he still lost. They had moved him into a cell with three other men, and David thought they had all murdered someone. The most likable of the men, Ace, had murdered his wife's sister. It was a twisted set of circumstances, but David's predicament wasn't much different.

He still couldn't remember how he'd ended up with the knife in his hands. His first clear memory after falling asleep was waking up with his eyes on Caroline. She seemed horrified, and when he took in his surroundings, he understood the reason for her distress.

When Ag saw their mother, she screamed until Caroline pulled her out of the room. David wanted to call emergency services, but his phone was upstairs. He yelled for someone to call them and went to work on trying to hold pressure on his mother's wounds.

Her eyes had been open, but instead of the accusal he deserved, they reflected fright. Her mouth moved, but no sound came out. He wanted to hear her voice and receive condemnation or forgiveness, but he encouraged her to save her strength.

He moved into the trance he adopted in the emergency room. He blocked out all other sights and sounds and concentrated on his patient. When the emergency technicians arrived, he recognized Tony Spumoni and gave him a rundown of the situation.

Tony didn't ask about the person who had inflicted the stab wound. The police took over that part.

Sheriff Murphy was off duty, and thankfully, Lewis wasn't among the police officers who gathered evidence. David was honest with them, and when they asked who had stabbed his mother, Caroline cut in and told them it had to have been an intruder.

The police checked the doors and windows, but there were no signs of forced entry. Because of his profession, no one had questioned the blood on David's hands until a culprit was absent.

David had stepped up and confessed to holding the knife. In retrospect, he could have argued the fingerprints on it and made up a story about a struggle with a potential burglar, but he told the truth. His conscience wouldn't afford a lie.

Now, he faced attempted murder charges that could elevate if his mother died from her injuries. He should have been worried about his freedom, but he focused on his guilt.

After a lot of consideration, he'd decided he'd been sleepwalking. *But what kind of dream would mislead him into killing his mother?*

"It's your go," Frank said gruffly. He had sharp teeth he had filed to a point and meaty hands. David was certain he didn't want to upset Frank by delaying the game.

"Look at your cards," Ace warned.

David wasn't certain how he could tell what David was holding in his hand, but he could always guess what David was going to play before he played it. Ace shifted his dark brown eyes at Houston, but the man laid down his hand.

"I fold. I gotta call the missus, and I don't have time to wait on Worm."

"Worm" was David's nickname. Frank had given it to him after David had lost his first game of poker, and David hadn't contradicted him.

"I need to call my girlfriend, too," Frank said, looking up at the show airing on the television to gauge the time. They didn't have a clock. Someone had smashed it after they'd received bad news, and the deputies hadn't replaced it.

"You have a phone card?" Ace asked Houston.

Houston flashed a cheap phone. "Naw. Sam went out on the road crew, snuck off for a few minutes to meet his girl and get some supplies, and put it in his suitcase."

David wrinkled his nose. For men in their position, a "suitcase" was a part of the human body David never imagined sticking a phone inside.

David laid down two cards and Ace let out a long sigh as he handed two fresh ones to him. "Boy, why did I bother teachin' ya if yer gonna make plays like that one?"

Frank's smile spread. "Wouldn't of mattered. I got a flush." He laid down a suit of clovers in descending order.

Ace laid down his cards without fanfare. "Royal flush."

Frank's face fell. "You're a liar."

Ace was a mild-mannered man, but there were some things he wouldn't let pass. He jumped up and grabbed Frank's neck.

"Say it again."

The two men stared at each other until Frank dropped his eyes. Frank's teeth were intimidating, but Ace's reputation as a wily fighter preceded him.

Frank crossed his arms, and Ace took up the cards. He held out his hand for David's cards and David gave them to him automatically.

Frank flashed his teeth, and David looked away. Satisfied that he'd exercised dominance over David, Frank went to his bunk and fished out a phone from under the mattress.

"You're not gonna make it if you don't pay attention," Ace told him.

David scrubbed his face with his hands. "I know. I'll do better."

Ace took a card off the pile. "This is the jack of spades. He knows how to adapt and learn anywhere." He pulled another card. "This is the jack of hearts, and this"—a queen of hearts followed—"is the queen of hearts." He gazed at the card. "That little burger will ruin anyone, but especially the jack of hearts."

David thought he understood the analogy. "Yeah, I know. I'm too soft."

Ace laughed at him. "Unless you listen to me, boy, you're gonna be someone's little darlin' in prison. Those boys have teeth and they're not afraid to bite."

Frank moved the phone away from his ear. "Hey, I bite!"

Ace scoffed. "Yeah, you bite chunks outta ninety-pound women."

Frank let it go, but Ace sized the man up like he planned to make him rethink his dismissal.

"Who's your queen of hearts?" Ace asked.

"I'm with a woman—"

"I didn't ask who you was with. I asked who has your heart."

David shook his head in his hands. "Caroline."

"Well, she must be a doozy with a name like that. There's a reason why women have songs named after them."

"I don't think this one is like JFK's daughter, though."

Ace either didn't know who the song was penned after or didn't care. "Have you spoken to her about how you feel?"

"I'm with another woman," he repeated.

Ace motioned to the surrounding walls. "You aren't really with anyone while you're here. Do you have plans to see the woman you're with while you're in prison?"

"She's pregnant with my baby," David told him.

Ace took out a clear plastic wrap with tobacco rolled inside it. He took out a pinch and stuck it inside his lower lip.

"Sounds like you've really screwed yourself."

David nodded.

Ace stared at him as if he were deciding on the best advice to give him. "You're staying with her just for the baby?"

"Yeah. She's a great girl, and—"

"Break up with her."

David was looking at his feet, but when Ace spoke, his head shot up. "What?"

"If she's a great girl, she'll find someone better to take care of her and the baby."

"But I need to be with her. It's the right thing to do."

Ace stared at him sideways. "The best thing to do would have been not to be with her while your heart belonged to another woman, but that's out the window." He spit tobacco juice into a cup. "But there are some things you need to ask yourself."

"Like what?"

Ace gritted what was left of his teeth and touched his swollen jaw where an abscessed tooth was causing him difficulty. "How long are you going to be in here? Can you provide comfort to her? Will the woman you love be there for you, and if she will, will it mean more to her for you to be with her?"

David sat back in his chair and crossed his arms. "I don't see how I can really be with either of them."

"Good answer."

Ace didn't clarify his response, and David was too impatient to wait for anything that followed. He jumped up and paced beside his chair.

"I told you. You're screwed." Ace chuckled.

David shot him a look, and Ace laughed. "Boy, even if you wouldn't have ended up here, you'd already done a number on your life."

David sat back down and pressed his thumb and forefinger to his temples. "I know. I just want to do the right thing."

Ace sighed and flipped up the jack of hearts. "Follow your heart."

The next card he revealed gave David the direction he needed.

Chapter 27

When Ag's phone rang and she accepted the charges, Celeste knew the call was from David. Ag talked to her brother for the full ten minutes, and then she excused herself for the next ten-minute phone call.

Before the call ended, she rushed out and placed the phone in Celeste's hand. Celeste took it and walked upstairs after gesturing to Ag to keep an eye on Emma.

"I don't think there's a lot of time left," David said. "How's Emma?"

Celeste's elation deflated. She'd thought David had wanted to talk to her, but he was only speaking to her to learn about their child.

"She's great," she said, holding back tears. "She's saying more words, and Mindy potty-trained her."

She could have kicked herself for mentioning Mindy's name.

A disembodied voice reminded them that there was one minute left in the conversation. David spoke quickly.

"I've had a lot of time to think about what I've done or haven't done while I've been here. There are people who are important to me, and I haven't treated them fairly."

"David," Celeste said softly, but she followed it with nothing.

"If you don't know anything else, know that you're a good mother, and I love you."

Celeste opened her mouth to return his sentiment, but the phone call ended. She waited for it to ring again, but no matter how hard she willed him to call back, Ag's phone stayed silent.

She walked down the stairs, defeated. Emma and Ag looked up at her.

"He loves me." She handed the phone to Ag and dropped onto the couch beside her.

Ag leaned back. "He never stopped."

Emma returned to feeding her baby doll, and Celeste threw up her hands. "What can I do about it, though?"

"I don't know," Ag said. "Honestly, I wouldn't do anything." She stood up swiftly and put her hands on her hips. "My brother's emotions are so wishy-washy that he'll probably want to push you away again tomorrow."

Celeste didn't know how to respond. She finally was true to her feelings.

"I have done a lot to hurt people, and I hurt David the most."

Ag scoffed. "That's arguable."

Celeste cringed. She wondered if Caroline's abortion was common knowledge.

"Anyway, David may feel mixed up about me."

Ag glared at her. "My brother is impulsive. He may be a great nurse, but his reactions in relationships..." She shook her head. "Do yourself a favor and forget about him."

Celeste's eyes filled with tears. "I can't."

Ag surprised her by speaking roughly. "Then you're an idiot." Her curls bounced as she shook her head. "What has he given to you since you've changed your life? A day together as a family? A roll or two in the sheets?"

Emma looked up, and Ag censored her tongue. "I just don't think it's worth it."

"I love him," Celeste reminded her.

Ag spoke softly, and Emma crawled to a different part of the room. "Stop chasing after my brother. You were a great couple before you left, but David's heart broke into bitter pieces, and he'll never stop resenting you for going back to Willie or for keeping Emma a secret for so long."

Celeste looked up sharply. She wanted to tell Ag the truth, but her fear won out. Ag wouldn't believe Celeste was from the future, and she still technically had custody of Emma, so Celeste remained silent.

Ag glanced over at her mother. "Maybe my brother was sleepwalking when he stabbed our mother, but I don't care. He's the reason she's going to die, and I'll never forgive him."

She burst into tears, and Celeste did her best to console her. She wrapped her in a hug, and Emma scooted over and lay against Ag's leg.

Mrs. Winsome's breathing picked up pace, and when Celeste looked over, the lady's dark eyes were boring into them. "Not his fault."

Ag flew to her mother's side, and Emma moved to Celeste's leg. Mrs. Winsome's eyes were trained on Celeste. Ag patted her mother's hand, hoping to get her attention, but it was no use.

"Tell her," Mrs. Winsome demanded.

"Tell me what?" Ag asked, truly bewildered.

"Ask her who she is," Mrs. Winsome said, finally looking at her daughter. "And ask her who sent her."

Chapter 28

Celeste rang the doorbell, and Dalton's footsteps pounded down the hall. He swung open the door.

"It's her!" he screamed into the house. To Celeste, he said, "You can put the baby anywhere. We'll play with her after our show is over."

He plodded upstairs, leaving Celeste to show herself into Mindy's beautiful home. Aside from some toy guns scattered in the hall, the house was a showplace. Celeste did not know how Mindy could work twelve-hour shifts, raise two boys, and keep her house immaculate.

She called Mindy, but she received no response. Cameron came to the edge of the steps.

"Where's your mom?"

"She's asleep," he said.

Celeste considered leaving the house, but Cameron beckoned her upstairs. "Do you want to see something cool?"

Celeste didn't want to disappoint the boy, so she followed him upstairs and into Mindy's room. Even though Cameron had invited her, Celeste felt like it was a huge intrusion.

Mindy lay under a thin yellow sheet. Her hair cascaded off the pillow on either side of her head, and she had folded her hands peacefully over her belly.

"Watch this," Cameron said.

He walked up to the bed and screamed into Mindy's ear. She didn't move.

"Don't do that," Celeste commanded.

Cameron shrugged. "Why? She's not gonna wake up."

"I told my teacher about it, and she says that my mom must sleep like death," Dalton said as he entered the room.

His statement caused Celeste to panic, and she ran to Mindy's bedside to check her pulse. It was steady.

When she looked up, Dalton had the point of one of his dinosaur's tails indenting Mindy's leg. The space around the point was almost purple by the time Celeste moved his hand away.

"You shouldn't do that."

"She doesn't know," Dalton argued. "She'll just think it happened to her at work."

"She's your mother, and you shouldn't poke at her while she sleeps."

Celeste had a thought. "What do you do if you need something?" She looked down at Emma. "What happened when Emma cried out at night when your mother kept her?"

Dalton looked at the rug he stood on and tried to gather some of the fabric with his toes. "I got whatever she needed. She only woke up a couple of times, though."

Celeste had visions of Emma crying for hours until Dalton picked her up. She couldn't stand the idea of the child trying to balance her toddler as he struggled down the steps to get her something to eat or drink.

"David used to get us stuff while Mommy slept," Cameron chimed in.

"I'm big enough to take care of us now," Dalton said proudly.

"Of course you are," Celeste said, putting her hand on his shoulder. "Just remember who to call if there's a fire or someone is hurt."

Dalton rolled his eyes. "Yeah. I know. My mom tells me that every day."

They walked downstairs and Celeste made the children peanut butter crackers with celery boats. They munched happily, and the boys told Celeste and Emma about playing in a tee ball league.

"I don't know how your mom does it," she said. She works a lot, keeps a tidy house, and still manages to keep up with you guys."

Dalton and Cameron looked at each other.

"Nana takes us to all our practices and games," Dalton said. "Our mom hasn't even seen us play ball."

Celeste's heart went out to the boys. Her father had been her biggest fan when she was a child, and she hoped the boys' nana was as great with them as Celeste's father had been with her.

"I didn't know you were here," Mindy said. She pulled her hair up into what most women called a "messy bun", but it looked like every hair fell naturally into place.

"I haven't been here long," Celeste told her.

"Good," she said, grabbing an apple off the counter.

Celeste searched for polite conversation starters. "How's the baby?"

Mindy put one hand over her stomach. "The baby is doing great."

"When is your next appointment?"

Mindy looked at her strangely.

"When is your next appointment with the OBGYN?" Celeste clarified.

"Oh!" Mindy acknowledged, taking a bite of her apple. "I'm meeting with a midwife next week. I'm going to do a home birth. I think the sheriff will let me stream it so David can watch the birth."

Celeste couldn't think of anything to say.

"I know it may seem strange, but I want David to be part of the experience in any way possible."

Celeste tried a smile that fell flat. "I think it's great." She wanted to add further encouragement, but she couldn't find anything else to back it up.

Mindy held her hands out for Emma, and the toddler looked back at Celeste. She nodded to her daughter and handed her to Mindy.

"She's so heavy," Mindy commented, struggling to hold her. She balanced Emma on the counter. "How old is she now?"

It was a question Celeste liked to avoid. Emma's birthday fell during a different season, but everyone who knew them thought Emma had turned one a couple of months ago.

"She's about sixteen months."

Mindy's eyes widened. "She looks like she's between two and three years old. If it weren't for the DNA test, I'd say the pregnancy didn't match with the time you were with David."

It may have been the cattiest thing Mindy had ever said to her, but she covered it with smiles and hospitality. "Do you want to have coffee in the living room?"

"I'll take water," Celeste said agreeably.

They settled on Mindy's new sectional couch. Even though there were three seats she could have taken, Mindy sat next to Celeste. They were so close their legs touched.

Mindy spoke to Emma, but she talked down to her. Celeste's father had treated her like an adult, and she had responded with respect. She treated Emma the same, and she was convinced it was one reason for Emma's advanced speech. After all, her grandfather may have been right about her accelerated growth, but Emma's intelligence wouldn't have expanded without nurturing.

"Have you spoken to David lately?"

Celeste surveyed Mindy. She didn't look at her when she asked, but it was clear the woman was fishing for news about her boyfriend.

"He called Ag yesterday."

"That's wonderful!" Mindy said. "Did you have time to talk to him?"

Celeste didn't like to lie. She avoided it whenever possible, but she had a feeling she shouldn't tell Mindy the truth. At the very least, it could hurt her feelings.

"No."

Mindy perked up, rubbing Emma's cheek with her nose. "Well, I'm glad he had the chance to talk to his sister."

The women got through another half hour of strained civilities before the boys involved them in a board game. Cameron's meltdown after a loss was the cue Celeste had been looking for to help her leave gracefully.

"Are you sure you can't stay?" Mindy asked, feigning a friendly tone.

"No," Celeste replied. "I need to help get dinner ready for Mrs. Winsome."

Mindy touched Celeste's arm. "I've been praying for her. She has the First Baptist Church in her corner."

Celeste thanked her for her kindness.

"You and Emma could go to church with us on Sunday."

Celeste considered the idea. She loved the people at the church, but they liked her better when she had been "Emma" or Hailey Hall. Some of them had very strong feelings against Caroline.

"I'll probably stay with Mrs. Winsome so Ag and Emma can go." Church was supposed to be a safe place, and Celeste didn't want to be the reason someone felt uncomfortable in their place of worship.

Celeste wished she hadn't suggested weekly get-togethers with David's girlfriend. It was hard on Mindy and her, and Celeste could only hope it would get easier as they spent more time together.

Celeste felt a change in the atmosphere as soon as she pulled into the driveway. She never had feelings, other than brief glancings of intuition, but the idea something had altered worried her.

She practically ripped off her seatbelt and pushed the button on her daughter's five-point harness. Emma watched her carefully.

What if Mrs. Winsome had died? The lady had seemed fine, but they'd been cautioned that she could pass away at any time.

Celeste ran up the porch steps and fumbled with her keys. Emma hugged herself to her neck to keep Celeste from putting her down.

The closer she was to opening the door, the more Celeste knew something had happened while she'd been gone. She flung open the door, and it bounced off the wall.

Mrs. Winsome was sitting up in her hospital bed eating the yogurt Ag spooned to her. Ag looked up at Celeste, puzzled by her exaggerated entrance.

After she had spoken to Celeste the previous night, Mrs. Winsome seemed to improve dramatically. She was still frail, but it was easier for her to remain conscious and speak clearly.

She wanted to ask *What's wrong?* but everything appeared to be fine. Celeste closed the door and sat Emma at the edge of Mrs. Winsome's bed.

"Pretty baby," Mrs. Winsome said as she looked at the toddler.

"That's Emma," Ag told her.

Mrs. Winsome rolled her eyes. "I know my own granddaughter, Agony. I knew it way before you."

Celeste expected her panicky feeling to go away, but it only intensified. *Was her grandfather putting stress on her original body in his time frame?*

She decided it wasn't likely, as she'd had no sign Caroline had been using her body for the months before she discovered her grandfather's plan. It had to be something in her current situation.

She sat on the couch and put her head in her hands.

"Is something wrong?" Ag asked.

Celeste looked up, ready to tell her about the feeling, when there was a knock at the door. Ag and Celeste looked at each other, silently affirming that neither one of them expected company.

Ag stood up, but Celeste raced to the door. She was ready to face whatever was on the other side.

Her hand trembled as she turned the knob, but her sweaty hands allowed her to pull the door open. She gasped when she saw who was on the other side.

Sheriff Murphy looked down at her. His face was sober, and his green eyes seemed sad.

Was he there to tell them something had happened to David?

He surprised her by putting his hand on her shoulder. After a brief squeeze, he moved to the side. David dropped two plastic bags on the porch and held his arms out to her.

<h1 style="text-align:center">Chapter 29</h1>

Celeste ran into David's arms. As they held each other, nothing else mattered, and a part of her relaxed she hadn't known was tense.

When she looked at him, she was surprised to find that she was crying. "Did they let you go?"

He shook his head. He held her with one arm and pointed to Sheriff Murphy.

The hardened police chief said nothing.

"It was a R/O Bond," David explained. "The sheriff put up his property so I could get my affairs in order."

"But Mrs. Winsome is going to live," Celeste argued. "Everything will be okay." She leaned into him. "I don't think your mother is going to press charges against you."

"That's not who I have to worry about."

Celeste followed his gaze. Ag stood in the middle of the room with her arms crossed.

"Ag has power of attorney over Mama," he told her. "And she hasn't forgiven me."

David waited at the door, staring at his sister. Ag's features never changed. Her thoughts were unclear.

"Get in the house," Mrs. Winsome called. "It's not a Mexican stand-off."

Her mother's words startled Ag. "Mama! You can't say that anymore."

Mrs. Winsome threw her fist down on the bed. "Jesus wept, Agony! What am I supposed to say?"

Ag made several noises. "Er, I guess you just call it a stand-off."

"Is that what this is, Ag?" David stepped away from Celeste. "Are you against me?"

Ag broke eye contact. "David—"

"Because you could never hate me more than I hate myself for what I've done."

Ag glared at him. "Oh, I'd say you're wrong about that one."

"I won't have it!" Mrs. Winsome declared. "I won't have my children fighting." She looked from her daughter to her son. "Now, what happened?"

Ag rounded on her. "He tried to kill you!"

Mrs. Winsome's face wrinkled in disbelief. "That wasn't him."

"Who else was standing there holding a bloody knife over you?"

Mrs. Winsome muttered something. It took Ag a moment to get her to speak clearly.

"I keep telling you who it was, but you won't listen."

Sheriff Murphy stepped through the door. "Who was it?"

Sheriff Murphy had validated her, and Mrs. Winsome's voice rose proudly. "It was the man who was in my son's body."

The sheriff looked back at Celeste and David. Celeste had paled, but David put his head in his hand.

Ag's fists flew to her sides. "You *will* serve time for trying to kill my mother."

Sheriff Murphy held out his hands, palms down. "David won't go to trial unless Mrs. Wiinsome presses charges."

It was a surprise to hear the seasoned officer address Eleanor Winsome so formally. To Celeste's knowledge, he called everyone else by their first name—even Kerry Shelton, who had to be near Mrs. Winsome's age.

"She isn't able to make those types of decisions," Ag countered.

Mrs. Winsome clapped her hands for attention, but the weak sound hardly registered in the room. "I have my wits about me, and I'm not pressing charges." She looked at the sheriff. "You can let him go now."

Sheriff Murphy nodded.

Ag raised her hand, and a smug expression crossed her features. "Actually, I don't think my mama can say that."

"I love you, girl, but no one cares what you think right now. My boy needs to get in out of the weather," Mrs. Winsome said.

"No," Ag argued. "He doesn't deserve to be here after what he did." She pointed to her mother, her hand shaking. "I have a power of attorney over you, and I say the charges will stick. David will pay for what he did."

"That's not a Christian action," her mother countered. "He said he didn't do it, and I said he didn't do it. You don't rule the roost, girl. I want my son to come into our home."

Ag's mouth moved, but nothing came out.

"That girl reminds me so much of—"

She stopped, obviously remembering her company. Celeste doubted Mrs. Winsome was referring to Bill or herself, and she wondered about whose actions Ag's mirrored.

She stared at David, her brown eyes showing more emotion than Celeste had ever seen from her. "You're home, David."

David didn't need a formal invitation. All he wanted was his mother's forgiveness. He ran to her side, and after a moment where he assessed the best way to embrace her, he wrapped her frail shoulders in a hug. His body followed his arms, and he lay mostly on the bed.

When David's back shook as he cried over his mother, Sheriff Murphy excused himself. He tipped his hat to Celeste and shut the door on his way out.

The scene before her drew Celeste, but Emma tugged at her leg. She realized that the best place for them was outside.

It was a warm night, and Emma scooted across the porch. Celeste worried her daughter might pick up a splinter on her bare legs, but the toddler navigated the porch without incident.

After a stretch of time, David walked outside. He sat beside her and put his arm around her shoulders. Celeste could have stayed in that moment forever as they sat on the porch steps. She wished instead of moving back and forth in time that she could just freeze it.

"I'm eventually going to prison."

Celeste grabbed his free hand and wound her fingers through his. "It seems that way."

He glanced at Emma, who scooted in his direction. "I won't see her grow up."

Celeste tugged his fingers. "We'll visit. You can see her—"

"No. Emma doesn't deserve that. If it wouldn't be even more confusing for her, I'd say you should tell her you didn't know her father."

"Da," Emma said, placing a well-timed hand on David's arm.

He looked behind him as if he were just noticing her. "Emma! How's my baby girl? You've gotten so big!"

It was a common way to greet a child, but his words rang true. Emma had grown a lot since he'd last seen her.

He pulled Emma into his arms, and she giggled as he rubbed his coarse beard against her skin. These moments were the ones Celeste treasured the most. The two people who had stolen her heart were laughing and playing as she watched.

Emma settled against him, and David rubbed her arms. "It's getting cooler. We should take her inside."

Once indoors, David asked Celeste to get Emma's bed out of Ag's room. "Once you get it into the kitchen, I'll take it upstairs." He put her hand over his arm. "I've been working out."

Celeste laughed as he waggled his eyebrows. Their playfulness caused Mrs. Winsome to stir in her sleep.

She hated to ruin the moment, but she had to maintain some self-respect. "Maybe tomorrow."

David's face fell. "Is this about Mindy?"

Celeste nodded. "I can't sleep with you before you break up with her."

She had spoken boldly, as she didn't know his intentions. She relaxed when he planted a soft kiss on her cheek.

"You're right. I need to break things off with her. I just hope she'll still let me be a part of her pregnancy."

Celeste mulled it over. "She seems like a reasonable person. I think you'll be okay."

David's eyebrows drew together. "You haven't seen her when she gets mad." He held up his arm and pointed to a scar. "I thought I was going to need stitches over that one."

Celeste brushed her fingers over the mark. "It's not like you to put up with abuse."

"She threw a plate at me," he said. "It happened once." He shrugged. "Besides, we were arguing over you, and everyone who knows you seems to have strong feelings about you."

"I can't imagine why," she deadpanned.

"You're an idiot."

They turned toward the voice. Mrs. Winsome was awake and watching them.

David pushed his hair back and chuckled. "I know, Mama."

She let out a puff of air. "You, too, boy, but the girl needs to tell you who she really is."

Mrs. Winsome's direction inspired Celeste, even though she couldn't trust the effects of the woman's aphasia. "I've told him a couple of times."

Mrs. Winsome surveyed her. There was a long silence before she spoke again.

"Then he doesn't deserve you."

She slipped back into sleep. David was unaffected by the scene, as he thought Celeste was only humoring his mother.

Celeste and David readied Emma for bed. David zipped her sleep suit, careful not to pinch her delicate skin.

"This is all I ever wanted," David said as he patted Emma's back. "I just wish I could have been there from the beginning."

He didn't lay the blame at her feet that time, but she could feel it coming from him. She tried to change the subject.

"I've been sleeping in your mother's room—"

She stopped talking when his head jerked in her direction. He kept his voice low, but she could imagine his disbelief.

"How could you sleep in that room after what happened?"

"It was hard, at first, but after working all night, and—" She stopped when he shook his head. "Ag told me it was best."

"Of course she did." He squeezed his eyes like the act would erase his words. "Never mind. That wasn't nice."

He switched conversational gears. "It looks like this young lady is asleep, so where do you want me to put her?"

Celeste patted the couch, and David placed her on it. They lined the floor with pillows before David pulled Celeste to his room. She stopped him at his door.

He didn't wait for her to speak. He devoured her kisses and pressed her against him.

"I don't have a lot of time, and I don't want to waste a second of it."

Celeste gave in to his advances, and he pushed open the door to his room. They stumbled across the rug and laughed.

David looked down at her seriously. "I love you, Caroline. You're all I thought about while I was gone."

It should have softened her remaining will, but the sound of another woman's name shocked her into reality. She pressed her hand lightly to his chest and took a step away.

"What's wrong?" David asked. "What did I do wrong?"

Celeste stared at him, willing him to realize that she was Celeste and not Caroline, but it wasn't possible. He couldn't read her mind, and she couldn't provide him with the proof he needed to show him she was telling the truth.

"Nothing," she lied. "I'm just not comfortable being together before you talk to Mindy."

He ran a hand through his hair, and Celeste was glad to see he was letting it grow out a little more. "Yeah. That's not a conversation I'm looking forward to."

She let him kiss her one more time before she left his room. She climbed on the couch beside Emma, opting not to go to Mrs. Winsome's room to sleep.

It proved difficult to rest, as Mrs. Winsome liked to sleep with the living room lamp on. After her ordeal, Celeste understood why the lady would want to see her surroundings immediately upon waking.

"You told him?"

Celeste raised her head. Mrs. Winsome had opened her eyes, and she was staring in her direction. Ag had brushed her mother's hair, and the golden glints against the dull brown gave it a healthier glow. It was hard to believe the woman was still knocking on death's door.

"I told him, but he doesn't believe me."

Mrs. Winsome pointed at her. "I won't be here forever, girl, so you'll have to *make* him believe."

Mrs. Winsome's condition had caused her to speak openly about things she thought were true. Celeste understood she was referencing her fictional writing, but part of her needed to talk plainly. She used the lady's deteriorating brain to her advantage as she tried to find comfort.

Celeste struggled to maneuver around Emma without waking her. "How? Everything I say sounds completely unbelievable."

Mrs. Winsome's head turned to her bedroom door. "Agony said you've been reading my journals."

"I have."

She smiled. "What do you think of them?"

"At first, I thought they were real, but Ag told me it was a made-up story—"

Mrs. Winsome's eyes flashed. "You know they're true."

If you're going to have this conversation, you're going to have to commit to it, Celeste thought.

"I think your journals are eye-opening."

Mrs. Winsome's stiff wrinkles softened. "It's not like anything you'll see in the movies. The people who write my shows can't even come close."

Celeste disagreed, but she said nothing. There were plenty of shows and movies about time travel, and there were a few that were eerily similar to the process she had used. Fact wasn't always too far from fiction.

"I definitely enjoyed reading them."

She folded her hands over the thin blanket. "Where did you get to?"

Celeste thought back. "I think Steve had come back, and you guys were building another machine."

The thin smile she had been holding fell. "That idiot." She shook her head. "We were all idiots."

"A group of college kids discovered time travel. I'd say you were ahead of your time."

Mrs. Winsome didn't accept her compliment. "Everyone in our group had extremely high IQs. That's what drew us together. We could talk about the sciences and none of our peers understood. Nothing we developed is beyond reach. Even now, someone with the right knowledge, skill, and a lot of money could build the same device."

Celeste guessed she had slipped into her character. Mrs. Winsome never spoke that way.

"I wish I could have read more about your adventures," Celeste volunteered.

Mrs. Winsome motioned to her room. "They're all in there. You can read them anytime." Her mouth twitched at the corners. "This time you have my permission."

Celeste colored. Mrs. Winsome was right. She had gone through her host's personal journals without asking.

A chuckle cracked across the room. "It's okay. I don't mind, even if you are a blonde woman."

Celeste was relieved. She'd thought she'd offended her ex-mother-in-law.

"What's your name?" she asked.

Celeste hesitated. It was one thing to feed into Mrs. Winsome's condition, but it was another to add herself to the mix. If she told Ag or David about their conversation, Celeste could lose Emma.

Mrs. Winsome read her misgivings. "I'm not gonna share it with my overprotective daughter and wishy-washy son. It's up to you to tell them."

"Again," Celeste said.

Mrs. Winsome's eyebrows drew together. "What'd you say?"

"I said 'again'. I told David my name was Celeste when I came back the last time."

The lady brought her hand up to her head and touched her temple. "Did you bring something to prove it, Celeste?"

Celeste shook her head. "The only thing that transferred with me was Emma and the blanket I wrapped her in."

Mrs. Winsome threw up her hands. "Did you stuff a newspaper in the blanket?"

"We don't have newspapers. Everything is online."

Mrs. Winsome rolled her eyes. "Of course it is. Generations will lose centuries of information to make it more user-friendly." She put rabbit ears around her last two words.

Celeste couldn't help adding her view. "It saves trees and a lot of unnecessary waste."

"The world will be here long after the scourge of humans has been swiped off the planet."

After the war, Slover's disease, and infertility issues in her time, Celeste couldn't disagree. The diminishing human population was on its way to extinction.

"Why are you here, Celeste?"

She was unaccustomed to hearing her name in her current time frame, and she didn't think it should be said so often. She decided Mrs. Winsome called her by name because she wished to familiarize herself with it.

"I came back to stop the Great War."

Mrs. Winsome stared at her silently. For a long moment, the lady did not show she was going to speak or had even heard her.

Celeste wanted to look away, but she held Mrs. Winsome's gaze. She blinked and released Celeste from whatever hold she'd had on her.

Mrs. Winsome stared at her hands in her lap. "War. It's always war that creates the desire to elicit change. We go through our lives without care until a dictator shakes up the snow globe of the world and destruction rains down like snowflakes over our heads."

It was poetic and true. She wanted to tell Mrs. Winsome more, but she let her words settle over the silence of the night.

"You know, you won't be able to stop the war," she told her. "No matter how hard you try, someone else will extinguish millions of innocent lives." She looked at Celeste. "Don't let that weight fall on your shoulders."

Tears rolled down Celeste's cheeks. "I had to try, and I think it worked."

Mrs. Winsome smiled sadly. "I thought that at one time. But I was wrong, too."

Chapter 30

We approached our project with new confidence. Steve had already traveled back in time once, and we knew he could do it again.

Danny was sure he had done his job and Linda's, so everything seemed to be in place.

Steve was sad when we led him to the machine. He missed Linda, but he wouldn't call her before his jump into the past. I kept expecting her to run through the door, and I even left it unlocked for her, but our little group wasn't in a fictional tale. She didn't know the date we planned to send Steve into the past again, and if she did, she was too busy with her family responsibilities to pull herself away.

The send-off was anti-climatic. Steve was there one moment, lying on a leather couch, but the next second he was gone, leaving behind a slight wind and a nominal electrical charge.

Liz, Danny, and I hung around Steve's house for the next few weeks. He had given us free rein of his large home, and we'd moved in. It had helped me the most, as I had been struggling to keep my apartment.

Danny went out on the weekends and sometimes didn't return until early in the morning or late the next day. I should have been upset about the female company he was likely keeping, but I was indifferent to it.

Liz and I cooked, cleaned, and played cards. She was a good friend, but she seemed two-dimensional to me. She didn't seem to have hopes or dreams that went beyond her task. No matter how well I thought I knew her, I wondered if I really knew her at all.

Steve didn't come back on the day he was set to return. He came back sooner.

He ran into the house, picked me up, and twirled me around. I laughed with him.

"Did you hear?" he asked us.

We hadn't been out of the house all day, and the radio had been silent.

"Is the war over?" Danny said eagerly.

He nodded his head. "The war is over, and it's been over for two years."

Vertigo threatened to send me crashing to the ground. "What do you mean? I just heard President Truman's address last night. He's going to try a new tactic."

"It never happened," he practically squealed.

Steve and Danny disappeared into the basement, and Liz ran to the phone. She went into her room, pulling the long cord behind her.

Danny and Steve emerged from the basement, carrying champagne and glasses. Danny tripped and one fell from his grasp, breaking against the ground.

"That was my glass," Steve said, and he laughed and slapped Danny on the back when Danny's face fell.

We toasted Steve's success, even though I was still reeling from the possibilities. My mind raced, and instead of calming it down, the alcohol sped up my anxiety.

I stepped outside and took in the wind whispering through the trees. *The war had been over for two years.*

I walked two blocks into town and noted the changes. Storefronts gleamed and more people walked past them. Men stood at the doors, either greeting patrons or carrying on conversations with neighbors. Some of them bore the marks of war, while others carried their scars inside.

I marveled at the sight of the men who had returned home. *How many of them would have died in the two years I'd just lived through?*

Another question occurred to me. *Why did I remember the last two years?* Steve had been the only one who had traveled back in time, so how did Liz, Danny, and I know about what had never happened? And worse, why weren't the last two years of our lives changed? *Had we lived in some sort of bubble created by the charge Steve had left behind?*

A man bumped into me. He apologized, and I smiled at him, noticing the cane he used for balance.

Bill.

If the war had ended two years ago, would Bill be alive?

I couldn't wait to get back to Danny's house. I ran into a soda shop and begged to use their phone. The girl behind the counter hesitated, but she led me to a back room and watched over me as I waited for the operator to connect me to my parent's number.

I didn't wait for my father to say more than a greeting. "Is Bill okay?"

He muttered something I couldn't hear, but then he said, "I think so. He seemed to be the last time I saw him."

If I hadn't already been sitting, my legs would have given out. "He didn't die in the war?"

My father is a practical man, so he was firm with me. "What is this about Eleanor? Bill is crippled, but he works every day at the Feed and Seed."

"He's not at the church?" I had always thought he'd be a preacher.

"No, he turned down the job to spend more time with his daughter. Becky has expensive taste, and she wanted a three-bedroom house in town. He owes her father $5,500 dollars for that one, so he has to work every day the store's open."

I was still reeling from the news that Bill was alive. "That's too bad."

"It's a cryin' shame," my father agreed. "He would have made a good preacher."

"He's alive."

My father missed my breathlessness. "Yes. So many boys, like your brother, lost their lives."

That struck a chord with me. Steve had erased the war deaths of the last two years, but he hadn't gone back far enough to wipe away the event that caused my brother's death.

I rushed through the rest of the conversation and avoided the shop girl's questions when I left. As I stepped into the sunshine, Danny accosted me, but it wasn't the same person who I'd left at his house. This Danny was much older, and he grabbed my arms with such urgency that I cried out.

Lines traced paths around his eyes and mouth, proof that he'd had some good times. At least the middle-aged Danny in front of me hadn't suffered for the crimes we'd committed against the government and the natural order of things.

A gentleman looked in our direction, but I eased his worry with my smile. "What do you need?"

Danny didn't mince words. "We have to get the machine out of the house."

I didn't ask him questions. I ran behind him, tossing off my low heels to keep up. When we got to the house, a red truck was parked in the driveway.

"Is that your truck?" I asked.

"It is today," he told me. "We have to load all the equipment into it."

We snuck through the back door, carefully staying quiet while Liz, Steve, and the younger Danny laughed in another room. It was far too easy to smuggle out the equipment, and I asked Danny for advice about the state of the world in his time before he left.

"I can't upset the course of history too much."

I crossed my arms, and he chuckled. "The outcome of the war was a one-time thing."

I raised my eyebrows.

"Look, if you make it through your new life, you can find help at this address." He scribbled on the back of an envelope.

I placed it in the pocket of my dress.

"I have some notebooks," I told him. "Could you take them with you?"

A break in the notebook and the change of color in the pen showed that the next part had been recorded later. Mrs. Winsome wrote it as if she'd continued her entry on the same day.

I didn't wait for Danny's stolen truck to rumble to life. I ran inside and distracted my friends from the sound.

I shared another glass of champagne with them, and we sang a song I didn't know. The war was over, Bill was alive, and the world was healing.

There were things I wanted back. If I had been in Steve's place, I would have found a way to save my brother's life, and Bill and I would have been married. We'd stay with my parents so he could pursue his dream, and I'd have a baseball team of children for him.

No knock sounded when they came in. Liz was the first to notice, and her face drained of all the color it usually held. The supervisor from the Secret City asked his men to scour the house for our equipment, and they were disappointed to report that it was gone.

Al stepped into the room, exercising his new authority. "Then take them with you. They rebuilt it once, they can do it again."

My heart sank with his betrayal, but his next words broke me.

"They stole my idea, and they'll have to suffer for it."

Chapter 31

Celeste had stayed up reading most of the night. She caught a few hours of sleep before David woke her up by combing his fingers through her hair.

"Good morning."

She sat up and wiped the sleep from her eyes. "I guess it would be to someone who got a lot of sleep last night." She laughed to lighten her statement.

David nodded to his mother, who was still sleeping in her hospital bed. "Did she keep you up last night?"

He meant it as a joke, but it was Mrs. Winsome's words that had caused her to toss and turn long after she'd laid down.

"I made bagels, and there's cream cheese in the refrigerator," Ag announced as she carried Emma to the bathroom.

After she came back out, she handed Emma to Celeste, and David tried a jab at his sister. "You didn't make the bagels or the house would be on fire."

Unamused, Ag glided into the kitchen.

David's smile quickly left his face, and Celeste felt the need to encourage him. "It'll just take some time. She still loves you."

He shook his head. "She always loved Mama the most. She cared about all of us, but Mama was her world."

"I'm still here," Mrs. Winsome croaked.

David flew to her side. "Of course you are, Mama."

"I was just biddin' my time until you two quit sucking each other's faces—"

David patted her arm. "We didn't kiss, Mama."

She allowed him to place a pillow behind her back. "Well, before you know it, I'll be a grandmother again."

She'd meant that she thought David and Celeste were going to make another baby, but Celeste's mind flew to Mindy's pregnancy. David must have had similar thoughts, as he lowered his eyes.

"I can smell beans cookin' for supper, but does anyone eat breakfast here?"

Ag answered her call by bringing in a bagel with cream cheese melting over it. "Here, Mama. I know you like them."

Mrs. Winsome's appetite was encouraging, and Celeste let herself hope that her recovery was progressing. She asked for collard greens with her beans, and Ag made a note to make them as a side dish.

David played with Emma all morning, and Celeste took the time to take a shower. She thought she heard voices raised when the water stopped running, and she ran downstairs when she heard Emma cry.

"Stop fussin' around that baby," Mrs. Winsome said as loudly as her lungs would allow.

David put Emma on the floor, and she crawled to Celeste. David and Ag faced each other. Her hands were at her hips and his were in fists at his sides.

"I'm not a killer," he yelled.

She mocked him. "No, I guess you're an *attempted* murderer."

David walked away, brushing past Celeste. "I don't have to put up with this."

He slammed the door on his way out.

Celeste hated to think he was on his way to Mindy's house, but she knew he would go there. He might have every intention of telling her they were over, but if Mindy cried, he was likely to cave. He didn't feel welcome in his own home, so if she opened hers to him, she might win him over.

It took every ounce of Celeste's willpower to keep from running after him. No good ever came from chasing after someone with fickle emotions.

Instead, she tried to calm Ag. Ag stiffened when she tried to hug her, so she waited until Emma's nap to speak to her.

"Ins," Emma said sweetly. "I sleep with you?"

The lines on Mrs. Winsome's face softened as she held out her hands to her granddaughter. "My sweet grand, you always have a place with me."

"Don't you mean *granddaughter*?" Ag corrected.

"I said what I said," Mrs. Winsome replied without taking her eyes off Emma.

Celeste helped her daughter settle beside Mrs. Winsome. Even though she wasn't a fan of the early afternoon television programs that scrolled across the Teleboard, Emma was asleep in minutes, so it was likely that she hadn't absorbed it.

She found Ag in her room. She was typing furiously on her laptop, but when Celeste entered the room, her productivity slowed to a trickle.

"Are you still consulting?"

Ag nodded and grabbed a coffee cup on her bedside table. "Not as much as I used to, but I still have some loyal clients."

"I didn't know if you'd still work after everything that happened."

Ag held her hands up. "Someone has to pay to make the repairs around here."

"I have some money—"

Ag interrupted her. "I don't want your money."

Celeste felt chastised. She'd been saving to move into another place, but she wanted to help the Winsomes.

Ag sighed. "I want my brother to help. I don't want him to do everything, but this is our family home. If he's not going to help pay for the repairs, he can at least help put on some of the siding in the garage or look at the pipes."

"There's a garage?"

Ag pointed in the direction of the backyard. An old barn-like building stood there, but Celeste had thought that it belonged to their neighbor.

"It's where Daddy used to keep his old Camero. David and I weren't allowed to go in there. Even Daddy raised his voice if we played too close to the building."

"I'm sorry about David. Maybe I could talk to him."

Ag scoffed. "David has two babies to take care of now. He can't help his family."

Celeste looked at her hands and wound one finger over another. Ag noticed her awkwardness and patted her hands.

"It has nothing to do with you. Mama and I want you and Emma to stay, but David needs to help support Emma and give Mindy money for their baby until he goes to prison."

"He doesn't have to go to prison," Celeste said hopefully. "You could drop—"

Ag shook her head violently. "No."

There was very little to say after Ag's refusal. Celeste could talk to her all day, but she wouldn't change her feelings.

After Emma's nap, Ag served Mrs. Winsome soup beans. The family gathered in the living room with their bowls until Mrs. Winsome barked at them to get to the table and keep crumbs off her floor.

"And that baby doesn't need to get used to eating in front of a screen," she called from the living room.

They were midway through their meal when Mrs. Winsome piped up again. "Where's my greens?"

Ag's eyes widened. "I forgot to put on the greens."

She delivered raw spinach to Mrs. Winsome, who barely voiced a complaint while she ate it. Ag flashed the empty bowls at Celeste when she collected them.

"She's getting her appetite back," Celeste observed.

It was hard to wait for David after dinner. Celeste cleaned the floor and stacked blocks with Emma, but his absence distracted her. *Was he with Mindy, and was she providing him with the comfort Celeste had refused him?*

Her longing glances at the door hadn't gone unnoticed by Mrs. Winsome. "He'll be back. He doesn't look at that other blonde woman the way he looks at you."

"I don't want him to bounce between us."

Mrs. Winsome steepled her frail fingers. "My boy's emotions are all over the place. You have to understand why he'd be a little mixed up. When people mess with the natural course of time—"

"Stop it!" Ag stepped into the room and pointed her finger between them. "I'm tired of hearing about jumps through time and body swapping. I'll get your journals if you want to add more to your books, but don't act like outside forces were responsible for David's attack."

"Agony—"

Ag returned her mother's contemptuous stare. The ladies would have stayed locked in an ocular battle if Emma wouldn't have climbed up Ag's leg, balancing her cast against the floor.

Ag picked Emma up and took her upstairs for her bath. Without her daughter to distract her, Celeste was left with nothing to do.

She scrolled through some social media, trying to look up Braedan and Macey, but they had blocked her account. She found Hailey and Braeden's mother, and she read some posts that dated back to the car wreck. Mrs. Hall had begged her friends to pray for her family and updated them on Macey's progress.

"Research?" Mrs. Winsome asked.

"Kind of."

Celeste valued her time alone with Mrs. Winsome. Even though the lady's mind had deteriorated and she thought Celeste was a character in one of her journals, it was nice to drop her pretenses.

"What do you want to do?"

Celeste turned off her phone. "I want to stay here with David and Emma, but my grandfather can pull me back at any moment. Somehow, Braeden is mixed up in what my grandfather wants to accomplish, so if I find a way to work at that angle, maybe I can stay."

She closed her eyes. When she opened them, she spoke softly to Celeste. "You've read my notebooks. There's no way you can stay. Eventually, you'll have to go back to your body."

Celeste argued her point. "But Caroline is in my body, and she seems happy about—"

"That's not it." Her wrinkles folded over each other on her forehead. "How much of my journal have you read?"

Ag brought Emma downstairs, and their conversation died. Emma placed a kiss on Mrs. Winsome's cheek, and the lady cried out when her hand slipped to her stomach.

"What is it, Mama?" Ag put Emma down and placed a hand on her mother's head.

"It's just my side hurtin'. I think supper gave me some gas."

Ag fixed her mother some warm milk, and Mrs. Winsome was asleep in twenty minutes. Emma soon followed, and Ag went to bed early.

The house was quiet, and Celeste snuck into Mrs. Winsome's room to read more of her journal. What she read changed her view on everything she thought she knew.

Chapter 32

They didn't get our equipment. And our lives didn't change when we went to sleep. When we dozed out, we woke back up in the same cold room. Maybe that charge really had done something that kept us from fully belonging to the new world.

I kept reminding myself that whatever happened, another version of Danny had gotten our machine before the government touched it. It was hard to focus when Al ordered them to torture me, and I lost one of my fingernails, but I kept my mouth shut.

They rounded us into a twelve-by-twelve room and sat us in a circle. A patch of Liz's hair had been ripped out by the roots, Danny was nursing broken fingers, and Steve's upper body was soaked. I'd heard of waterboarding a prisoner, but I'd never seen it in practice. His eyes were bloodshot and snot poured over his upper lip.

We were all emotionally spent, but we reawakened when they carried Linda into the room. The skin over her left foot was darkening, making a purple-black stain.

Steve tried to get up, but he was chained to the wall like the rest of us. The soldier who brought her into the room looked disgusted as he fixed her restraints. He wouldn't look at any of us, and I was unsure if he was disgusted with us because he thought we were traitors or if he didn't like torturing a woman.

Steve moved his foot as far as it would go, and Linda touched it with the tips of her fingers. She took breaths in gasps as she reached for her lover. The extension proved too much, and she lost consciousness.

When the soldier left, Steve looked around the room, staring pointedly at the mirror behind Liz. "They're going to listen to everything we say." His voice was almost too raspy to understand.

"Then they'll hear exactly what I told them!" Danny shouted at the mirror.

"Save your strength," I told him. I didn't know what they planned to do with us, but we weren't dead yet, so I had hope that they would keep us alive.

"Did anyone say anything?" Liz's eyes floated, and I wondered if her torturers had drugged her.

We all shook our heads.

Linda's arm twitched, and she shot up, grabbing her ankle. Her dark hair fell over her leg as she massaged her swollen skin. "I think my foot is broken."

"It looks like it," Steve agreed. Then, more tenderly, he added, "I missed you."

"Me too," she returned. Her gaze fell to her lap. "I'm sorry about all this."

"It's not your fault," Liz said, rubbing her temples. "Al knew what we were up to. I don't know if he was unaffected by the shift in events because he was with us the first time we sent Steve, or—"

"I told him," Linda said.

"What?" Steve croaked.

Tears rolled off Linda's cheeks as she explained that Al's soldiers grabbed her and tortured her for days. She rolled up the sleeves of her dress and angry purple, green, and brown bruises dotted her arms.

"There's more on my stomach and back," she told them. "I've lost count of the days I've been here, but today was the worst. Al broke my foot himself."

"Then I'll break him," Steve vowed.

Linda glanced over at him before she hung her head. "But I told them. I told them everything I knew and everything I suspected."

After her admission, the door opened. Al walked in with a smug expression.

He folded his hands before he spoke. "This could have been so different. All you had to do was live out your mundane lives—"

"Oh, shut up!" Liz said. "No one wants to hear your nonsense."

Color rushed to Al's face, but he smiled. "Some of the Native Americans scalped their adversaries. I wonder if you'd like to be afforded that privilege."

"Yeah," Liz returned, touching the bleeding spot on her scalp. "After this, I'd love to scalp you."

Al spat on her, and Danny and Steve moved against their restraints. They were no match for the metal that held them in place.

"I never liked you," Al said.

"The feeling is mutual," Liz returned, staring at him until he looked away.

Al turned his back on her. "Now, I don't know all the specifics, but I have a good idea what your little group was up to."

"Just leave us alone," Linda begged. "You said you would stop harassing us if I told you what I knew."

Al chuckled. "I lied." He kicked Steve's shoe. "I think you've had some experience with liars, so you shouldn't be surprised."

He took a breath. "Well, look at us. We're all together again. He received their glares with pride. "It seems you were successful, so now we're going to continue your missions."

"Missions?" I asked.

He pointed at me. "Yes, my sweet Eleanor. We are going to work together to erase history." He tilted his head to the side and placed a finger on his chin. "At least the parts the government doesn't like."

I understood his plan a little faster than my friends. When they recognized what it meant for each of them, they understood the repercussions of our last mission.

We had saved millions of lives, but now the government—and most importantly, Alexander Maze—had control over ours.

Chapter 33

Celeste lost her breath. She read and reread the name, willing the letters to change, but they remained the same.

She rushed into the living room. Mrs. Winsome had been asleep, and she grimace in pain when Celeste shook her awake.

"What is it, girl? Is something wrong with David?"

Celeste shook her head. "You know my grandfather. His name is in your book."

"Which one was your grandfather?"

"It was Dr. Maze. You called him Al."

She chuckled. "So, he fancies himself a doctor now."

Celeste thought back to what she'd read about him. In Mrs. Winsome's journals, he hadn't pursued a medical degree or finished his undergraduate degree, but people had been putting their faith in him for years. He'd had a lot of success, but there were times when community members died at his hands. She wondered if it was due to his inexperience.

Mrs. Winsome sighed. "I wondered how well you knew him, but I never guessed you were his blood. I thought the good Lord would prevent his seed from speadin' after all the harm he'd caused."

"My father was a good man," Celeste defended.

Mrs. Winsome met her eyes. "I shouldn't have said that. Sometimes the apple doesn't fall far from the tree, but a replanted seed can grow into a beautiful garden."

Celeste didn't have time for metaphors. "I thought our talks about the past were because you had dementia."

A sly smile inched up her face. "I'm sure I'm not doing as well as most seventy-year-olds, but I still have my wits about me."

Celeste went through several possibilities in her mind. "Are the timelines blurring?"

She nodded. "Every time it happens, I see two tracks." She shook her head once. "That may not make sense to some people—"

"I get it. You have two different sets of memories for the same time."

Mrs. Winsome looked at her gravely. "Yes. But I have so many times like that. Sometimes, I don't know which one is the right one, but when Ag or David look at me funny, I know I'm following the wrong path."

"Does it affect you when he sends other people?"

She closed her eyes and let out a breath. "I don't know, child."

Something else she'd said piqued Celeste's interest. "I thought you were in your eighties."

She smiled. "A lady never reveals her age."

Celeste knew her discovery was important, but she didn't have time to explore it. Keys rattled in the door, and David walked into the room.

"We need to talk."

Mrs. Winsome lightened her voice. "My live-in soap opera is back!"

David rolled his eyes. "Can you watch over Emma for a minute?"

The older lady cackled. "Just be sure to talk near the vent so I can hear you."

David flicked the keys into the dish by the door and climbed the stairs. He glanced back at her once, but she couldn't read his expression.

"No fornicating!" she called after them as they ascended the stairs.

As Celeste followed him to his room, she was overcome with doubts. *Had he seen Mindy? Had he broken up with her, or did he come back to let Celeste know he was going to stay with her?*

She was full of emotion, and when she closed the door behind them, she couldn't hold it back. Celeste didn't believe she was weak, but her love for David and the frustration she felt over the ruin of their romance was overwhelming. She didn't want to hear another one of David's speeches about duty and loyalty. She was more aware of them than he could understand.

David noticed her tears and took her into his arms. "What's wrong? Did Mama say something?"

She shook her head on his shoulder.

He tried to pull her away so he could look at her, but she dodged his eyes. She was ashamed of her tears and she didn't want to explain them.

"What's wrong, sweetheart?"

The term of endearment brought on a fresh wave of tears, but after they receded, she could tell him why her feelings had swelled. "You went to Mindy's house, didn't you?"

He chuckled and caressed her cheek, cupping her chin before he wrapped his arm back around her. "No. I can honestly say I had no intention of going there."

The next beat of her heart skipped with hope. "Really? I thought you'd—"

"I actually drank a couple of beers at Lewis's house."

The breath caught in her throat. "I thought you two didn't get along."

He pressed his forehead to hers briefly, and she could smell the hops on his breath. She should have noticed the difference in his walk, but the things she thought had happened had preoccupied her.

"We got along tonight," he answered. "I don't think we're gonna see each other every week, but I might catch a game with him now and then."

"Is that what you did tonight?"

"Actually, I thought he was going to arrest me."

Celeste's eyes went wide. "What did you do?"

David looked at her sheepishly. "I almost got into a wreck."

"Wrecks don't get you arrested." Something occurred to her. "You weren't drinking, were you?"

"I was in traffic at a stoplight." He pointed toward Erwin. "I was on the phone with Amber, but she couldn't meet me because she was going out with her husband."

Celeste nodded.

"The light turned green, and I didn't move right away," David continued. "This guy sped until he was right against my bumper and yelled, and I recognized him."

"Who was it?"

David's jaw clenched. He looked away before he spoke. "Grady."

Celeste had wondered if Grady had crossed paths with David over Caroline. It seemed Caroline had been with Willie when Grady had made advances on her, but David had heard about it, and he despised him for trying to take advantage of her.

"You had bruises up and down your arms, but because of who his father is—" David was almost purple with rage.

Celeste put her hand on his chest. "What happened?"

"I put the car in park, got out, and I tried to pull him through his window."

Celeste's hand went to her mouth. "You didn't almost get into a wreck. You almost got into a fight."

"I almost wrecked his face," David chuckled.

Celeste stared at him, wondering about his temper. *Had his short time in jail changed his usual mild-manner responses?* She decided it may have had some effect on him, but David's frustration had been building since her grandfather had pulled her from Caroline's body the first time, and her time meddling hadn't improved it.

"I didn't punch him or anything," David informed her, "but Lewis was on me pretty fast. He'd been picking up a pizza across the street, and he'd run to get to us before everything got too out of hand."

"I'd say it got out of hand when you got out of the vehicle."

David forced a laugh. "Yeah. I was pretty heated, but Lewis dragged me back to the SUV and talked me out of going after him."

"Didn't Grady press charges?" Celeste thought he seemed like the type of person who would stretch an offense to its maximum.

"I think he wanted to, but Lewis knows some stuff about his family, and he talked him out of it."

Celeste patted his shoulder. "So, Lewis kept you from going back to jail, and now the two of you are best buddies."

"I wouldn't say that, but he invited me back to his house, and we talked for a while."

Her eyebrows went up. "You bonded over Grady?"

He shrugged. "You know, the enemy of the guy I don't like makes us not want to kill each other."

Celeste smiled at his joke.

His eyes widened. "Did you know Lewis has a gun range in his basement?"

Celeste answered negatively, as she had been inside Hailey Hall's body when she'd shot a gun in Lewis's basement. She brought him back from his distracted observations.

"So, you told him about Ag?"

He led her over to the bed and they sat down. "Yeah. He doesn't believe that I tried to kill my mother on purpose. Don't tell anyone I talked to him about it, though. He said they could question him at the trial over it."

Celeste moved on to a subject that was bothering her. "What about Mindy? Did you break things off with her?"

David dropped her hand. "After I'd had a few beers, or 'liquid courage' as Lewis calls it, I called her. I don't know what I said, but she didn't seem upset. She told me she wished me the best."

Celeste was satisfied that he'd ended his relationship with Mindy, but it didn't sit well with her. "Why didn't you tell her in person?"

David popped off the bed and ran a hand through his hair. "I wanted to. I really did. But she always finds a way to make me feel guilty or get me into her bed. Usually both."

"Oh."

David sat with her and grabbed her hands. "I know what I can handle, and if she would have hugged me and talked about the baby, I would have caved."

Celeste said nothing.

"I think I know what you're thinking, and it makes me look bad. I know my willpower isn't strong after I've been with someone, but I know how to control it. I just don't go around the person."

Celeste felt her heart drop, and it was reflected in her voice. "How does that work when you'll have to see Mindy for the next eighteen years?"

He cupped her face. "Because you'll be with me. I won't see her without you, and after a month or so, it won't matter, because when I'm with you—truly with you—I don't see the other women in the world."

Celeste kissed him. She didn't care that he tasted like the beer he'd shared with Lewis or that he'd broken up with his last girlfriend over the phone. All she knew was that she had found her soul mate. Even though he'd been born decades before her, she knew he was the only one in the past, present, and future for her.

He leaned her back on the bed and moved his hands across her body. She responded to his touch and undressed him quickly. As he kissed her neck, he whispered in her ear, "I love you, Caroline."

Her desire dried up instantly. The world came back into focus and tears stung her eyes.

Sensing the change, David pulled back. "Are you okay?"

"You don't know me," she said.

He cupped her face. "I know you love classic rock, the color green, pizza, long walks, and hopefully, me."

"I love you so much." Her voice cracked on every word.

David's tone grew softer and more serious. "Sweetheart, what is it?"

"You know all these things about me, but you can't put them together." She jumped up, fixing her wrinkled pajamas. "You don't make the connections between me and—"

She almost said Hailey, but she stopped herself.

David sat up on the bed. "You're not making any sense."

Celeste tried to think about her outburst from David's perspective. He was trying to make amends with his ex-wife and express his love for her, and she was the woman he loved.

She approached it from another angle. "I don't think we should do this tonight. Your mother is listening, and she can't care for Emma if she wakes up."

Most of David's passion had been doused when she'd popped out of bed. "I guess you're right." He grabbed his boxers. "Let me walk you back to the couch."

Celeste giggled. "Not in boxers with tousled hair."

He agreed, and she crept downstairs. Emma slept in the same position, and Mrs. Winsome's breaths echoed off the walls.

Just as Celeste entered a comfortable doze, Mrs. Winsome moved on her bed. "Don't forget about DOVE."

"Okay," she responded automatically.

"Promise me you'll read about it, but that you'll never use it."

Celeste didn't make a promise and Mrs. Winsome's snores filled the room again.

Just before morning, a cry echoed out that changed their lives.

Chapter 34

The first moan didn't wake Emma, but Celeste shot up. She flew to Mrs. Winsome's bedside, and the woman grabbed her hand.

"Please. Make it stop."

The early morning light filtered into the room and Celeste's eyes followed Mrs. Winsome's hands as she directed her to the pain.

"It's your stomach?"

The lady nodded as another pain seized her. Celeste called for Ag, and she rushed into the living room.

"What's wrong with Mama?"

"Her stomach hurts."

Mrs. Winsome held up a shaking hand. "It's been hurtin' since just after dinner, but"—she took a breath—"I thought it might go away."

"I think we need to call an ambulance," Celeste said. She grabbed her phone and ran upstairs to wake up David.

He mistook Celeste's soft prodding and tried to pull her into bed with him. He stopped after she began a conversation with emergency services.

He sat up abruptly. She ignored his questions and concentrated on giving the operator the information he needed. David assessed his mother's pain, and he concluded. "I think it's an obstruction."

He didn't elaborate, and the emergency crew didn't say more as they loaded up Mrs. Winsome. Their motion woke Emma, and Celeste picked her up.

"Ins," she said, stretching her small hand to her grandmother.

The woman stared back at her, but she couldn't move. The pain was too intense.

Mrs. Winsome's eyes shifted to David. "Help. Help."

Celeste didn't want to leave the room, but Emma didn't need to be part of the scene. She elected to go to Ag's room, where she could be close by, but Emma wouldn't hear the commotion.

Emma's bed was still in the corner of Ag's room. A small princess with a purple dress and a magic necklace stared back from the pillowcase.

"Do you want to lie down in your big girl bed?" Celeste suggested.

Emma crossed her arms. "Want Ins."

She brushed through her blonde curls with her fingers. "I know, honey. Maybe after Ins gets back, we'll have a special time for the two of you."

Ag breezed into the room, throwing her phone, laptop, and a book into a large bag. "I'm riding in the ambulance with Mama," she said and ran out the door.

Celeste waited, hoping David would fill her in on what was happening, and he came into Ag's room with red-rimmed eyes.

"Da!" Emma cried, holding up her arms for him.

He picked her up and hugged her, but he put her back on the bed. "I'm going to talk to Mommy for a minute, okay?"

Emma didn't acknowledge his request. She turned her head and pouted.

"I love you," he said, squatting down to look into her eyes. "I'm sorry Daddy has to leave, but I'll be back as soon as I find out what's wrong with Ins."

"Daddy's always gone."

He cradled her to him, and emotion lined his voice. "I know it seems that way, but I'm never away from you because I want to be. Ins is sick, and she needs me, or I'd be getting ready to have breakfast with you in a couple of hours."

Emma returned his affection and climbed onto her bed. David led Celeste out of the room.

"I may be at the hospital for a while. Will you be okay?"

His concern touched Celeste. It reminded her of a time before he thought she'd intentionally hurt him.

"We'll be okay."

He glanced at Ag's door. "Do you think she knows I love her?"

Celeste nodded. "She just wants you to be here." She wrapped her arms around him. "We both do."

He gave her a gentle kiss, but it was short-lived. "If I hurry, I'll get there in time to meet Ag in the waiting room."

"Don't speed," she cautioned.

He threw a hand up on his way out, making no promises.

It was hard to wait for David's call. Celeste laid down on Ag's bed, as Emma had fallen asleep on her bed. The lighting and smells differed from the ones in the living room and Mrs. Winsome's room, so she only dozed. After half an hour, she rose and filtered into the living room.

She stared at Mrs. Winsome's bed. Celeste had noticed the woman holding her stomach, but she'd thought it had been gas. She wished she would have known more about Mrs. Winsome's condition so she could have helped her avoid the pain.

She stepped past the bed with its tautly pulled sheets and deeply indented pillows and edged her way to Mrs. Winsome's bedroom door. She crossed her legs and laid her phone beside her.

David's text lit up her screen. He told her he had been right about the obstruction, and due to the position and seriousness, the doctor had called a surgeon.

Celeste said a prayer for Mrs. Winsome. She opened the journal she'd read from recently and turned to the next entry.

I think I figured out a way to go deeper into the past without affecting the other changes we've made. So, if I make certain accommodations to my formula, Danny can plug it into the program, and the US Government can keep its wartime victory and add to its conquests.

They eliminated certain threats before they became threats, pushing Steve into dangerous and terrifying situations. His only solace was in Linda. They didn't even hide their fornications after he returned from his missions, and none of us had the heart to speak against his comforts.

He asked her to marry him, and Al allowed the chaplain to hear their vows. Linda was upset that her family couldn't see the proceedings, but we were prisoners, so they only allowed certain privileges.

Linda and Steve were married for about a week when Al came into our lab with liquor on his breath. I hid behind Danny as Al grabbed the chalkboard.

"It's time for another mission," he announced without looking at us.

Al had the power to make our lives unbearable, so we stared at him without speaking. "I've been talking to—" He weighed his words. "—someone. He thinks we need to do something special for ourselves."

He turned to Danny. "You need to make a program that will bounce into the future and reach into the early 1920s."

"I did that a month ago," Danny told him. "Steve killed some guy in Russia—"

"It was a family," Steve said. "They had me murder kids." There was enough venom behind his words to kill everyone responsible for his forced act.

Al waved away his words. "You had no problem killing the dictator and his pregnant girl-friend."

"That was different," he responded gruffly.

"That baby had the potential to grow up and take away the freedoms of millions of people. You, your wife, and your children could have been among them."

Steve hung his head. "You could have had me kill him when he was a man."

Al shook his head. "We've already been over this. He would have had too much influence."

"But he would have had a chance to make different choices."

Al flipped his hand in the air. "He was led into the political arena, and he would have remained on that path." He slammed a book on the table. "I'm not here for the government. Tonight, I'm here because we're going to right a few wrongs in *our* lives."

Liz glared at him. "*You're* the wrong in *my* life."

He laughed as if she'd told a joke. "The feeling is mutual, but this can benefit all of us." He held up an X-ray.

"This is a picture of Steve's internal organs before and after each jump."

We all gathered around to look at it.

"Now, I've only had a couple of medical classes, but look at this." He pointed to an obvious sign of age on the liver and lungs. "Each time we send him, it gets worse." He pointed to Steve's eyes. "I can see the deeper lines around his eyes."

"You and your buddies aren't really giving me a chance to sleep," Steve cut in.

"Maybe not, but you have age spots."

Steve looked at his hands. "It's sun damage."

I had seen the signs. No twenty-five-year-old man should have looked like Steve.

"Time travel is aging you."

Steve stared at him. I kept waiting for him to punch Al, but he didn't move.

"I think if you spend a little time in the past, it may reverse the changes."

He brought out another set of X-rays. "This is an X-ray from your last mission, and this one"—he pulled up the other X-ray—"shows your organs after a trip before you were born."

The difference was noteworthy.

Danny took the X-ray out of his hands with an odd look on his face. "You may have found the fountain of youth."

"You could go back with him," Al suggested.

Steve shook his head violently.

"I don't want anyone else to have to suffer through—"

Al tsked. "You want to keep it all to yourself. I understand."

"It's not that. I just—"

"His feelings don't matter to me," Danny said, leaving Steve and Linda with wounded expressions. "I'll go if I want to go."

"But who will man the computer?" I asked.

"You will," Danny replied. "I'll teach you everything you need to know about the program, and you can send us both back."

Al smiled at the dissension in our group. "It sounds like a great plan!"

Before he left, he took Danny and Steve into Steve's room. Whatever they discussed made Danny white as a sheet when he came out. Steve was contemplative, but he seemed vindicated.

Whatever Al had asked of the men was going to push Danny to his limits. Specifically, Al requested something from him, because Danny kept muttering about Al as we worked together, saying things like, "Does he really expect things to change?" and "Why can't Steve do it?"

He finally fell into a chair and rubbed his eyes. "I just don't think I can do it."

I let him have those moments without questioning him. Danny's trip into the past could
guarantee a long, more fruitful life for him,
but it came at a huge cost.

Al gave no one anything unless his benefit from
it outweighed theirs.

Celeste stopped reading to look at another text from David.
He said the hospital had transferred his mother to Johnson City
Medical Center, and she was scheduled for emergency surgery as
soon as the operating room could be prepared.

Celeste checked on Emma, and finding her still asleep, she read
more in Mrs. Winsome's journal. From the look of it, it was her last
entry in her oldest journal, and Celeste absorbed every word.

Steve and Danny were gone for three months.
During that time, we waited. I made some
improvements to the machine and learned the
basics of computer programming. Taking what
Danny had shown me, I worked backward. Danny
was a brilliant man, and if my IQ had been below
his, I never would have figured out his work. I
saved it on disks that only the government knew
about, and I put it in a crack I had discovered
in my closet. I put my new journals there, too.

When Steve and Danny came back, they were
notably younger, and Al had a new title. He was
still in a high-ranking position, but everyone
around him referred to him as a doctor.

When I asked him about it, he said Danny
had helped him make a change to his childhood
circumstances, and he had gone on to obtain a
medical degree at a young age. He flashed his
eyes at me.

"Who knows? The next time I send someone back,
I could be running for president." He grabbed

my fingers, but I jerked them away. "Or maybe I'll find the wife I've always wanted."

I shuddered, and he smiled. "I'm not *that* bad."

"You're a murderer," I spat at him, and he didn't contradict me.

Steve and Linda stayed secluded after his return. When we saw them, Steve looked younger but worn.

It wasn't long before Al assigned them another mission. "It's time to see if our missions are truly successful."

We were all too battle-worn to respond.

"We're going into the future," he announced with outstretched hands.

"You mean *I'm* going into the future," Steve deadpanned.

Al nodded. "Well, at first it will be just you, but after a few successful missions, I think we can all go. To stay."

Everyone was shocked. "All of us?"

"I feel sorry for you, and in my pity, I've decided to help you leave." He motioned around him. "I think you know the government will never let you go."

The thought had crossed my mind when I wasn't allowed to write to my parents.

"The choice is yours."

Steve jumped into the future the following Friday. And he never came back.

Chapter 35

Celeste stopped reading when Emma woke up. They made it through the morning with periodic texts from David. The surgeon they'd wanted was unavailable for the surgery, so they had to wait for the hospital to prepare a surgeon on call. The nurses controlled Mrs. Winsome's pain, but just barely, and David got more nervous the longer they had to wait.

Celeste couldn't function after one o'clock, and she worried about getting through work. She was exhausted and upset, but she didn't have anyone to keep Emma.

She worried Mindy didn't like her since David was unaware of what he said when he broke up with her, but she was her only option. Mindy answered on the third ring.

Celeste launched into a spiel about Mrs. Winsome's obstruction and her predicament. When she finished, Mindy agreed to watch Emma so Celeste could go to work.

"You'll have to bring her to the hospital in Johnson City. I'm here with David, but I can keep an eye on her, too."

Celeste felt the wind suck out of her. "What?"

She hadn't wanted to sound weak, but she'd been completely blindsided. *How had Mindy ended up with David? If Mindy could keep her at the hospital, why couldn't Celeste and Emma have gone with David when he left?*

"I was getting ready to clock in when they brought in David's mother, so I asked Rowena if I could take the day off. I rode with David when Mrs. Winsome was transferred to Johnson City."

Mindy was sweet when she spoke. No one would have guessed that her explanation was hurting Celeste.

Celeste knew it was her turn to speak, but she couldn't think of an appropriate thing to say. Mindy thought the line had been disconnected.

"Caroline?"

Celeste heard David repeat her name in the background and she hung up. She sat with the phone in her hand for several minutes, wondering what to do.

David told her he loved her, and he kissed her before he left. It seemed like he wanted to be with her, but only when they were together.

Mindy wasn't to blame, as she was following the man she loved, and he probably hadn't mentioned her when he broke up with Mindy over the phone. David was the one whose feelings were mixed.

Had he even mentioned her in his last phone call with Mindy? Celeste doubted it. He wouldn't want to hurt Mindy's feelings.

Celeste had turned on the television, more for background noise than entertainment, and she noticed tanks rolling over unfamiliar terrain. She thought about the emotional war she had been fighting for David. *What was she fighting for?*

David had been completely devoted to her when they were first together. She never doubted his fidelity when they were married, and she had felt a connection deeper than her desire for Movey or her obligation to Zam.

Something had changed when her grandfather pulled her back the first time. Caroline's rejection hurt David, and he carried resentment over it. Even though she hadn't left him, David thought she was responsible for his broken heart, so he treated her feelings carelessly.

"It's over," she said aloud.

Emma didn't hear her. She continued to play with her toys.

Celeste decided she would go back and assume her body. She'd make a deal with her grandfather to keep Emma and her safe, and she'd eliminate all of her ties to Zam.

In her time, it was more difficult to sever a union, but she couldn't stay married to a monster. She would wait out a year and hope that the court granted her request.

Her mind darted to Movey. She still had feelings for him, and he'd be happy to let her explore them, but it couldn't work out. He was always way more in love with her than she was with him, and he'd resent her when she couldn't give him her whole heart.

Her heart still belonged to David, and she didn't know how long it would take to get over him. After her conversation with Mindy, she knew it was time to move on. She had to be a good example for her daughter, and Emma didn't need to see her bouncing to David every time he thought he loved her.

It had been one thing for him to have seen Mindy in the emergency room. That had been unavoidable, but taking her with him to the hospital in Johnson City...

Celeste pulled some plastic shopping bags from under the sink and started packing. Halfway through, she thought about what she was doing.

She could go back to the future with Emma, but why would she need any of her toys or clothes? Everything could stay in the past where it belonged.

With tears in her eyes, she ran upstairs. She threw open David's bedroom door and slung herself onto his bed.

She cried, beating the pillows and kicking away the sheets. Her hand hit something, and it distracted her from her fit.

Under one of David's pillows was a picture of them on the beach. It had been a quick weekend trip, and they held hands as David's paid photographer followed them on their walk.

Celeste hadn't understood why a man was several feet behind them with a camera until David dropped to one knee and proposed to her. She fell on the sand and front of him and kissed him. She forgot to say *yes*, but her answer was clear.

He'd already proposed to her, but his romantic gesture delighted her. David was so happy to be with her he proposed to her twice more in other locations.

David had a picture of them kissing on the sand on his bed. It had been under one of his back pillows, but the fingerprints on the metal frame showed that he'd looked at it often.

It didn't change her mind, but it quietened her emotions.

Celeste made David's bed, carefully wiping the frame and putting it on the bed. She didn't hide it under a pillow. She wanted him to know she saw it and still left him.

Celeste penned a quick note to her grandfather. In it, she told him she would agree to any circumstances—aside from those that may harm Emma—he set for her as long as he pulled her back to their current time.

She didn't want Caroline to pop back into her body at the Winsome's house, so she hid their house key under the floor mat in her car and waited by the river. David had taken her to the area when she had lived her life as Emma, a woman who didn't know her name or have memories.

She longed for the moments they'd shared, but she pitied Hailey. Hailey Hall had been her host during that time, and even though she would have died soon after Celeste led her to her death, Celeste was still upset over the ordeal. Her grandfather hadn't fully explained the situation when he'd sent her on that mission, and he'd been responsible for wiping her memories.

Unknowingly, Celeste had damaged Hailey's relationships with her mother, sister-in-law, and fiancé. Most of her family never had closure, as they thought Hailey had died without caring for them. She may not have been able to help the situation without the knowledge of her life as Celeste, but it was one of her biggest regrets.

Emma slept peacefully in her arms. From that angle, Celeste could tell her daughter had experienced another growth spurt. Maybe it would stop if Emma went back to her original time frame. She'd miss her father, grandmother, and aunt, but she could live a fuller life without the risk of dying before her time.

Celeste held Emma close to her, as she didn't want them to be apart when her grandfather opened the letter. She'd marked the day and time to open the envelope, and it was five minutes away.

Celeste wanted to soak in the scene and think of David during that time, but she thought about her responsibility. She called the hospital about finding a replacement for a night. Celeste's conscience would be clear, and Caroline could take the job if she was mature enough to handle it.

She looked up the number and dialed it. She wouldn't have been able to go to work anyway, so it was best to alert them.

Grady picked up, and Celeste recognized his voice. He must have been called in to replace Mindy.

She tried to sound as bright and cheery as possible. "Hey, Grady! Is Rowena still there?"

Rowena handled the nurses on the day shift, but she could help Celeste find a replacement.

"She's gone," he said through a mouthful of food.

Celeste glanced at the clock on her dash. "Are you saying she left two hours early today?"

He repeated himself. "I haven't seen her."

Celeste thanked him, even though she had to swallow her pride, and prepared to call Amber. Before she hung up, he spoke again.

"Tell Mindy's boyfriend that I'll press charges the next time he grabs me by my throat. I have marks, you know."

Celeste tried to look over the way he referenced David and chose to address the latter part of his statement. "You shouldn't have been so impatient at the stoplight. David has been going through a lot lately."

He scoffed. "What red light? I saw him at the gas station."

Celeste didn't know what to say. David had told her he had almost punched Grady at a red light.

"All I said was that he shouldn't let a slut sleep in the same house as his mom."

Celeste almost hung up on him, but she tried to keep her voice even. Caroline had done some terrible things in her life, and she may have wronged Grady grievously.

"I can't blame him for standing up for the mother of his child."

"Yeah, I don't know whose baby you have, but it's not David's."

"We had a DNA test," she said simply.

"So, you slept with him after the divorce?"

Celeste was having a hard time keeping up with their conversation. "What are you talking about?"

He let out an airy sigh. "You were the one who came to my door. I'd always had a thing for you, but you never gave me the time of day until you needed my help."

Celeste was completely lost. She thought he may have made something up.

"You slept with me once, but then you went back to Willie."

That made better sense, as it was in line with Caroline's character, but what had she needed from Grady?

"You knew I'd logged time at the clinic, and—"

Celeste's vision blurred as she thought about what he was about to say. *Did Caroline lie to her?*

After Willie had beaten her when Hailey was her host, Celeste had gone to the hospital. Caroline tagged along in the backseat, as she was attempting to escape her circumstances. When they were alone, she'd told Celeste that she had never been pregnant.

Celeste assumed that David's baby had traveled with her, and that had to be true, as the DNA test had confirmed it. *But what if Emma hadn't been the* only *baby?*

Was Caroline really so terrible? Had she aborted Lewis's *and* David's babies?

"You owe me," he said to her. "I've told you about what I'd do if you don't give me what I want."

Celeste swallowed hard. "What do you want?"

"I want you."

After her disconcerting phone call with Grady, it was hard to call Amber. Amber took her phone to Rowena, but before Celeste could tell her about her situation, Rowena stopped her.

"I have been meaning to call you, but it's been so busy around here. I thought I'd just catch you on your way in, but since you called, we need to talk."

Celeste was confused. She tried to remember if she'd made a mistake or violated a HIPPA agreement, but she drew a blank.

"The hospital runs a check on healthcare certifications, and you're not certified as an LPN. They couldn't even find a CNA license."

Celeste's blood went cold.

"You were hired based on a photocopied certificate, but unless you can provide us with a certificate that can be validated, I'll have to let you go."

Celeste told her she'd look for her certificate, but it was a lie. She'd never been an LPN, but she'd thought she'd be able to continue the ruse.

Now jobless and loveless, Celeste counted down the seconds until her grandfather pulled her back into her own body.

Chapter 36

It didn't happen.

Celeste waited for two hours, but he didn't take her. She returned to the Winsomes' home, as it was obvious her grandfather had ignored her request. She'd pack her bags and leave. She could take some of the money she'd saved and live in a hotel until she got another job.

Mindy called her, but she ignored it. She didn't want to explain to her she'd lost her job.

She retrieved the key from under her floor mat and opened the door. If she shared custody with David or Ag, it wouldn't be the last time she saw the house, but she felt like she was leaving her home. The apartment she'd shared with her father hadn't had the same feeling since he'd died.

She grabbed plastic shopping bags and filled them with everything that belonged to Emma and her. She made Emma's bed, gave her a bath, hung her dresses in Ag's closet, and cleaned the house.

Celeste felt completely drained. *Had the love she'd shared with David powered her through the times she'd not rested? Was the dopamine from their connection enough to sustain her until she realized it was over?*

Emma played with David's old blocks. Celeste planned to leave them behind, even though Emma played with them every day. They were *his* blocks, and she wanted Emma to have something she enjoyed when she visited. She'd buy her a set of blocks when they found a place to stay.

Celeste planned to leave when Emma fell asleep. It would be an emotional time, and she didn't want her toddler to see her cry. Emma's cognition had increased with her physical development, and she'd displayed signs of empathy. It wasn't Emma's job to comfort her as they left their home.

Celeste needed something to occupy her mind. The news was detailing the president's trip to a foreign country to smooth out a misunderstanding, but she had no interest in political ties. Everything that happened to her was happening in her heart.

She grabbed the next journal from Mrs. Winsome's room. They weren't dated, but the wear on them helped show which one was next. She sat next to Emma and immersed herself in Mrs. Winsome's past.

Steve and Danny were hooked up to the equipment in less than two weeks. I held Danny's hand, and he looked up at me with wide eyes.

"Steve says it won't hurt," he said.

I patted his arm with my other hand. "Then it won't hurt."

"I wish you would have married me."

I tried to think of something that might make him feel better about the uncertainty he faced. "Maybe you'll find someone in the past."

He chuckled. "And then I'd get younger, and she'd be twenty years older when I got back. No thanks."

I laughed at his joke, and I congratulated myself on refusing his proposal. Love knows no bounds through time and space, and age doesn't matter. If Danny was only interested in the aesthetic appeal, he would never find a true partner.

Linda sobbed on Steve's chest before he sat in the chair that was meant to take him away. He talked to her as if she were the one who had to face the mission.

"You're going to be okay," he told her. "You can play cards with the girls and ask the supervisor if you can redesign your room."

"What good is changing a striped design to floral if you're not there to share it with me?"

Linda brushed Steve's hair with her silver hairbrush. She lovingly applied each stroke, as his hair had grown in the time we'd been confined to our quarters.

Steve stopped her efforts and stood to face his wife. He caressed her hair, pulling it back as he combed his fingers through it. "I'll do everything I can to get back to you."

"What if you can't?"

"Then I hope you'll try to find an old man later on. Maybe he'd be dead by the time we met again."

The future date would have placed Linda in her late fifties. By then, she would have lived her life with someone else, especially if she wanted to get married and have children.

Al came to the lab to watch us send off the boys. He and Liz had to hold Linda back, as she was unwilling to let Steve go. It was harder on her than the other times he had traveled through time, and I couldn't put my finger on it.

Celeste flipped through a few entries that talked about playing cards and going through daily routines. Linda was depressed, and she cried over the smallest things. Celeste stopped scanning when she found an entry that interested her.

We're getting a little more freedom. Al must think the remaining members of our team are weaker since we're the fairer sex, so he's allowed us to go to the cafeteria for meals.

Last night, Linda didn't join us, but she'd been sick that week. I'd heard her in the bathroom every morning, and I'd kept my distance. I like for my meals to stay in my stomach, and I didn't want to catch a bug.

Liz stayed in the cafeteria to talk to some of her friends, and I walked back to our lab alone. Someone sidled up beside me, and I thought it was Al, so I steeled my nerves. I looked to my right, and Steve stared back at me.

Unlike how he'd left, and certainly not younger, his eyes crinkled when I recognized him. "It's always fun to surprise you."

"What happened?" From our last experience, I knew his visits were brief and had something to do with a personal mission.

His features turned serious. "We need to get to Linda."

I quickened my pace. "What's wrong?"

"She's going to try to jump forward to me."

"Doesn't she make it?"

We were at a full-scale run, and he didn't answer me. I pushed the buttons to unlock the door to our lab and living quarters, and something struck me.

"You were able to do both?" I asked excitedly. "You jumped to the past and then to the future?"

He nodded.

"Why didn't you jump directly to Linda?"

"I had to sneak in here," he admitted. "I think the government put up something that blocks us from coming back."

"What about Danny?"

Steve didn't answer me and pushed his way through the door.

The equipment was on, and I could hear it whirling in the lab. Linda had herself hooked up in a chair, and she was holding the transfer button. Her fearful face softened when she saw Steve with me.

"I'm going to you."

"You can't," he said, taking small steps around the field of equipment.

I started looking for the main power source. That was Liz's job, and I'd seen her focus on a certain side of the room, so I started there.

"You'll die."

Linda's breath caught. "You mean we'll die." She put her other hand over her stomach.

I hadn't noticed the small bulge, but it made sense. I'd heard about emotional women who had morning sickness, and Linda had been both.

"I need you to stay here and have the baby," Steve told her.

Linda shook her head. "It's better for my family to think I'm dead than to know I'm with child without a father around. It would kill my daddy."

"Are you willing to risk the baby's life?" I asked.

Linda looked down at her growing belly. For a second, I thought I had helped her.

"I'll risk everything to be with the man I love."

She pushed the button.

Steve yelled her name, and I think I cried out. After Steve told her she'd die, watching her go was like witnessing her death.

I cried against his chest as he rocked me, but when I looked at his face, it was dry.

"I won't waste our time by telling you lies," he said. "Linda made it to me."

I beat his chest with my fists. "Why did you say she'd die?" I yelled each word between punches.

He grabbed my wrists. "I wanted her to be too scared to go. At least here she would have a chance."

"What happens?"

He breathed a sigh that carried the weight of all his actions.

"Linda made it to me. But unlike Al thought, Danny and I didn't grow younger. He's trying to find a way to reverse the age difference, but he's not there yet."

He scrubbed his face and sat. "Linda found me, and we have a beautiful baby boy."

"Congratulations," I said automatically.

He gave me a thin smile. "It was wonderful, but for every year he grew, we seemed to jump ahead three. It was almost like our bodies were trying to catch up to the years we skipped in the time jump."

His voice cracked. "Linda died before our boy was twenty."

Hearing about her death made it seem real to me, as in some other time, it had already happened.

"The best I can tell, she died of old age, but she would have been in her forties." He put fingers to his face and glided them down his chin. "Her wrinkles were deeper, like an almost seventy-year-old woman instead of one a little over half her age."

"I'm so sorry."

He wiped his hands across his face. "I have several purposes for coming back here." He ran to my room and went straight to the place where I kept my old journal and the disk with the blueprints for the machine.

"What are you doing?" I shrieked.
"You told me to get this stuff."
"I did not!" I yelled at him.
He didn't pause in his work. "Eleanor, I pop in to see you a lot, and you told me to grab this stuff, so now I've done it." He turned his bloodshot eyes on me. "Do you doubt it?"
I hung my head. "No."
It sounded like something I would do. I'd want to keep our project safe.
"What else are you supposed to do while you're here?"
Steve's jaw clenched before he spoke. "Where's Al?"
He stormed into the hall, pulling something shiny out of his pocket. It glinted in the brighter lights.
I grabbed his arm and dragged him to the nearest corner. "You can't kill him!" I whispered harshly.
Steve's face remained expressionless.
I felt an electrical charge in the air. It lifted the hair on my arms.
"Did you leave the machine on?"
"No," he replied, waving away my answer. "Is there anything else you want me to take?"
"Wait a moment," I told him.
I wrote this part of the story to send with him. He was impatient while I wrote it, and I'm sure he'll break away and run to murder Al as soon as I finish.
I can't save everyone, and I don't even know if I care if Al lives another day.

The color of the pen changed, and Celeste thought the last part of the entry was added later and in a rush.

The electrical charge I felt wasn't in my imagination. It was Al.

We tried to stop him, but he zoomed somewhere in time before we could stop him.

I hope he dies there.

Chapter 37

That was how her grandfather made it to the future. He had run away cowardly before Steve could kill him.

But what happened to Steve and Danny?

More questions popped up from the answers she had, and it seemed like it was a never-ending cycle. *Would she ever know the truth?*

A car crunched the gravel, and Celeste glanced outside. David helped Ag out of the car, practically carrying her up the steps.

Celeste opened the door for them. She stared at David for an explanation, but he looked past her. They both sat on the couch, and Celeste curled up in front of them, rubbing their fingers.

The action did nothing to gain their attention, as the siblings were lost in their own thoughts.

Celeste glanced over at Emma to check on her welfare, and the toddler stared back. It seemed like Emma was trying to express something without words, but Celeste couldn't grasp it.

She crawled over to them and placed a hand on David's leg. "Daddy?"

David noticed her right away. He lifted her into his arms and held her there as if she were his only comfort.

Celeste chanced a question. "What's happened?"

He almost didn't answer her as he choked back tears. He squeezed his eyes shut. "She's gone."

Celeste felt like a cold bucket of water had been splashed on her. "No."

He nodded his head until the tears flowed down his face. "Mama's gone."

Celeste didn't know how she made it through the night. David and Ag had more of a right to their tears than Celeste, but she was still upset over Mrs. Winsome's death.

It was hard for her to understand. In her time, intestinal surgeries were rarely done, but they had almost been perfected. Even emergency surgeries only required two days of hospitalization before the patient was released. They stayed on a liquid diet for a few days, but no one died.

David said feces had made its way into Mrs. Winsome's bloodstream during the surgery. It sounded like a terrible way to die, but Mrs. Winsome had been under the effects of anesthesia, so she had slipped away from life without her knowledge.

It made Celeste think about her vulnerability. Caroline was walking around inside her body in another time. If she was involved in an accident, Celeste would no longer have her own body, and she'd be stuck as Caroline forever. She wasn't ready to accept that fate, especially since David's feelings shifted as easily as water ran through the endless creeks in Unicoi County.

David kept his arms around Ag, and she allowed it until she went to bed. She said nothing to either of them. She grabbed a pillow and the blanket from Mrs. Winsome's hospital-issued bed and took them to her room.

David stared after her. "I always knew she'd take it the hardest."

Emma climbed into his lap and stroked his hair. "Love Daddy."

He buried his head in her blonde curls. "I love you, too. You and your mommy are all I have now."

Celeste glanced at the pile of bags by the door and wondered how long David would take to notice them. He had seen them, but he waited until Emma fell asleep to address the issue.

Emma's head was over his heart, and her arms fell from his shoulders. David moved her into a more comfortable position on his lap, and he stared at the Teleboard. Two men were debating the effects of a presidential decision, but their voices were muted.

"Are you leaving me again?"

"Yes." After her conversation with Mindy, Celeste didn't feel like she owed him much more.

"Sounds about right." His eyes glazed over, but the tears didn't fall. "If it weren't for Emma, I'd tell you to leave tonight, but I'm not sure about the custody arrangement since I went to jail." He glanced toward his sister's room. "And she's in no condition to care for Emma."

His words stung, but she pushed them aside. "I'll stay here while you and your sister make arrangements, but I'm filing for custody of Emma. The order was drawn up when I was kidnapped, and it was only temporary. You and Ag will still have visitation rights. I'll have to work, and you can—"

"You're a cold-hearted—"

His sister's bedroom door interrupted him. They were quiet as she used the bathroom, and on her way back she stared at them with almost empty eyes.

"No fighting around that baby," she said. Her mother had spoken the same words.

David allowed Ag to pick up Emma. Whether it was Emma's recent growth, or the toll grief had taken on her body, it was more difficult for Ag to lift the toddler.

Once David and Emma were alone, he seemed a little less spiteful. "You weren't going to take her away from me again?"

Celeste shook her head.

He was silent for a long moment that seemed to stretch out for an eternity. Celeste watched him, waiting for him to speak, and hating herself for her desperation to continue their conversation.

"I didn't want you around." He rubbed an eye, and the action looked almost painful. "I knew you would leave, but I couldn't keep myself away."

"I didn't plan to leave."

David exaggerated an eye roll. "Yeah, I'm sure you just couldn't help it." He shot up from the couch. "I've got news for you. I'm done!" He threw up his hands. "I can't make you love me the way I should be loved, so I'm going to let you go."

He pointed to the bags at the door. "Thanks for making it easy on me."

Why did he get to claim the moral high ground? He was the one who had cheated on her.

Celeste stood up, and her hands flew to her hips. "Well, maybe if I didn't have to worry about whose bed you'd be in every six seconds, then I would have stayed."

David was completely baffled. "I've stayed in my bed—alone—since I've been out of jail."

"But you took Mindy to the hospital with you." She didn't want to cry, but she felt the tears coming. "And you left Emma and me here."

Watching her emotions take hold of her softened David. "I didn't think the hospital would be a good place for Emma."

"It wasn't," Celeste agreed. "But you didn't have to take Mindy with you."

He rubbed his hands over his face. "Anyone could have climbed into the car with me, and I wouldn't have known it."

"Did she hold your hand on the way?"

He stared off, trying to remember. "I don't know."

"Of course she did," Celeste sobbed. "And you let her think she had every right to be with you—"

"She does!" he shouted. "You may not like it, but Mindy is carrying my baby. She knew Mama, too, and she was concerned about her."

"Really?" Celeste coughed back some of her feelings. "Did she visit your mother in the hospital? Did she check on Ag? But now that you've ended things with her, she's interested in your family."

David didn't want to concede the point, but he'd rather avoid the conversation than admit he was wrong. "Look, my mother just died, and—"

"It's always something with you," she said.

His jaw clenched, and he raised a finger. She didn't give him the chance to speak.

"I crossed time for you, David. Not once, but three times—even though I didn't know why I was doing it the first time. I know in my heart that you are my soul mate, but I will not let you hurt me." She pointed to Ag's room, where Emma lay sleeping. "That little girl deserves a better example from both parents."

David ignored her reference to time travel and picked up on her last statement. He crossed the distance between them.

At first, he stared at her, as if he was having an internal debate. His eyebrows went down, and he touched her arm. Seeing that she didn't pull away emboldened him, and he wrapped his arms around her, cradling her lower back.

"I choose you," he said. "I only want you, and I'll do nothing but show it from now on."

She tried to look away, but the golden flecks in his eyes drew her back. They seemed to intensify, and she took it as a sign of his sincerity.

Celeste may have hated herself for the pull she felt toward David, but she couldn't deny his hold on her. *How could a man who was born in the past be her soul mate?* They were from different times and it shouldn't have worked at all. But it did.

That night, she didn't resist when he led her to his room. They sought comfort in each other's arms, and in the morning, their hearts still belonged to each other.

Chapter 38

Everyone slept in the next morning. Even though Emma was usually up after the sun cleared the mountains, she continued to stay quiet in Ag's room.

Celeste was the first to wake up. She prepared a pot of coffee for David and Ag and waited for Emma to rise before she had breakfast. Since the last time her grandfather whisked her away, just before it was time for her to eat breakfast with Emma, she always made a point of having breakfast with her daughter.

She stared at Mrs. Winsome's empty hospital bed and then opened her door and looked at where she had been sleeping when she'd almost been killed. She couldn't sleep there now. The lady was dead, and somehow that made the bed almost haunted.

Even though it seemed the woman had known about her grandfather, Celeste wasn't sure her story made sense. There were a lot of holes in it that only a writer would forget. After all, if Eleanor Winsome had helped develop a time machine, why wasn't she rich, famous, or dead at a young age? The government would have wanted to bury that knowledge if she hadn't wanted to work for them.

Celeste resolved it was a story. Alexander was a common name, and the surname could have been a coincidence. It was easier to accept than the other possibility: her grandfather had a vendetta against Mrs. Winsome, so all Celeste's missions were tied together in such a way as to study her or cause her pain.

With the former idea in mind, Celeste picked up another journal. Mrs. Winsome had filled it with David's first steps and Ag's teenage misfortunes, so she selected another one. It seemed to pick up where the last one had left off.

I have altered events twice by going back in time. Liz helped me.

I asked her if she wanted to right a wrong in her past, but she didn't want to do it. She's afraid God will be angry with us for tinkering with His master plan. She may be right.

I can't speak for God or His feelings about what we've done. On one hand, if He were against it, wouldn't He have kept the materials for the equipment out of reach? But our knowledge has always been there, waiting to be tapped, so free will has more to do with it than anything else.

If that's the case, Liz is as doomed as the rest of us. I suppose the only sin she'll be free from is the act of time travel in her body.

As for me, I've felt the pull start from my head and jerk me through rapidly swirling colors. I expected to see stars, but only reds, yellows, and oranges surrounded me, making me feel like I was consumed by fire.

I landed in a field next to my house. I could see my father's car, and my brother's bicycle was propped against the door to the building. I'd have to move it in the building before winter or the tires would lose pressure.

I'd chosen the day for a reason. I'd been staying with my friend, Patsy, so the real me wouldn't get in the way.

I crept up the steps, minding the creaky ones, and I opened the door.

My dad was sitting in his favorite leather chair reading the newspaper, and my mom was in the kitchen with her back turned to me. When I opened the door, my dad lowered his paper and raised his eyebrows.

"Did you decide not to stay with Patsy tonight?"

I did my best to stay calm, recounting what I'd rehearsed to Liz. "I stopped by to grab something. I'll be gone in a minute."

My mother walked into the living room, wiping her hands on her apron. "Where's Patsy? Did her father drop you off?"

"Patsy rode with her father to the hardware store. They're going to pick me up on their way back through."

My mother's mouth formed a thin line. She didn't think it was proper for Patsy's father to let me out in the driveway without walking me to the door. I ran upstairs before they could ask more questions.

In David's room, I pulled out the number for Patty. I dialed her and asked how to get in touch with David.

She told me that the only way she knew to talk to him was by post. I worried that there wasn't enough time for a letter to reach him.

I sat down and penned a few short lines in my room, worrying that it wouldn't be enough. I went back through my note and underlined several parts, especially the part where I told him how much I loved him.

I ran downstairs to ask my mother for a stamp. She handed me one from my dad's mahogany desk. She stared at me while I put it on the envelope.

"You look different, and I've never seen you in those clothes."

I had done my best to recreate the teen I had been before my brother's death. Liz trimmed my hair, and I put it in a ponytail. We shopped at a good Samaritan store, but we couldn't find clothes that would have matched mine. We ended up buying something an older woman might have worn in the 1940s.

"I spilled water on myself," I lied. "Patsy's mom lent me some of her clothes."

"Why didn't you change into your own clothes?"

My mind worked fast, and I put my hand on my mother's arm. "It's fun to play dress up sometimes."

She stared at me for a long moment before she turned around and headed to the kitchen, calling over her shoulder. "You can dress up. Just don't go and try to grow up too soon!"

I had to mail the letter, and the nearest post office was at least a mile away. I was going to tell my parents that I'd wait out on the porch, but the phone rang.

My parents had been the last children in a long line of siblings, but their brothers and sisters had been many years older than them. As a result, they didn't have many family members, so people seldom called the house.

I almost jumped out of my skin. *Could it be David?*

I'd thought about somehow intercepting the last phone call I'd shared with my brother, but it would have taken a great deal of skill to have lured the younger me away from the house. I risked shocking my former self, and I needed the transition to be as seamless as possible.

My mother answered the phone. Her eyebrows drew together, and her head darted in my direction.

"Eleanor?"

I almost jumped out of my seat from the shock. The younger me had called my mother from Patsy's house!

Why hadn't I remembered that I'd forgotten my church dress?

I flew into action. I ran to my mother, jerking the phone from her hand.

My father caught my act and issued a warning. "Eleanor!"

I laughed nervously as I addressed the younger version of myself. "You're so funny, Patsy! I hope you and your dad are going to pick me back up soon."

I hung up the phone, but when I did, I positioned it a little off the cradle to keep it from ringing again. I forgot about the off-the-hook noise, and it beeped loudly after a minute. I pretended to hang it up again, unplugging the cord from the receiver.

"It was you," my mother said.

My hands were sweating rivers, but I wiped them on my skirt and tried to play it cool. "Don't be ridiculous. That was Patsy playing a prank. She called from the hardware store."

My mother crossed her arms. "I don't think Mr. Johnson would let her use his phone for such mischief."

My father had stopped reading to survey us. I only had one other angle I could work.

"I'm standing right here, Mama," I looked at my father. "You see me, right?"

"A young lady shouldn't take that tone with her parents," he scolded, but he went back to reading.

My mother returned to cutting tomatoes. "I'm going to have to talk with Patsy's mother about this. I don't know if the two of you should be together if you're going to act this way."

I spotted David's bicycle through the kitchen window. "I'm going to put up David's bicycle."

My mother exaggerated her surprise. "Why would you—"

I didn't wait for her to finish. I stuffed the letter in my coat pocket and ran outside.

I pushed the bicycle into the building and ran down the hill. I thought I heard my father call after me, but I wasn't certain.

I walked to the post office with my hands in my pockets. November was a chilly time in my region, and I'd worn a jacket, but I needed a coat. The bitter wind pushed against me as I walked.

I heard a car behind me, and I ducked into a bush. My father's car sped past, and I congratulated myself on my foresight. My younger self would probably be grounded for a month, but I might get my brother back.

I mailed the letter at the post office. The building was closed for the day, and it was hours before Liz was supposed to try to pull me back, so I prayed David would get my letter.

He had the option to take his Christmas leave early, and I had begged him to do it. I said I had something special for him.

Liz pulled me back, and we talked about what I'd experienced. Nothing had seemed to change, but I couldn't call my mother to find out if my brother was still alive. If he was alive, I'd find out in time, but if he was still dead, I wanted to prolong the moment before I learned the outcome of my experience.

By the time I lay down for the night, it all seemed like a dream. I tossed and turned for hours, hoping to erase the failed attempt from my mind. Finally, sleep found me.

I woke up in Bill Winsome's bed.

Chapter 39

People from all walks of life attended Eleanor Winsome's viewing. The line of mourners stretched out the door, and everyone stayed for her funeral.

David stood near the coffin, accepting condolences on behalf of his family. Almost everyone shook his hand, but a few of the older people snubbed him. Celeste assumed it was because they believed he was completely responsible for the injury that had led to his mother's death.

David tried to keep his features neutral, but he stared after a couple of the townsfolk with a pained expression.

Ag couldn't stand. She looked at her mother as if she were willing her to get up and start berating people. She held on to the edge of the pew, crying softly at times and shaking her head at others. She looked at the people who approached her, but she didn't see them.

Families from the First Baptist Church passed by the coffin slowly, but Dot Bailey paused, staring at a woman she may have seen as her nemesis. It shocked Celeste when she leaned down and kissed her cheek. She spoke something into Mrs. Winsome's ear, but Mrs. Winsome had passed beyond the reach of her words. Whatever she said brought a wave of emotion over Dot, and her son, Sam, had to steady her as she walked back to her seat.

Celeste didn't know most of the people who attended the funeral. Caroline had been raised in Erwin, but Celeste had only lived there under the guise of other people.

Kerry Shelton and some of the older men walked up to the coffin just before the start of the service. He approached Celeste as she was watching Sheriff Murphy give his condolences to David.

"Are you doin' okay?" he asked her.

She nodded her head. Ag insisted Celeste should sit with Emma in the front pew, but almost everyone ignored her. Some had smiled sadly as they walked past, but she didn't know if they were sympathizing with her or Emma.

"I'm okay," she said.

He patted her hand. "Let me know if I can do anything."

Just before the viewing closed, two boys ran up the aisle. Cameron tried to climb into the casket while Dalton pulled at his legs.

"Mom's gonna take away your game!" he shouted in the mostly quiet sanctuary.

Cameron continued to laugh. David calmed the boys with one look. He was upset, but he didn't yell at them. He simply pointed to the end of the aisle where Mindy was running to catch up to them.

She'd worn three-inch black pumps with a loser-fitting black dress. The dress hid her pregnancy, and while in her home church without a husband, Celeste understood Mindy's desire to keep that part of her life private until she had to admit she was carrying David's baby.

Cameron and Dalton ran back to her, and she covered her face. They approached the casket together, Mindy holding a child's hand in each of her own.

They moved over to David's area, and he waved away her apology. Mindy glanced over at the first pew, and her mouth set in a firm line when she noticed that David's ex-wife had been invited to sit in the family's pew, but she had to find her own seat.

Celeste felt moved to offer her a place on the pew, as she knew Mindy would have done the same for her. She patted the seat next to her. "Sit with us."

Mindy almost wrestled the boys into the pew. She seemed frustrated, but not tired. "Thanks," she muttered a little too brightly.

David sat next to Emma during the service. He didn't even glance in Mindy's direction. "I saw Kerry come by."

Celeste nodded. "It was nice of him. Was he friends with your mother?"

David looked at her strangely. "I imagined he came here for you. Wasn't he friends with your dad?"

Celeste felt like someone had splashed a bucket of cold water on her. "What?"

David put his arm around Emma but kept his puzzled look. "I'm pretty sure they were close. You called him Uncle Kerry."

Celeste's mind raced. *Why had Kerry acted like he hadn't known her?* She shrugged to herself, realizing that it explained his willingness to help her when he had given her a job at his pawn shop.

As the preacher readied himself to speak, Celeste glanced around the room. She tried to locate Kerry, but her eyes fell on someone else.

Aunt Lynn and a man she assumed was her husband sat in the second pew behind her. When she noticed Celeste, she waved and nodded knowingly.

Celeste's confusion pounded through her mind and ruined most of the emotion she would have felt during the service. She wanted to talk to Kerry and Aunt Lynn, but it wasn't the right time.

As the preacher reviewed Mrs. Winsome's many accomplishments, Celeste didn't hear him mention that she'd been to college or worked on a special project. He talked about her parents and her brother, and he said they'd preceded her in death.

It was just as Celeste had thought. Mrs. Winsome's journals were fiction. The reference to her grandfather had been purely coincidental.

David had elected to have the viewing, funeral, and interment on the same day. Celeste was glad for it, as she didn't think Ag could face another day of forced interaction while she was grieving for her mother.

They rode in a limousine and arrived at a small graveyard between the Nolichucky River and an academy on the hill. David helped Celeste out of the car, and he practically carried his sister to the gravesite.

As Celeste made her way behind them, Emma wiggled. She tried to hold her up, but Emma's cast was gone and she was eager to run on the road beside the graveyard.

"Can I help you with her?" a familiar voice asked.

Marcia picked up Emma and twirled her around. "This road is too dangerous for you," she told Emma.

She saw the look of shock on Celeste's face. "You don't know me, but I was once—"

"—with Ag." Celeste finished.

Marcia raised her eyebrows.

When Hailey was her host, David and Celeste had attended classes at an art studio Marcia's mother owned. Caroline had never met Marcia, so Celeste had to come up with a reason for her knowledge.

"Ag talks about you a lot, so it feels like we've already met."

Her mouth lifted to the side, revealing her sparkling teeth. "She does?"

Was it coincidental that an art teacher had given birth to a daughter with perfectly symmetrical features? From her radiant brown eyes to her rounded chin, nothing was out of place. Marcia wore clothes that complemented her light skin, and even her black work suit made her look trim and fit.

Celeste nodded.

"That's how I knew you, too," Marcia confessed. "Ag talked about you and posted pictures of this little princess." She readjusted Emma's weight on her hip. "I didn't expect her to be this big."

Marcia shook her amber-colored hair. "I probably should have stayed away, but Ag meant more to me than she'll ever realize."

"I'm glad you're here."

Marcia cast a look toward her lost love. "I couldn't have stayed away. If she needs me, I'll be here, even though she's pushed me away."

"What happened?" Celeste asked before she could stop herself. She put her hand to her mouth. "I'm sorry. You don't have to answer that."

"It's okay." She glanced at Emma and tickled her. Emma tried to tickle her back.

"As far as I knew, everything was fine. I called her every night, and we got together over the weekends, but after we'd been together for a couple of months, our weekends together became overnight trips or just quick dinners. It wasn't long before Ag just slipped away from me."

She shook her head. "I should have seen the signs, but I was so busy with my art studio, and my father was ill." She smiled apologetically. "Before I knew it, there was complete silence from her. I reached out a couple of times, but"—she nodded her head in Ag's direction—"you know how she can be about forced interaction. It just causes her to pull away more."

Marcia laughed almost to herself. "In a lot of ways, she reminds me of my mother." She cocked her head to the side. "Well, maybe that's not exactly true. Ag seems like an old soul stuck in a rapidly progressing world."

Celeste had to admit that she'd felt the same about Ag. The woman had adapted to technology, but social interactions were a challenge for her. She wondered if it had something to do with the occasional homophobic comments and unwanted advances from men she still had to endure.

David glanced back at them, and his eyes widened momentarily before he turned his attention to steady his sister down the steep embankment to his mother's grave. There were rows of metal chairs under a canopy that protected them from the afternoon sun, and a light breeze blew through from the river, creating a balanced temperature.

David waved her over, but Marcia didn't join them. Instead, she sat behind Ag, looking completely miserable as she watched her cry. She reached out once, but her hand fell just short of Ag's chair before she withdrew it.

The preacher said a few words over the casket and recited a well-known Psalm, but his message was brief. When he finished, he left quickly, walking in long strides up the embankment.

Celeste looked after him, wondering if he was uncomfortable or if his hasty exit was a common practice. In her time, the dead were burned, and only those who knew them carried their memory. No gravestones or markers showed their life and death, but online databases kept a record of the names of the living and deceased for genealogical purposes.

During the interment, Celeste held Emma in one arm and grabbed David's hand in hers. He put his arm around Ag, but she didn't seem to know he was there.

Ag understood when the service was over, and she fell in front of the casket, weeping bitterly. David fell on his knees with her.

"No!" Ag cried. "Please wake up, Mama." She grabbed the handles on the casket, her voice rising as people either stared or hurried away. "Tell me I can do better! I'm not ready for you to go! PLEASE!"

Her body shook so hard Celeste thought she was going to convulse. Watching her reaction to her mother's burial made Celeste cry, and Emma tried to wipe her tears away.

Marcia rushed to Ag, enveloping her in her arms. Ag made no move to disengage from her embrace, and Marcia whispered in her ear.

"You should probably get Emma out of here," David called back to Celeste.

Celeste's car was in the Winsomes' driveway, so she was stuck. She hurried out from under the canopy, but after she was away from the scene, she didn't know what to do.

She stared at the mourners as they trickled past her, but she didn't recognize any of them. Some of them exchanged polite smiles, but no one spoke to her.

She looked down at her feet, and a tiny gravestone caught her eye. A lamb was etched above the name Lilly Bell Martin.

Celeste was pretty sure Mrs. Winsome's last name had been Martin, but she'd said there were two sets of families with the same surname. It must have been the stillborn baby of one of Mrs. Winsome's relatives, as there was only one date on the stone.

She moved through the other rows of gravestones, seeming to move through time as she walked. The newer graves, like Lilly Bell's and Mrs. Winsome's, were closer to the road, but the older graves were near the tree line.

An expanse of forest that stretched as far as she could see limited her vantage point. She read names like Willa, John, Jacob, Samson, and his wife, Katrina, but one name stopped her in her tracks. It wasn't the name as much as it was the date under it.

David Regal Winsome stared back at her in block letters.

Celeste had expected the date to read sometime around December 7, 1941, but the date of his death was different.

David's uncle had died only five years ago.

Chapter 40

Celeste stared at the grave for a long time. Emma wiggled against her, causing her to shift her position.

Mrs. Winsome's brother had died during the attack on Pearl Harbor, so why was the date of his death listed as five years ago? He had lived well beyond the war and married. Patty Winsome was buried next to him, her name sharing the broad, slate tombstone.

She shook her head to clear it. She had been thinking about Mrs. Winsome's writings. Of course, her brother hadn't perished during the war.

Why didn't that thought seem right, though?

She trudged back to Mrs. Winsome's grave, hopeful that Ag had calmed enough to get back into the car. Maybe Marcia could go with them. It would take some of the pressure off David and give Ag someone to love again.

As she got closer, she noticed David was behind the tent. He held his face in his hand, and she couldn't tell if he was crying. She resolved to get to him quickly, in case he needed her. He had been strong for his sister, but there would be a time when he'd break down over his mother's death.

Before she could approach him, Mindy came up behind him. She wrapped her arms around him and laid her head on his back.

It hadn't been easy for her to peel herself away from her boys. They ran around the graves, causing the remaining mourners to cast weary looks in their directions.

In her time, they buried no one, but her father had taught her to respect the ground over those who had been placed in it. She cringed as Cameron ran over a woman's freshly packed grave and Dalton played hopscotch over tombstones.

Her heart took a nosedive into her stomach when she watched Mindy give David the attention she should have been present to give him. He looked down at her hands and grabbed them.

Celeste wanted to leave. She wished she had brought her car. She could have run to the nearest post office and begged her grandfather to take her back to her timeframe. She'd start dissolving her fake union with Zam, and she'd stay with Movey Shelton.

Movey was safe. He'd never hurt her, and he'd love Emma. He'd always wanted a child.

David turned around and met Mindy's eyes, but instead of desire, Celeste saw pain and frustration. He pushed Mindy's hands away and dropped them. Celeste wasn't close enough to hear their exchange, but after David spoke, Mindy said something that made his jaw clench. She stormed away, calling to her sons as they ignored her.

Celeste stood in place, and it only took seconds before David saw her. He moved across the uneven ground, but when he got to her, he only slid his arm around her shoulders.

Celeste didn't press the issue. David hadn't known she had been watching him, but he had kept his word to her. For now, that was enough.

Marcia came back to the Winsomes' house.

She looked around at the walls as if she had never been inside, and Celeste was almost certain she'd never met Ag's mother. She followed Ag to her room, and they stayed there for several hours.

David plopped onto the couch and held Emma as she napped. Celeste laid out dishes that church members had dropped off. She couldn't eat, but she hoped the other people in the house would deplete some of the food that was overloading the refrigerator and freezer.

She sat next to David, laying her head on his shoulder. He fell asleep watching the news.

Celeste couldn't stay still, and she kept hearing sounds from Ag's room, so she crept into Mrs. Winsome's room and pulled out one of her journals.

Now that the lady had passed away, her words had new meaning. They certainly held more significance, even though her writings only outlined stories that seemed to be based on her life.

I did it. I really did it.

I thought my efforts were for nothing. After my trip into the past, Liz and I played cards into the night. Nothing happened, and when our wine was gone, we retired.

I'd been writing in my journal, and I fell asleep with it pressed to my chest. When I woke up, my ears were ringing, and the corners of the book poked me in the ribs.

But the light was different, and the smells weren't the same. I had no light in the room that joined the lab, but bright sunshine lit up my eyelids, almost allowing me to see the veins in them before I opened my eyes. The scent of sandalwood laced the air.

I rose carefully, afraid that my head would be hung over from drinking the previous night. As I lifted, the sheet fell away and exposed naked flesh. I'd always worn clothes to bed unless I'd had an unmanageable sunburn, so I was shocked. But I was in for an even bigger surprise, as a man was snoring next to me.

I let out a blood-curdling scream.

Bill Winsome shot up from the bed. After he assessed that there was no immediate danger, he held me to him. It felt odd to be held

by anyone, as I had spent the last few years
avoiding romantic ties, but he was compassionate
and seemed familiar in a way I had never known
him. His kindness stretched beyond the feelings
we'd shared and hovered around a permanence I
wanted to preserve.

"What's wrong, sweetheart? Did you have a bad
dream?"

A thousand thoughts flooded my mind, but
at that moment, it hit me. I had changed
everything.

I had to make sure. I spoke breathlessly
against his shoulder. "I had a bad dream about
David. I dreamed he died in the war."

He cupped my chin. "No, sweetheart. He's at
home with Patty and their new baby."

I looked down at my finger, and a gold wedding
band stared back. Of course, I had married Bill.
Without my grief pushing me away from him, we
had moved forward with our plans.

As if in answer, a flood of memories washed
over me.

Bill sat in a pew at church to propose to
me, as his leg had been taken by a bomb. Our
marriage had been a lovely church affair, and he
had started preaching at the church soon after.

I looked at Bill Winsome and I found everything
I needed. Sure, I'd miss the camaraderie I'd had
with my friends, and I wasn't sure about the
fate of Steve and Danny in their futures. If I
was honest, I didn't care about Al. I hoped he
had died somewhere.

I saw *my* future in Bill's eyes.

I cried. Most of my tears were happy, and
he mistook them as the leftover trauma from
a nightmare, so he held me close. Afterward,

I experienced love in a new way, and I never wanted to let it go.

Celeste wished she'd stopped reading there. It was a great ending to a love story that she knew spanned decades. But she moved on to the next page.

Bill isn't happy. He seems satisfied with everything in life, but something is missing.

The start of my feminine cycle excites him, but he mopes around when he learns about my monthly visitor. I know he wants a baby, but for whatever reason, I'm not getting pregnant.

My mother feeds me sweet potatoes, as she sees the looks on our faces when my father asks about our family plans. She says that I might have twins because they're supposed to make a woman very fertile.

Bill is a great husband, but I feel he somehow mourns for the child he lost when I changed history. The other day, he passed a doll, and I saw him reach out to touch the embroidered design on the dress. A light smile touched his lips before he dropped his hand, his happiness forgotten.

When you love someone, you want them to be happy, and after eight months of feeling like I'd failed my husband, I was ready to adopt. I spoke about it with Bill and my parents, and they were happy about my decision. David was less enthusiastic.

"You're just stressed out," he told me. "Go on a trip and relax. That's how Patty and I ended up with Jacob."

I considered his idea. Bill was scheduled to go to a conference, and I could tag along. Several members planned to build a missionary church in another country, and Bill needed to go over the ministerial plans. The conference was in Florida, so I could lie by the pool and be ready to fill my husband's needs.

I decided to go with him, but before I could inform Bill, I heard a knock at the door. I ran to open it, and I saw Steve on the other side.

Celeste thought she heard Emma stir, but it had only been the television. Tensions were escalating in the Middle East, but that was almost constant. One country attacked another, and after several months, there would be a truce, and two different countries would go to war.

Steve ran past me, surveying the house to make sure we were alone. Bill was making his hospital rounds, so I'd been by myself before my friend's arrival.

"I put it in your garage." He shook his aging head. "I guess it's more of a building."

I was struck dumb. "What did you put in the building?"

He ran a hand through his hair and stared at me with wild, bloodshot eyes. "The equipment! You know, DOVE."

My heart dropped at the sound of the name. We had given it to the machine he and I had built. He scrubbed his unshaven face. "They know I have it. Al found Linda and me—"

"Linda's still alive?"

He cocked his head. "Linda is fine. Well, not really." He massaged his temples. "She's aging, like me."

I chuckled. "We all get older. In fact, I—"

"Not like that, Eleanor. We're aging almost twice—if not three times—as fast. It's like our bodies are trying to catch up to the years we skipped."

My world had been consumed by thoughts of pregnancy, so my mind went straight to the baby. "Did Linda deliver—"

He waved a hand in the air. "Yeah, he's is fine. He was born in that time, so the time difference doesn't seem to affect him."

My scientific brain wanted to ask more questions, but Steve was already in my kitchen. On his way out the back door, he grabbed a piece of my tomato soup cake.

"I miss these," he said, taking a big bite. "We don't have them in my time."

I followed him to the building and helped him get ready. He grabbed my hand.

"After I leave, never use it again," he warned. "We've done enough, and they're about to catch up to Danny, Linda, and me. I have to lead two separate lives, and I know if they don't get me, Al will."

"Who's *they*?" I asked. "Have you seen Al? I thought he went to the past?"

He stared at me a moment, as if deciding whether he was going to answer me. "It's best that you don't know. All I'll say is that they see every time jump, and the more you do, the more they'll be onto you."

We said our goodbyes, and only after he was gone did I think of all the things I should have asked about the future. If tomato soup cakes were gone, what else wasn't around anymore? Did he know when I died, and could I have prevented it?

I put one of my dad's locks on the building, and I palmed the key. They'd left the house for Bill and me to keep up after they decided to explore the country in an RV. They'd been gone for three months, and they showed no signs of

returning, so I wouldn't have to worry about my
dad getting anything out of the building.

Bill would be a problem, but he was going on
a trip, so I could use the time to cover the
equipment with some junk my dad had collected.
If I positioned it just right, Bill would never
notice it.

Confident with my plan, I spent a pleasurable
evening with my husband. That night, he touched
my shoulder, a clear indication that he wanted
to be intimate.

"My monthly visitor arrived early," I told him.

He retreated and rolled over. Deep in the
night, I heard him crying. He said "Danielle"
in his sleep.

*Wasn't that the name of the daughter he'd
shared with Becky?*

I couldn't rest, but I pretended to be asleep
when Bill left. A minister from Johnson City
picked him up before the sun rose. By the time
the day cast its full light on our valley, I
was a new mother.

Celeste dropped the book. Mrs. Winsome's words were so powerful, and everything added up. It seemed too real to be fiction, but if Mrs. Winsome's journal were true, then it meant that one of her children didn't really belong to her.

How did I go back to a time that no longer
existed? It wasn't easy.

Steve had placed our data and my old journals
beside DOVE before he left. I had the program
from Danny's work, but I altered it. So many
things could have happened, but I set the time
and jumped back before I could talk myself out
of it.

I stayed days in the other time frame. First, I stole a car, then I nabbed the baby while her parents were sleeping. I drove to Steve's house and arrived just before the future Steve took the equipment. Liz held onto the baby as I wrote the letter that saved my brother's life, and before time could catch up to me, I zoomed back, and Liz sent the baby and me back to an hour after Bill left for his ministry meeting.

I loved the baby instantly. She was my child, and I thought of her as belonging to Becky, Bill, and me. I played with her and dressed her in the dresses my mama had saved from when I was a baby. Every day, though, she seemed to get a little bigger. It wasn't long before I realized she was going through the aging Steve had described.

I did the calculation in my head. She had gone three years into the future. She would be five before it leveled off, and at her rate of growth, it would take a couple of months.

I had to tell Bill. He would have to know about everything from my rejection of him the night before he left to the abduction of his baby. Of course, in this time frame, he wouldn't remember having Danielle, but would he still love me after he knew what I'd done?

Of course, at first, he'd think I was touched, but after he witnessed the baby's accelerated growth, he'd know. *What was I going to do?*

That's when God answered my prayers. A week passed, and Bill informed me they needed him to go to Africa and set up the church. He wanted me to go with him, but I refused.

In those months, the baby grew into a toddler and settled into a young child. She knew me as her mother, and everything she did delighted me.

I saw Dot in the store and I asked about Becky.
She slapped me.

I was shocked until my mother called and I told
her about the experience. "How could you do that
to Dot? You know how she loved her sister."

"Loved?"

"Eleanor, what is wrong with you? You went to
Becky's funeral after the car wreck."

I dropped the phone, and I don't know how
long I sat crouched on the floor. Worse still,
Becky's child, the one I had stolen from her
in the other time, was the one to comfort me.
I held her and cried. I decided Dot had every
reason to hate me, and I'd let her do it for
the rest of my life.

Celeste reflected on the friction between Mrs. Winsome and Dot
Bailey. She definitely understood the reason for it. Except, Mrs.
Winsome's story had never happened. Well, parts of it were true,
so maybe that was a section that was based on real events.

I wish I could have gone back in time and erased
the car wreck. I thought about instructing
Becky's daughter about the way to bring me back,
but I didn't want to put that kind of pressure on
a child who was already struggling to understand
the world at an accelerated speed. *What if she
couldn't bring me back?* Anything could happen
to her, and without me to tell them, no one
would realize the child's place.

What's more, Steve had told me about the
mysterious "they" who watch time jumps. After
bouncing through time with a baby, I may have
picked up some attention, so any subsequent time
jumps could give away my location.

Becky would have to remain dead, and I would
be the only one who knew it was my fault.

Bill returned several weeks after I didn't see any measurable growth from our child. I gave him the story about adopting her from a couple in Johnson City who moved away, and I thought he wasn't going to believe me.

"Is this my daddy?" the child asked. She'd peeked into the room where we'd been talking.

Bill never missed a beat. He took her in his arms and played with her until she fell asleep. Seeing them together made me realize his daughter was truly what my husband had been missing.

"I didn't want to ask while she was awake, since she thinks I'm her father, but what did you name her?"

I'd given it a lot of thought, and I had decided to name the child as a reminder of what I had done. I was responsible for Bill's happiness and David's life, but I was also responsible for Becky's death.

"Agony."

Bill startled. "Agony? That's no name for a child. We'll call her Ag." I put a hand on his arm, and he stared at it. "Do you want to give her a middle name?"

He ran a hand through his hair and clenched his jaw. I'd get to keep the name I'd chosen, but I would have to agree to any middle name he picked.

"Danielle," he said. "I've always liked that name."

Chapter 41

Celeste was completely overwhelmed.

Ag was a product of Bill and Mrs. Winsome's marriage, right? Everything she'd read was fiction. Even Ag had confirmed it.

Why didn't it seem right to Celeste? Why did she have a nagging feeling the words were true? She just couldn't shake the reference to her grandfather. There's no way Mrs. Winsome could have plucked Alexander Maze's name from the air.

There was only one thing to do to prove it to herself.

Celeste crept out of Mrs. Winsome's room and eased the back door open. It creaked twice, but the noise didn't seem to bother the sleeping souls in the house.

Once outside, she jogged to the building, certain that she could swing the doors open. She saw the lock before she touched the double doors. She pressed her hand against the wood, and white paint chipped into her hands as she pushed. They moved inward, just enough for her to squeeze herself through.

Once inside, Celeste stared into complete darkness. The only light was behind her, and the crack in the door only allowed a sliver of sunshine to fall onto the floor.

She'd had the foresight to bring her phone. She'd grabbed it with the idea that she could take pictures, but the flashlight feature could help her find a light.

She quickly abandoned her search for a light, as she felt pressed for time. A light bulb didn't dangle from overhead, and her phone swept the area well enough.

The building seemed larger on the inside, even though junk littered every angle. Spiders scurried away from her light and a lone snake skin caused Celeste to make her steps more careful and deliberate. The smell of forgotten machinery lingered. The deeper she went into the building, the more she lost the scent of motor oil and starter fluid and picked up notes of earth.

A loft rested at the back of the building, and ladder-like stairs led to it. Celeste placed her hand on the creaking wood, but before she took her first step, something caught her eye. A blue tarp hung loosely underneath the loft. Jagged forms poked from beneath it, making the covered items unrecognizable.

Celeste forgot about the threat of vermin and reptiles. She bolted to the tarp and jerked it away. A fine sheet of dust flew into the air, obscuring her view and causing her to cough.

"There you are," she said to the empty building.

Celeste stared at the equipment. At best, it was the most basic form of the time machine she had designed. The components were there, from the computing technology to the chair on which a traveler sat, but it looked more like a living rough sketch than her vision of a time machine.

A bird chirped outside, and it reminded her she needed to go inside before she raised more questions. She took pictures of the equipment and covered it with the tarp.

Celeste hurried indoors, preparing her story as she flew inside. There was no need to worry, as everyone was still sleeping.

She prepared pancakes, and by the time the last golden disk touched the plate, Emma was awake and reaching for her. She lifted the child and laid plates on the table, choosing a plastic one for her toddler. Emma insisted on holding her plate until she sat with her food.

Ag, Marcia, and David filtered into the kitchen. David raised his eyebrows at his sister, hoping to engage her in conversation, but Ag didn't speak to him. Even though she had depended on him for physical and emotional support during their mother's funeral and interment, Ag wouldn't acknowledge her brother.

Marcia noticed the difference and tried to extend her condolences to David. Ag interrupted her efforts with a sharp look. Marcia made it through the uncomfortable breakfast, but she left shortly afterward. Ag kissed her lightly and promised to call her.

David helped wash the dishes, and a message dinged on his phone. He uttered a curse and returned it to his pocket.

Celeste couldn't contain her curiosity. "What was that about?"

David grabbed the edge of the counter and clenched his jaw. "Mindy sent me a text about the baby's heart rate and growth."

Celeste's eyebrows drew together. "What's wrong with that?"

David closed his eyes and took a deep breath before opening them again. "I asked her to let me know when she was going to see her doctor. I wanted to be there." He took out his phone and flashed the picture Mindy had sent him of the front of the obstetrician's building with the baby's information in plain white text. "It looks like she didn't listen. Again."

"I'm sorry you didn't get to go," Celeste said.

Emma crawled into the living room. Celeste followed her and turned on a show with babies and an unruly preschooler. Emma shook her head and stared at Mrs. Winsome's hospital bed. Ag and David would sell it soon, but it still sat vertically to the television.

"It's time for her shows, isn't it?" she asked her daughter.

Emma looked down. She was young, but she felt the grief in the house.

Celeste found an early soap opera, and she turned it down most of the way. Tomorrow, she would stop putting the show on, but Emma needed to hear it in the background. It provided the comfort she craved.

When Celeste went back to the kitchen, Ag was laughing. "You're the stupidest man I know."

David was already seething from the part of their argument Celeste hadn't heard. He called his sister a name that most people associate with a female dog.

Celeste shushed him and pointed in Emma's direction. "Don't you think that's enough?"

David glared at her. "Fine. Take her side."

"I'm not taking—"

"Yes, you are," he interrupted. "You're thinking it, too."

Celeste lifted her eyebrows. "Thinking what?"

"You think Mindy should have the baby without me!"

"I—"

"That's not what I said, David," Ag voiced. "I told you that you were clueless. If you—"

David's eyes narrowed. "I'm clueless? What about you?" His hand flew in the direction Marcia was traveling. "You have a wonderful girlfriend who loves you, but you keep pushing her away."

"That's none of your business!" Ag shouted.

Celeste cringed, but a quick look confirmed Emma hadn't heard them. "Guys, think of Emma."

They were both too heated to hear her.

"Besides," Ag said, "I don't take advice from men who kill their mothers."

David's jaw was so tight Celeste could hear his teeth pressing together. "I didn't kill her."

A self-satisfied grin spread across Ag's face when she realized she'd hit a nerve. "You killed my mother, and I'll never stop hating you."

The conviction with which she said it left no doubt.

Ag's venom fueled David. "If you were a man, we'd be walking outside."

Ag stood up and slung her chair into the table. "No need to stand on ceremony." She waited for a beat and added, "Mother-killer."

Their eyes locked, and neither sibling backed down. David wouldn't hit her, but he was too angry to walk away.

Celeste opened her mouth to diffuse the situation, but a cry carried into the kitchen. Three heads turned to the living room.

Celeste was the first one to reach Emma and quickly assessed that she was unharmed. Emma pointed to the television, and Celeste's heart dropped somewhere near the pit of her stomach.

Ag was the first to react. "Oh, my god!"

David slumped against the doorframe. His eyes were wide in shock, and all the vitriol from his fight with Ag disappeared.

Celeste sat down, but she didn't remember doing it. She stared at the screen, willing it not to reflect the events before her.

"I thought I stopped it," she whispered. No one heard her.

The Willis Tower, or what remained of it, rained down debris as it fell to the ground. It had been decades, but the attack on September eleventh was still in the minds of many, and Celeste couldn't help comparing the two instances, especially when the scene shifted to other buildings around the world in a similar state. On the screen, the image changed to two somber news anchors, while the live coverage moved to the upper right-hand corner of the screen.

The Teleboard was turned down, so they couldn't hear the news that anchors relayed. Celeste didn't need to hear them to know what they were saying.

She had spent many hours in class going over this day. It was a day they marked but never celebrated.

One hundred people walked into one hundred buildings with undetectable bombs strapped to them. After a decade, another country's intelligence finally unraveled how they could get past the security, but Celeste had never absorbed the information. It wasn't important for her mission.

The ticker tape showed the words she thought she'd never see again. `Officials agree the Great War has begun.`

Chapter 42

"I stopped it," Celeste mumbled again.

David and Ag weren't listening to her. They were as lost in their own thoughts as she was in hers.

Celeste wasn't certain what event had shown on her grandfather's Predictor, but he had assured her that her missions had been successful. After her first mission, the catalyst for the Great War started a couple of years from her current time. She had fixed it when she went back in Hailey Hall's body, or so she'd thought.

Why did Hailey make a difference? It was one memory her grandfather had sought to erase, but just like new memories surfacing after a timeline shift, the horror of the news report had triggered something she was certain her grandfather wanted to keep buried. She remembered the reason he chose Hailey Hall as her host.

One man had made the difference. Prior to the Great War and with no one's knowledge, he studied weapons and developed strategies for a secret company, and his work spurred the attack on the world.

Celeste racked her brain. *Why would the war have started sooner, though? Why had the timeline for the Great War accelerated?* Her mind felt compressed under the implications.

It came down to grief and loss. Important members of the man's family had been taken away, and instead of understanding the value of all life, the experiences spurred him to work harder to find weapons that protected the ones he had left. He didn't know that a woman at his company was waiting to sell his developments to the highest global bidder.

A thought invaded her mind, ripping apart her feelings. When he realized what he'd done, he committed suicide.

It wasn't long after the initial attack when the man's wife found him in a pool of blood. She was unbalanced from a recent loss and overdosed a month later.

Wait. Celeste hadn't learned that in school.

Had his wife taken her life in the original timeline? Celeste struggled with her memories, but every time she thought she saw the truth, another thought replaced it. It was like trying to pull two magnets apart after they had been drawn together.

She wrestled to remember the truth, but a new truth existed, and she had changed the course of another life. Again.

She popped off the couch and picked up Emma. Without announcing her intentions, she ran to the door.

She had a life to save. Or two.

During the drive, she worried that she'd be too late.

David placed his hand over hers. She fought the urge to pull it away.

He had run out of the house behind her and gotten into the car. She rationalized it would be good to bring him along, as he could stay with Emma while she assessed the situation, but his attentiveness unnerved her. She reminded herself that he was experiencing the shock of the Great War for the first time, and they had attacked twelve of the cities in his nation.

David needed her, but she couldn't be there for him. It was within her power to save a life—maybe two—and she was ready to try.

He must have thought she needed to take a drive to clear her head. He watched the scenery go by and only looked at her once when she turned into a subdivision.

"Where are we going?" he asked.

She ignored him. She could see her destination looming before her and her nerves were on edge.

She hardly took the time to jerk up the emergency brake when they stopped in front of the house. David tried to hold her back and yelled something at her, but her mind focused on the solid white door.

Celeste didn't stand on ceremony. She burst into the house—thankful for the unlocked door—and charged to the bedroom.

When Braeden saw her, he jumped. He'd already made a cut on his wrist, but it was horizontal. She had stopped him from making a vertical one.

She remembered the love and acceptance he'd showered on her when he'd thought she was his sister. He was a good man, and even though he lied to his family about his profession, he thought he was helping keep his loved ones safe.

Braeden didn't see his sister or Celeste's true form. He saw Caroline.

"Why are *you* here?" he yelled at her.

Celeste thought he'd jump off the bed, but he remained in place. She backed away a step when he pointed his knife at her.

"Look, Braeden, I know you don't believe me, but things will be worse if you kill yourself."

Looking at the knife in his hand, Braeden shook his head. "I'm a traitor to my country."

He probably thought she'd ask why, but Celeste didn't have time to play dumb. "The plans you drafted got into the wrong hands. You didn't sell them."

He brought the knife down, stabbing into the mattress. "They couldn't have snuck bombs into the buildings without my cloaking device."

Celeste could smell the liquor in the room, but she couldn't place the type. Whatever he'd consumed had left its mark on him.

"You can't think that way," she said, taking a step.

"What am I supposed to think?" he snapped. He looked from the floor to her eyes, and she saw the conviction in them. "I'm just as responsible for the deaths of all those people as the men who carried the bombs into the buildings."

Celeste could have argued that there were women involved in the attack. She could have told Braeden that his heart was in the right place as he constructed the devices, but she couldn't get the words past her lips. She found she had blamed him for the war.

In her time, Braeden Hall's name had been smeared. Everyone had felt the effects of the war, and they all blamed him for the cause. Celeste had hated him, too, until she had been the recipient of his love. Braeden adored his sister, and Celeste believed it was her death and his son's disappearance that led him to develop weapons of mass destruction and a device to camouflage them.

Celeste tried another angle. "Where's Macey?"

"Why does it matter to you?"

"It should matter to *you*. Who do you think will find you?"

He hopped off the bed like he'd been stung. Celeste followed him down the hall, but he tripped, barely catching himself.

"You're too weak to drive," she commented.

"Shut up," he tried to yell, but it came out in a strained whisper.

Celeste took out her phone and dialed the emergency services. When Braeden realized what she was doing, he tried to bat the phone away.

Celeste stopped her call long enough to say to him, "You will live. You're going to be here for Macey, so she doesn't overdose from the pain of your death. You're going to live, and you're going to help your country."

He pretended not to hear her, averting his eyes while she spoke. He eased against the wall and settled into a slump.

Even though she knew she shouldn't do it, once she was certain an ambulance was on its way, Celeste hung up on the emergency operator. She took the opportunity to look around the house. She grabbed a towel to apply pressure to the cut on Braeden's wrist and picked up his phone.

It wasn't password protected, so she easily located Macey's number and sent her a message.

"I want to see my sister."

"Your sister is dead," Celeste shot back. She had tried to be kind, but images of the ones who suffered in the Great War flashed through her mind. *It's not really Braeden's fault*, she kept repeating to herself.

"They killed her," he went on.

"Willie Jones killed her."

"No!" he yelled. The effort took almost all the strength he had in reserve, and he deflated. "She was gone way before she met him."

"She just lost her memory—"

"No," he seethed. "My sister would have known me. She would have remembered the love of her life, but she turned him away."

He shook his head, and it rolled against the wall. "No. The military was using her for some sort of tests." He jerked his thumb to his chest, but he only made it a fraction of the way. Celeste was still holding pressure on his wrist, so she held him in place. "She wouldn't have lived much longer."

Celeste didn't respond. Her grandfather had related the same information to her.

"They used me, they used my sister, and I'm almost certain they took my brother away."

Braeden's mother had shared the possibility of an illegitimate brother with her when Hailey was her host. It seemed his father had been living with another family. She took advantage of Braeden's condition to sate her curiosity.

"*Who* took him away?"

"Someone who knew how smart he was," Braeden answered. "All I know is that Hailey and I could talk to him before Dad died, but he seemed to drop off the face of the earth after he called for someone to help with Dad."

Celeste nodded along. She tried to seem apathetic, but Braeden wouldn't have pinpointed her interest. He was too far gone.

"Where do you think they took him?"

Braeden's shoulder jerked like he was trying to shrug it. "Who knows?"

Celeste wound up her courage and asked what she wanted to know. "What was his name?"

She didn't think he was going to answer her. Braeden kept his eyes closed, and the only thing she could see was the rise and fall of his chest. Just as she had given up, his lips moved.

"Gable."

Within minutes, a car pulled into the driveway.

Macey hurried in and rushed to Braeden. Celeste put her hands over the towel on his wrist and rose from the floor.

"What's going on?" she pleaded, looking from Celeste to Braeden.

Braeden was drunk and weak, but he answered her. "I did it."

"Did what?" she asked, bewildered. She cast eyes of molten lava at Celeste.

Did she think her husband slept with me? Celeste wondered. She had to admit, her presence and Caroline's reputation pointed to the possibility, but David and Emma were in the car. Surely, Macey wouldn't think she'd leave her family outside while she was unfaithful.

"I killed millions of people," he told her.

It wasn't the admission Macey had been expecting. She dropped her posture and released a sigh. Even though she didn't understand, soon, she'd know every secret her husband had kept from her.

Celeste slipped away. When she got back to the car, an ambulance pulled up to the curb. They shouted at her, but she got into her car and drove away.

David looked from the ambulance to her. Emma slept peacefully in the back seat.

"What was that?" he shouted in a whisper. "What did you do?"

"I saved two people," she said simply.

"You left me in the car with the baby."

She shrugged. "I couldn't take either of you in there with me."

David hit the door, and it startled her. "I'm trying my best to understand you, but every time I think I have you figured out—"

Exhausted from the events of the day, she was uninterested in easing his emotions. "I've already told you. I'm from the future."

"I don't want to hear that bull—"

"Fine!" she shouted. "I won't tell you about Braeden Hall's attempted suicide or remind you about the war."

"What about the war?"

"I told you we were headed for a war, and here it is."

"But you said it would be here later."

"I changed the timeline somehow, and—"

"You're insane," he said, aghast. "I didn't want to believe it, but—"

"Shut up, David." She took a cleansing breath. "Ask me a question. Pick something that I can answer quickly."

Just then, the radio announced two baseball teams who were scheduled to play the next day.

"The Sox will win by three points."

"It could be a lucky guess. They're a good team."

"Okay. Just before the third inning, a girl from the audience, Meryl Johnson, will lead the spectators in an impromptu singing of Amazing Grace." Celeste's father loved baseball, and the Red Sox were his favorite team. It was a moment recorded in history, as Americans were suffering from the attack on their homeland.

"Take me home, Caroline."

They didn't speak for the rest of the drive. Celeste wasn't caught off-guard when David left, announcing that he was going to Mindy's house.

It didn't surprise her, but she was hurt. Maybe she could save a life, but she couldn't save her heart.

<h1 style="text-align:center">Chapter 43</h1>

Emma played joyfully on the kitchen floor, and Ag dragged Celeste into her bedroom by her elbow. "What's going on?"

Celeste and David had left Ag to deal with her grief, and there was evidence of the pain in her eyes. She backed away a step when Celeste reached out to her.

"I don't need your pity," she barked. "I want an explanation."

Celeste's eyes darted to a crack in the door, worried that Emma had heard her aunt's outburst. The child continued to play, either uncaring or oblivious. Celeste assumed it was the latter, as her daughter seemed highly empathetic.

Celeste sat on Ag's bed and patted the bedspread. Ag accepted the invitation to sit next to her, but the distance between them was much wider than it would have been before she left with David.

"I'm from the future," Celeste told her.

Ag laughed. The sound was more nervous energy than mirth, but Celeste jumped at her disbelief.

"Yeah. You and my mother, too."

"Your mother is not from the future."

Ag rolled her eyes. "No, she was from the past." She shook her head. "At least, according to her, she got to go back to the past, so I guess that makes her—"

"A time jumper," Celeste provided.

Ag set her jaw and dropped her head into her hands, massaging her tired eyes. "Caroline, I've known you for years. I'll admit you've changed, but there's no way you could be from the future and live an entire life before you realize it."

Celeste racked her brain for ways to prove herself to Ag. She repeated the information about the Red Sox game, but Ag's condescending smile remained. There was only one thing left to do, and she really didn't want to do it.

"Eleanor Winsome is not your mother."

Ag slapped her. Celeste's hand went to her cheek, feeling the heat of the sting.

Ag's lips pulled into a snarl. "Get out!"

The happy sounds in the kitchen stopped. "Mommy?" Emma called uncertainly.

Celeste pushed her tears away to answer her daughter. "I'm fine. Auntie Ag and I were just talking."

Her niece's interruption did not soften Ag's resolve. "Leave."

Celeste held her hands up, showing that she had no intention of retaliating. "Ag, I know you're upset, but look at the facts—"

Ag's eyes narrowed to slits. "If you don't get out of my house, I will never let you see Emma again."

Celeste was tired of Ag and David using her child against her. Given the circumstances, Celeste thought she was an exceptional mother, but there was no way to prove it to people who were grieving the loss of a loved one and experiencing the upheaval a new war brings as it begins.

"Okay. I'll go. Just read your mother's diaries."

Ag tore the alarm clock from her nightstand and slung it at Celeste, hitting her in the chest. Celeste backed away toward the door.

"Those notebooks are fiction!" Ag screamed. "My mother and father loved me."

Celeste realized it had more to do with the insinuation behind her statement than the words themselves, but she couldn't erase what she'd said. "I never said that. Mrs. Winsome traveled across time to—"

A book flew in her direction, nearly missing her head. Ag released a primal cry.

Celeste inched open the bedroom door, unsure if she needed to dodge another projectile. She grabbed Emma off the floor, grunting at her increased weight as she struggled to move quickly. She grabbed her keys and jogged to her car without bothering to shut the door. Celeste had just buckled Emma when Ag appeared in the doorway.

"Bring Emma to me," she demanded. "I'll call the police if you leave with her."

Ignoring the threat, Celeste backed the car out of the driveway. A thud jolted her as gravel rained across her windshield.

"She threw rocks?" Celeste questioned, glancing in the review mirror at her toddler.

Emma's blonde eyebrows traveled up, and her mouth hung open. She craned her neck, but the car seat didn't allow her to see out the back window. Ag shook her fist and yelled as Celeste drove away, but she didn't throw anything else at the vehicle.

"Auntie Ag is having a bad day," Celeste told her child.

Emma nodded her head.

Celeste drove around a drive-thru and picked up a cheap pizza. She took it to the river, intending to eat it with Emma as the soothing sounds of the water rushed past them.

She hoped her favorite picnic table was free. It didn't provide a great view of the river, but it was the furthest one from the trashcans, and it was the same one David had shown her when Hailey Hall had been her host and he thought her name was Emma. Part of her wished she could go back to the simple moments she had shared with David that day, but then Emma wouldn't be with her.

It's a fair trade, she thought, glancing back at her daughter.

Her phone chirped, and she was surprised to see David's message on the screen.

`Come to Mindy's.`

That was all it said. She didn't understand why he'd want her there.

Was he going to rub his rekindled romance with Mindy in Celeste's face? She doubted it. The likelihood she'd have Emma with her was too strong for that type of drama.

Celeste didn't bother typing a response. "Change of plans," she told Emma as they backed away from the water.

David opened the door and waved her inside. She didn't see his face, but his posture was closed.

Mindy's boys were playing in the living room. Dalton grabbed Emma from her and plopped her down next to Cameron.

Celeste laid the pizza box on the table. "You guys can have some pizza."

She washed her hands and tore a pizza slice into bite-sized pieces for Emma. After she'd put it on the table, Celeste went upstairs, certain that was the direction in which David wanted her to go.

Mindy's room was at the end of the hall, and as she passed the boys' room, she noticed it was in complete disarray. Either Cameron and Dalton had been busier than usual, or they needed more attention than Mindy could provide in her condition.

Mindy's room smelled sweeter than the scents drifting in the hall, and it was much cleaner. The wood gleamed in the light, and the carpet looked new.

Mindy didn't look up when Celeste entered the room. She sat on the bed, staring out the window as David patted her back absentmindedly.

Mindy was lost in her own thoughts, and David had an odd expression. She'd seen it on the soldiers who'd returned from the war, and "shell shock" is what her father had called it.

"David?"

He jerked to attention and opened his mouth. Celeste waited, but no words followed.

"Hey, Celeste."

Celeste's eyes shot to Mindy, expecting a mocking glare. Instead, she saw sympathy and concern.

Celeste tried to keep her head level. At one time, David had spoken her name, but it had proved to be another person's manipulation.

Mindy sighed. "I know it must seem weird, but I've told David about your time jump."

Celeste swayed. She used a gleaming chest of drawers to steady her.

"She told me the same things you told me," David affirmed.

Celeste looked between them. *Was she dreaming? Had she slipped into an alternate reality?*

"How?" she squeaked out.

Mindy's lips formed a thin line. "I thought you'd know. I left some hints, and we used to be such good friends."

Celeste studied Mindy, trying to see her for the first time. The woman in front of her dropped her shoulders and her eye twitched.

It hit Celeste, and the wind went out of her body. In all the time she'd been around Mindy, she hadn't picked up on the similarities to her friend. She'd only met Mindy—the true Mindy—once, so she hadn't known her mannerisms to distinguish them from another person's.

She watched the realization dawn on Celeste's face and nodded. It was enough encouragement for Celeste to say her name.

"Timberly."

Chapter 44

"How long?" Celeste asked.

Timberly glanced away. "I've been kind of moonlighting in Mindy's body for months. I go in and out around the times you and David will be around her."

Celeste analyzed the first time she came in contact with Mindy since she'd transferred into Caroline's body. She could remember little things that she didn't place at the time, but what stood out to her the most wasn't the time Timberly spent in Mindy's body but her means of entry to David's room in the future and the ease with which she'd given Celeste access to him.

"Why are you coming clean now?" she asked.

Timberly looked at her hands. "I'm pregnant."

"I know," Celeste said, "and I'm sure my grandfather planted you here to achieve that result."

She shrugged. "Not really. He wanted me to establish a relationship with David to keep you from getting close to him again."

"But he didn't know—" Celeste started, but Timberly cut her off.

"We all knew, Celeste. You were only fooling yourself."

Celeste glanced at David to see how he was taking all of it. He stared at the floor in disbelief.

"I love him," she admitted. "I don't know why, but I expect it has more to do with the life we shared when I was here the first time than it has been during any other time jump."

Timberly let out a puff of air and darted her eyes at him. "Yeah. He's a bit jaded now."

"So, is this part of my grandfather's big plan, or—"

Timberly held up her hand. "Your grandfather doesn't know I'm doing this."

"But he watches his Predictor like a hawk."

Timberly tilted her head back to the window. "There was a disruption at the facility."

Celeste couldn't imagine what had taken her grandfather away from the device that showed him the results of his time-jumping experiment, but she was sure Timberly was the cause of the disruption. Before she could ask anything else, a cry rang through the hall.

Celeste didn't wait for Timberly's explanation. She bolted in the direction of the sound, stopping at the boys' room.

Piles of clothes were scattered on the floor, but as she stepped inside, she saw they were folded and tossed out of a drawer. She approached the drawer cautiously, peering into its depth.

In the center lay an infant surrounded by rolled baby blankets that protected him from the hardness of the surrounding wood. Celeste picked him up, and at her touch, his eyes opened.

One green eye and one blue eye.

"He's going to kill you," Celeste said when Timberly shuffled into the room.

"Maybe, but I'm tired of standing by while he hurts people."

Celeste nodded to her stomach. "But he'll destroy everyone close to you—including that baby and your daughter."

"Tom, too," Timberly said remorsefully. "I probably didn't think about it all the way through, but you didn't see what they were doing to that baby."

Celeste stared at the child in her arms. He looked okay, but she moved his suit down and exposed two marks just below his shoulders. Celeste and Emma had the same marks. She'd thought they were birthmarks.

"He plans to raise him to time jump."

Timberly nodded. "He's going to use him and Emma, and he planned to use this baby until..." She held her hand over her stomach and trailed off, leaving Celeste to draw her own conclusion.

"Did you lose the baby?"

There were tests to determine the viability of a pregnancy. Due to the reduced number of births, the focus of many studies had centered on reproductive health.

Timberly's hand went to her pelvis. "No, I'm still pregnant."

"Then he'll use your baby, too." Celeste turned her attention back to Braeden and Macey's baby.

"It's not that simple," Timberly said.

David wandered into the room and sat roughly on the bed. His eyes pleaded with Celeste for something, but other than his broken view of reality, she couldn't settle on what he wanted from her.

"I took a DNA test," Timberly went on.

In the current time frame, only an amniocentesis would have concluded the paternity of the baby, but in the future, a simple swab of the mother's cervix was enough—as long as she had abstained from sex for several days.

Tom and Timberly had already had one child, but Tom had been deemed infertile after repeated tries produced no more offspring. Celeste had thought David's disinterest in prophylactics was the most likely reason for Timberly's condition until Timberly's leading statement.

David stirred as if he were just waking. "I'm not the father?"

"Okay," Celeste said. "Why is that such a big deal? A baby is a baby. It doesn't matter how it was created."

"Your grandfather won't feel that way," Timberly said. "Just to be sure, he's going to lock me away until the baby is born, and then he plans to take my baby anyway, even if it's not David's child."

Celeste shook her head. "He can't do that. You have rights."

Timberly walked over and touched a strand of the baby's hair. "I think we both know your grandfather doesn't follow the law or a moral code."

"Are you going back?" Celeste asked.

Timberly nodded. "I have to go back and get my body out of the facility before he realizes I took his newest project."

"He'll find you," Celeste warned.

"That's true," Timberly said. "Tom still has a few military connections, though, so we're going to try to get away."

"Good luck and Godspeed."

The women hugged over the baby, and when they parted, Timberly's eyes were moist. She pasted a smile on her face as she dried her tears.

"Get that little guy back to his mommy and daddy."

Celeste promised to return him, though she doubted he would see both of his parents. At the very least, Braeden would get carted off to a mental facility, and Macey would need a little time to absorb her husband's part in the war to come.

Chapter 45

Celeste moved with a force she couldn't explain. If asked, she may not have been able to trace how she had gotten back to the Winsome's garage. She had been too lost in her thoughts.

David intercepted Ag. Celeste didn't know what he said to her, but she left them alone and no harsh words echoed off the mountains as he trailed behind Celeste.

David followed her to the garage. He was stunned by the revelations of the afternoon, so he didn't speak as Celeste unwound codes and started the ancient prototype.

The baby cried in his arms, and he offered him a bottle from the bag Timberly had prepared. Emma swung her legs as she sat on the riding lawn mower. Nothing seemed out of the ordinary to her.

Celeste moved everything off the time machine, convinced she could rebuild any parts that had been corroded by time. It was in a dozen or more pieces, and without her previous experience, Celeste would never have been able to put it together to serve its original purpose.

She spoke sometimes, relaying part of a code or the need for a part to the onlookers. They had no idea what she meant.

Occasionally, David would clear his throat or open his mouth to speak, but he always ended up with his eyebrows drawn together and a faraway stare. He was still in shock.

That was fine with Celeste. She had already told him the answer to every question he could ask, and she was busy, finally using the skills she'd brought with her from the future.

Several hours later, the machine whirled to life, but it lacked certain updates that would make it safe. Celeste glanced up at her family. David was lying across a wooden bench, balancing the baby on his chest, and Emma had fallen asleep in the machine's chair.

The machine ran, but it wouldn't transfer her without a code. Celeste racked her mind for any clue she may have read in Mrs. Winsome's journal. Part of the first entry sparked a memory.

"DOVE," she said aloud.

"It was on your wall," Celeste remembered, addressing Mrs. Winsome's spirit.

Celeste took the baby from David and herded him and Emma inside. She put them in bed, and they embraced. Celeste wished she could take a picture of the way David's strong arms circled around their daughter as they drifted back to sleep, but she'd have to settle for the memory of Emma's slight smile.

She looked down at the baby in her arms. She'd love to join her family in their slumber, but she still had work to do.

Celeste sat in her car on the other end of the street, breathing heavily. She craned her neck, searching for movement through the long branches, wiping fiercely through the rushing wind. Thick curtains were drawn tightly over the windows, and Macey's car rested on the lawn in the same place she'd parked it when Celeste had confronted Braeden.

She'd brought the baby to Macey's steps, placing him on a blanket, before she rang the doorbell. She ran back to her car in long strides, expecting Macey to catch her or call the police. She had gotten to her car, but her legs still shook from her increased adrenaline.

Even though the sun was up, the outside light turned on, but the door didn't budge. Celeste worried Macey would go back to bed after she saw no one through her peephole, but a sharp cry from the baby put her in action. Macey almost hit the baby with the door as she swung it open, but Celeste had anticipated that possibility, so she came within inches of the baby.

Macey scooped him up and clutched him to her chest. She let out a wail of grief over their lost time and inhaled thankfulness over his return.

Celeste's car was still running, so she put it in gear and raced out of view. If Macey saw her car, it was only a streak of silver through her tears of happiness.

The early morning light traveled over the sleeping family. Emma and Celeste lay over opposite sides of David's chest, breathing peacefully with the rise and fall of his respirations. No one stirred until the sun was almost at its zenith.

David was the first to wriggle his way out of the pile. He could sense the heaviness of the day, but he considered avoiding it to lie back down.

The phone rang, and he grabbed it, taking it to the bathroom with him. He answered groggily.

"Am I waking you up?" Sheriff Murphy asked.

"No," David responded, immediately alert. "What's up?"

"I'm sending Lewis Novack to pick you up at six o'clock this evening."

David wanted to speak, but words failed him. Luckily, Sheriff Murphy had expected his response.

"The report came back on your mother's death. The obstruction was an indirect result of your attempt on her life."

"But I—"

The sheriff interrupted him. "You don't have to prove your case to me, boy. In fact, it's best if you don't say anything else. I'm givin' you enough time to get some of your affairs in order and spend some time with your daughter. Outside of that, you're on your own."

The sheriff hung up long before David took the phone away from his ear. When he turned, Celeste was standing at the door. In his haste to get to the bathroom, he'd forgotten to shut the door.

"Are you going to jail?" she asked.

"I'm going to prison," he replied.

Celeste sighed. "I may have a way to change that."

David's face darkened to a crimson. "You can take your time travel bull—"

Celeste stormed off, grabbing Emma off the bed. "I'm not the only one who told you about it!"

Emma woke and rubbed her eyes. Celeste felt bad for fighting around her, but David would either have to face his frayed sense of the fabric of time or stay tangled in it.

David stalked into the room, grabbing clothes for a shower. "You're crazy," he said, seeking to extend their disagreement.

Celeste didn't engage with him. She stomped downstairs and popped open the back door. After a thought, she walked back into the kitchen to grab Emma a bowl of dry cereal. She spent the next two hours adjusting the machine.

David poked his head into the garage just as Celeste hung her head over the computer. "Aren't you in the future yet?" He chuckled, and Celeste wanted to punch him.

She refused to speak to him. David wrapped his arms around her waist. "I'm sorry."

His apology caught her attention, and she spun around. David noticed her surprise.

"I want to spend my last couple of hours of freedom with you and Emma. I don't want anything to get in the way of it."

Celeste closed her eyes. "I need you to do something for me."

David kissed her forehead. "Name it."

"I need you to push a couple of buttons."

David squeezed her closer to him. "We may have to wait until Emma takes a nap," he growled, "but I definitely want to push all of your buttons."

Celeste sighed, and David released her. "Look, Caroline. I have to go to jail in four hours. Can you put whatever this—" he motioned to the machine—"is aside until I go?"

Celeste worked through a plan quickly. "Okay," she said amicably. "I'll make a deal with you. If you will push a few buttons when I ask, I'll go back inside with you when we're done."

David still seemed skeptical. "What if you're electrocuted?"

Celeste choked back a laugh. If she were honest with herself, it was a possibility.

"I'll be fine," she assured him.

Celeste picked up Emma and placed her on the mower. She hoped Emma would be far enough away in case anything happened.

David seemed struck by a thought. "The little baby—"

"I returned him to his mother last night," Celeste told him.

David nodded. "I can't understand what's going on, but at least he's back with his mother." He shrugged. "I guess I can figure it all out while I'm in prison for the rest of my life."

Celeste thought about arguing with him or bringing up the fact that he'd serve only twenty years for his crime, but she decided against it. David hadn't stabbed his mother, and Celeste was frustrated that he still believed he was responsible for her death.

Celeste lined up the machine and instructed David about the places to attach wires to her. With any luck, she'd pop into her body and David would take care of her host's form.

As David pushed the button, Celeste's vision darkened. When she could see, bright colors flashed through her field of vision.

She never expected to still be Caroline when she woke.

Chapter 46

She woke on a hill surrounded by flowers. She recognized the hill as one she'd been on before. In David's time, his two-story white house stood on the property, but in her time, the house had been demolished, and tufts of grass pushed through the nearly barren landscape.

She had traveled in Caroline's body, even though she'd thought the program was designed to place her back in her own body. Her tattoo was still visible, and it seemed a little brighter. The purple flowers were brilliant with silver lines, like dew on the ends of the petals.

Celeste turned her arm over, surveying the full image. "It didn't look like that when I got it," she marveled.

She allowed herself a few minutes to adjust to the jump in time. While she took in the mild day and smelled the limestone in the air, she thought about the machine that had taken her to her present location.

DOVE, she thought.

Mrs. Winsome and Steve had used the new version of their earlier concept. Both of them had jumped in their own bodies. Mrs. Winsome had noted Steve's disappearance after she pushed a button, and Liz had helped her fix her appearance so Mrs. Winsome could fool her parents.

Celeste had traveled in a prototype, but it was a better design than the one she and her grandfather had constructed. Celeste laughed.

Mrs. Winsome had been a genius, and everyone had thought she was a simple preacher's wife.

She stood and stretched. Without transferring into another body, she only felt a little dizzy. Her vertigo disappeared as she traveled down the hill and onto the road.

She couldn't traverse the distance to town. There would be too many wild animals with Slover's disease waiting for her to come close enough to the woods.

As expected, the first vehicle on the road slowed to a stop beside her. An older gentleman with a bright smile held up his fingers in a familiar greeting.

"I thought I knew everyone around here," he said.

"I'm visiting Celeste Maze," she replied simply. "I borrowed her grandfather's car to take a drive, but it broke down back there." She soured her face as she jerked her thumb behind her. "You know how finicky those gasoline-powered engines are."

He nodded his understanding. "Well, I'm Fulton Brown, and if you need a ride, I'd be happy to oblige." He made a show of tipping an invisible hat. "If it helps, I know Alexander Maze. He tried to help my bride with her fertility issues, but she passed away before she could deliver our baby girl."

"I'm sorry," Celeste said automatically. There were hundreds of similar stories. Ectopic pregnancies and fatal miscarriages claimed the lives of many women. Celeste's mother had been a casualty of childbirth. Since the war, most women hemorrhaged to some degree when they delivered a baby, but most of them died.

Dr. Alexander Maze had developed a serum that resolved that particular after-birth issue. Families revered him throughout the region, and several high-ranking regional military leaders honored him. Her grandfather had saved a lot of lives, but his nefarious vision of the future tainted her view of him.

"I met my Mellie after that," he said. "We've been married fifteen years and adopted a war orphan."

Many men were too proud to give up the opportunity to carry on their bloodline. Fulton Brown appeared to care more about his wife than his pride, and it won Celeste over. She hopped into his vehicle without another thought.

When they pulled next to her grandfather's driveway, she thanked him as she stepped quickly onto the concrete drive.

Celeste stared up at the massive house, wondering if she could talk to her grandfather, or if she'd have to kill him.

David blinked his eyes. The sun was almost blinding, shocking his eyes.

He gasped for air, not because the oxygen was thin, but because he was unsure if he could breathe. He stared from field to field, recognizing his county, but missing the familiar landmarks that usually dotted the landscape.

When Caroline had disappeared, his first thought was to follow her. He knew very little about the program she'd used, but his mother had encouraged him to pursue a technology minor while he earned his nursing degree.

After changing the schematics to accommodate Emma and him, David threw an old baseball at the button until it finally started the program. Even though he'd just watched Celeste dematerialize, he didn't expect to shoot through the lights and sounds of time like a bolt of lightning.

"Where are we?" he marveled.

"Home," Emma replied as she took his hand.

Celeste wasn't surprised the door was open. Her grandfather's Predictor gave her away as soon as she arrived.

She climbed the steps—each one holding her weight firmly but betraying her presence—and stopped at her old room. Gentle cries demanded her attention, and she slid the walnut door open.

Celeste had enjoyed the dancing ballerinas on the curtains and the carousels across the walls when she was in her youth. As an adult, though, the room made her fearful, as if it was a front for the true intentions of her caregivers.

A crib had been scooted to the far corner of the room. Her daybed, where she had rarely slept, was piled high with fluffy pillows, blankets, and stuffed animals, but the crib only had a simple sheet.

The small form on the mattress kicked and cried out again.

Celeste rushed over to the baby and picked him up. Harvey Fletcher hadn't changed a lot since she'd last seen him. His face was a little fuller, though, and it gave her some solace. At least they weren't trying to kill him.

Harvey cooed at her, and Celeste noticed a tooth in his lower gums. It had just breached the surface, but it changed the infant in her arms to an older baby.

Why wasn't Caroline with him? Celeste wondered. *How could she leave him in the care of a psychopath?*

"He's a good baby."

Celeste jumped, and it startled the baby. She hugged him to her chest.

"You can put him back in the crib or carry him with you, but we're going into my office," her grandfather directed.

His slender form seemed almost thinner in his pinstriped suit. Celeste wondered if he'd worn similar attire when he'd met Mrs. Winsome.

She fought the urge to issue a sarcastic remark. Celeste held Harvey securely as she followed Dr. Maze to his office across the hall.

The last time she'd been in the room, she'd found a picture of David's mother and stolen a gun out of her grandfather's desk drawer. She sat in the chair as the door shut, but she didn't look behind her. The real threat was staring at her without an expression.

Dr. Maze didn't wait for his granddaughter to get comfortable. "I'm glad to see you're back."

Celeste rolled her eyes. "I bet you are," she responded sarcastically. "Why do you want me to sit here?"

He rubbed his fingers down his bristly chin. "I am glad you are here, Celeste. I spent a lot of time and money on you, so I don't want to lose you."

She laughed dryly. "Yeah, your granddaughter, the science project."

Dr. Maze stared at her with only traces of expression. She thought he was angry, but his posture was relaxed, and his attitude was calm.

"You look different from the picture of Caroline."

"That's because I'm a different person."

He nodded thoughtfully. "You're probably right. A person's essence is more than a physical appearance."

She thought about her spirituality and wondered if her grandfather equated an essence with a soul.

She had to veer the conversation in a different direction if he was going to answer her question. There were so many things she wanted to know.

"Did you want Hailey Hall to die so you could speed up the start of the Great War?"

He leaned back in his chair, resting his eyes on her. "I think you know the answer."

Celeste willed the emotions over her past host to stay inside. "Was she really going to die?"

He considered her before he gave a brief nod. "She and Robert were scheduled to go on a mission. Hailey Hall would have been killed, and Robert would have blamed himself."

Celeste hadn't thought to check on Robert. She didn't know how he had handled Hailey's murder.

"You saved him from more pain."

Celeste clinched a fist but relaxed it when Harvey's head bobbed. "Don't do that."

His eyebrows shot up.

"Don't act like you tried to prevent harm," she said. "You caused the Great War."

He sighed. "Don't be dramatic. The Great War would have happened with or without my influence."

"You could have stopped it."

He glanced at a picture of David's mother and back at her. "Have you ever really loved someone?"

"Emma," she replied. "And David and his family, too." After another moment, she added, "My father and Movey."

He chuckled. "Your father."

Celeste narrowed her eyes. "Yes, I loved my father dearly."

"If you could call him that."

Celeste grew wearied of his vague statements. "Are you going to tell me what you mean, or am I supposed to guess?"

"You're a smart girl. Haven't you ever wondered about your mother?"

Celeste crossed her legs and balanced the baby on her thigh. "My father told me about her. He said you did everything you could do to keep them apart."

Dr. Maze leaned back in his chair and placed a hand on each armrest. "He told you what I wanted him to tell you."

Celeste rolled her eyes again. She didn't care that he had the power to destroy her. He would not ruin her vision of her father.

"I know you read Eleanor Winsome's diary."

She shrugged. "So what? You're from the past. What does it matter?"

His salt-and-pepper eyebrows shot up. "It should matter quite a bit to you."

Harvey cried out, and Fanta quickly brought a bottle. When Havey had settled, Celeste said, "I'm tired of your games. Just say what you have to say."

Her grandfather tsked, but he launched into a story that changed her life.

Chapter 47

David stood in the middle of his hometown, but he didn't recognize it. The old movie theater had been turned into a children's theater, the courthouse was some sort of medical facility, and a digital billboard had been erected near the railroad's roundhouse.

He and Emma had been lucky an older man had picked them up in a truck David thought looked like something from an apocalyptic movie. The man seemed genuinely bewildered by their presence, and David wondered if it had something to do with their clothes. He seemed to have on something close to the hospital scrubs David wore to work, but David and Emma were dressed in tee shirts and jeans.

The man took them to town, but he kept glancing at them as he drove. It made David uncomfortable, and he was glad when the vehicle stopped moving.

As if the automobile and the change in the town hadn't been enough to prove he was in another time, David was bombarded by images of wild animals and ads that supported a law prohibiting meat. Something called Slovar's Disease had infected the animals, and they were unfit for eating.

David tried to find a good place to start searching for Caroline, but his eyes kept darting to all the unfamiliar sights and sounds. He was glad he was in a small town because anything more would have overwhelmed him.

Emma seemed to have everything under control. Even though she should have been between one and two years old, she had the form of a preschooler and the maturity of an older child. David had known something was off with his family long before Caroline disappeared into the future, but his fragile mind only wanted to accept the parts that fit into his perception of reality. Before Emma came into his life, Caroline was nothing but a liar, time travel didn't exist, and he wasn't a father.

Looking at Emma made his heart swell with pride. She had his eyes, and when she reached for him, he wanted to protect her from every evil in the world. If all the bad things had to exist to keep his precious daughter, then he would embrace the sinister alongside her angelic spirit.

Emma led him to a building with a storefront and pointed.

The entry was decorated with the same purple flowers on Caroline's arm but entwined with orange and yellow leaves. The door swung open, and the images glittered as they caught the sun.

Emma dragged him inside. After he digested the men and women in various stages of dress as they received tattoos, he thought he may be in the wrong place with a toddler. He tried to pull her back to the door, but Emma marched confidently to the back of the building and knocked on a brightly painted door. The colors were so brilliant against the stark white walls of the room that David had to shield his eyes.

Movey Shelton opened the door with a big smile that only grew wider as Emma jumped into his arms.

"Babydoll!" he shouted. "What are you doing here?"

David extended his hand, but Movey only looked at it. After an uncomfortable moment, he tucked his hand into his pocket.

"I see Emma, but I don't see Celeste," Movey said, motioning them into his office. "What has she done now?"

David didn't pretend he was unfamiliar with the name, but he wanted to make his position clear. "I followed Caroline after she used some sort of time machine, and it brought me here. My daughter trusts you, so I have a feeling you can help us."

Movey stared at him with an amused expression. David decided he didn't like his cockiness, but he had no choice. He had to trust someone if he wanted any hope of finding Caroline.

Movey pulled up the sleeve of his Alice in Chains shirt, revealing a tattoo with purple flowers. It didn't have Emma's name, but it was clearly the same tattoo that wound around Caroline's wrist. And if David were honest with himself, it was the same tattoo he had seen on Hailey when they had shared tender moments.

"I'll do anything for Celeste and Emma," Movey said.

An uncomfortable silence followed. David considered the idea that he was way out of his element. At the same time, he tried to tear Movey apart, but even the man's white eyeshadow was expertly applied.

"I need to find Celeste," he said, but even as the name left his lips, it felt foreign, like he was talking about someone else.

Movey straightened. "Well, she's in one of three places: her apartment, the facility, or her grandfather's house. Knowing her, she's in the most dangerous place."

"Where's that?" David asked.

Movey pointed to a map of the town on his desk. "I think you'll need to go to Dr. Maze's house, and when you do, you better be ready to do whatever it takes to leave with Celeste."

"I thought she was the most beautiful girl in the world," her grandfather started. "She walked with a purpose, and she didn't let the rules of society define her."

Celeste decided he was talking about her grandmother. He had never spoken much about the woman whose likeness hung in the foyer, so she paid attention.

He emitted a rare chuckle. "She had a pet rock and a guinea pig named Hippie, but she could calculate large sums in her head and follow the line of any cultural conversation. She was a paradox."

"My grandmother sounds like a lovely woman."

He scoffed. "Your *grandmother*." He twirled a pen on his desk. "You don't have one. I'm talking about Eleanor Winsome."

She was jarred when he said she didn't have a grandmother. Sure, her grandmother had died before she was born, but he shouldn't make Celeste feel more alienated by taking her claim of kinship away.

"Silly girl. The portrait that hangs in the hall is nothing more than a likeness I created of Eleanor with a few calculated differences. Stuart Shelton painted it well."

Celeste's heart dropped. "Are you saying—"

He interrupted her. "I never married."

Celeste's mind whirled. *What about the necklace her grandfather wore? Had he told her it belonged to her grandmother or had she assumed it did?*

Celeste thought about her next question before she spoke it. She was afraid the answer would send her past the point of no return, and she wasn't ready to feel more ostracized. Even as she spoke the words, she couldn't believe she had dared to utter them.

"So, who is my father's mother?"

It only took Movey fifteen minutes to charm the receptionist and turn off the security at the back of the building. He rushed David and Emma inside.

"Tech is more Celeste's thing, but I've been with her when she's delivered serious blows to the leftover warmongers." He smiled sideways. "I saved a few tricks in case I needed them,"

David didn't know what they planned to accomplish at the facility. He wasn't a great fighter. A self-defense class and a few push-ups a week hardly equipped him for the challenges they could face.

On the other hand, Movey looked like he could take on a couple of people at once. His broad shoulders tensed, revealing sculpted muscles.

He's an artist and a hero, David thought. *I haven't got a chance.*

Movey had more than casually mentioned that he and "Celeste" had been lovers. David didn't want to think about who she'd choose if the woman he loved was faced with a decision.

He hadn't exactly been good to her. Sure, when their relationship had been pure, he had doted on Caroline. They had gone everywhere together, and he had prepared every meal that touched her lips. *What good were his recipes and the way he'd treated her in the past when he'd emotionally run her through the wringer?*

If he believed "Celeste" was from the future, he could justify Caroline's pattern of behavior. Of course, Caroline had been his compassionate wife while Celeste was in her body, but if that doctor had jerked her back here, then the former Caroline would have returned.

What did the real Caroline think when she woke up naked in his bed? Was she afraid David had drugged her, or Willie had sold her for drugs?

He sighed deeply, and Movey put a firm hand on his shoulder. He understood that David had been lost in his thoughts.

"I know, man. The people on this side—the ones who knew about Maze's experiments—we've had time to deal with it. How long have you known?"

David couldn't look him in the eye. "She tried to tell me months ago. I thought she was crazy."

Movey chuckled. "Yeah, I might've thought the same thing if someone had tried to tell me they were from the future, but Celeste is a straight shooter. If she says something, it's usually true."

"If that's right, then it means she was in the body of another woman I loved, too."

Movey shook his head. "If you loved the same woman in two different bodies, it sounds like you love her soul."

Movey swallowed like he was trying to rid himself of the lump in his throat. "I'll tell you one thing. It's easy to love her, but it's hard to let her go." David thought he had finished, but Movey added, "Even when she wants you to."

A pair of voices drifted to them. The couple's words bit into each other through hushed whispers. From their vantage point, David saw a man and a woman. The man was plain, but trim, with dark hair, and the female had raven-black hair and pale skin. David's heart did a double-beat when she flashed her ocean-colored eyes. Her freckles danced lazily across her skin in non-discernable patterns, making him want to trace lines from one group to the next, but there was something in her voice that stopped his lustful thoughts and soured his first impression of her.

"Speaking of body-hopping," Movey said. He ground his teeth as they watched the pair turn the corner.

"Is that—"

"Yeah," Movey answered. "That's your Caroline in Celeste's body."

"She's not *my* Caroline," he said and realized it was true. The woman he loved lived in Caroline's form. "Who was with her?"

"Zam. Do you know about him?" Movey looked back at him for an answer.

David shook his head.

"It's probably better that you don't."

David skipped the cryptics. "What are they doing here?"

Movey crossed his arms. "Either they're trying to pick up her baby or trying to get her pregnant."

David's eyebrows drew together. "What kind of place is this?"

Movey answered him as they raced down the hall, "Not one you want to get caught in."

He had expected her question. Her grandfather used his words to create a labyrinth, and Celeste had never reached the center.

"Linda Wilson," he answered simply.

Linda had been Steve's girlfriend in Mrs. Winsome's diaries. Celeste had read about her, but, surely, her father's biological mother was named after an ancestor, or it was a coincidence.

"When I went into the future," her grandfather went on, "I thought I was alone. I believed I would be forced to live hand-to-mouth, but I rebuilt an empire over a year that rivaled anything I'd accomplished in my youth. Even though I was successful, I hated Eleanor Winsome." He picked up her picture. "And I loved her."

He put it down on the desk. Celeste could no longer see Mrs. Winsome's straight smile or dark curls.

"I saw Steve by chance. He had aged, but it was clearly my old friend."

Her grandfather's lips curled back. "I scouted him out for a few days before I arranged a *chance* encounter. At first, he was worried about me, but when I showed him no ill will, he invited me home for dinner."

Celeste tried to study the room, but her grandfather caught her roaming eyes. He had once told her to find anything to use as a weapon if she ever felt ill at ease, and Celeste definitely felt cornered.

He stopped until he was certain he had her attention. "My investigators had learned that he had lived in the time frame for over a decade, and Linda had been with him for five years." He looked at her pointedly. "You already know what it's like to see people after a certain amount of time has passed for them, even though their image and mannerisms are fresh in your mind. Still, I pretended to be shocked when Linda greeted me. I embraced my friends with care, and in truth, I was glad they were with me."

He flicked the pen he had been twirling, and it landed at Celeste's feet. "Linda dropped a bomb on me over a plate of warm apple pie. They wanted me to make a new time machine to send them into the past. They aged three to five years for every year they spent in the future, and they wanted to go home."

He held up a spindly finger. "But there was another reason they needed to leave."

Celeste wished he would finish his story quickly. Sweat beaded across her skin and she nervously rocked the baby. It was unlike her to be scared, but she had the feeling that she was more expendable than she thought previously.

"They introduced me to their child, a strapping teen with an inquisitive smile." For a moment, her grandfather seemed proud, as if he had been the reason for the boy's physical appearance or disposition.

"Steve suffered from arthritis and arterial calcification," her grandfather said. "And the boy should have been five years old, but he developed at three times the natural rate."

Celeste thought of Emma. *That's how her grandfather had known about her toddler's predicament.*

Her grandfather kept talking as a myriad of thoughts ran through her mind. "Steve had been forced to marry a woman from that time frame, and before Linda joined him, he'd fathered two children with her."

Celeste stared at the Predictor. Nothing happened by chance. Her grandfather had orchestrated it all.

"Braeden and Hailey," she whispered.

He laughed. "I was afraid you wouldn't make the connection, but I raised you to solve riddles."

"That means that the teen who found Steve after his heart attack was—"

"Yes, it was his son, and Steve's death left them penniless and afraid. Linda's health was failing, and the boy kept aging rapidly, so they were running out of time."

He reached into a drawer in the desk and pulled out the schematics of a machine that looked similar to the one she'd recently used. He spread it out with one hand, inviting her to look at it.

"I agreed to make the machine and set to work right away. After its completion, Linda and her son met me at my building. She uploaded her contribution to the machine and waited for me to make the final adjustments. The plan was to send Linda and the boy to the past first, and then I would follow them. We were set to move ahead, but the boy's chair sparked, so Linda gave her chair to him."

He smiled, and Celeste thought it seemed out of place. *Shouldn't he have been upset when the equipment didn't work?*

"I fine-tuned the sparking chair, but Linda was afraid to sit in it. I offered to go first in case the chair malfunctioned."

Celeste could almost see the scene unravel in front of her. Linda, with her silver hairbrush and a bag filled with her memories of Steve, gently nudged her son into Dr. Maze's building. Her anxiety was already heightened, but when her son's chair sparked, she only thought of protecting him. She switched chairs with him, but she was afraid she might be killed if the chair malfunctioned, leaving her teen boy orphaned in a past he didn't understand. Her grandfather's scheme had worked flawlessly.

He saw Celeste's discomfort as she put the pieces together, and he delighted in it. "While we spoke, the boy's chair sparked, and he disappeared. On the monitor, it indicated he had gone to the future. I told Linda that I would go after him."

He laughed so hard that a tear formed at the edge of his eye. "She was a silly woman. She gave me her hairbrush and urged me to retrieve him quickly. She promised he would trust me if I brought the brush to him and told him the secret word: DOVE." He raised his eyebrows as if Celeste should see the hilarity of it. "I gave her some vague instructions about how to use the time machine, but I disabled a component to stop working after my jump. I followed the boy to the future and never turned back."

Celeste slapped the desk, but her grandfather didn't flinch. "You left her alone!"

Her grandfather shrugged and went on with his story. "I told the boy that his mother had died when our location was discovered by secret agents. I gave him her hairbrush and said she'd handed it over as she'd died."

Celeste could hear the blood marching through her ears. "You're a monster! You didn't even care about the boy. He's probably dead because of you!"

He waved away her admonishment and continued his story as if she hadn't spoken. "I admit that the boy was of no concern to me. He had served his purpose after I had used his mother's attachment to him to punish her for her friendship with Eleanor Winsome."

Celeste wondered how hard it would be to hold the baby while she stabbed the pen at her feet through her grandfather's eye. She wagered she could do it effortlessly, but taking on Fanto was a different story.

"I tried to make another time jump, but without Linda's program, I was unable to succeed. I knew the password to her design, but the device that stored it was beyond my reach."

"Thank God," Celeste said.

"But now, I have the program, and I'm ready to move forward with my plan."

Celeste felt the blood rise from her neck to her face. Her grandfather could destroy so many lives in his form, especially if he didn't have to worry about manipulating unsuspecting people, like Timberly and her, to do his bidding.

She didn't know how he got the program, but she assumed his methods were less than honorable. She hoped her grandfather would explain it, but he went back to chronologically retelling his experience in their current time frame.

"The boy stopped aging at an accelerated rate," he told her, softening his voice like his words were a peace offering. "I used his blood to develop a serum to help combat the rapid deterioration of my cells."

He held out his hand. "I still have the serum if you want it for Emma."

She glared in another direction, but she could still see him in her peripheral vision. Celeste wanted the serum, but she wouldn't take it from his hand.

He shrugged his shoulders as he withdrew his hand. Celeste turned her head as he tried to erase a smug smile.

"I made an alternate discovery," he told her.

"Don't tell me. You found more ways to ruin people's lives?"

He rolled around her words like a fine wine. "It depends on how you look at it. Do you think *you've* ruined lives?"

"What are you talking about?"

"*You* were my discovery. Well, not you exactly. I had to wait a little while on you."

Celeste got out of her chair.

"Where are you going?" her grandfather asked. Celeste was happy to hear a slight strain in his voice.

"I'm leaving. You're talking in circles, and you're referring to something I don't understand. I'll see you later."

She was almost at the door before he stopped her.

"If you go, you'll never know the identity of your real mother."

Celeste let her hand fall before it ever reached the knob.

Chapter 48

"When I arrived in the future, my head was still in the past," her grandfather continued as if Celeste had never threatened to leave. "I used the technology I understood and the same methods I'd worked through hundreds of times. When I saw the cloning technology, I was amazed.

"The scientific breakthrough helped people who were missing organs, but I saw its full potential. Other scientists were busy creating parts to preserve living people, but I could manufacture a full human. Better yet, I could make a person like my son, who would be impervious to the effects of time travel."

"Your *son*?" Celeste spat. "He wasn't your son! You stole him from Linda." She nodded at the Predictor that stood proudly on his desk, its screen only revealing the secrets of time to a psychotic manipulator.

A sad smile touched his lips. "Gable may not have been of my loins, but he was every bit my son. As you know, he had one green eye and one blue eye, and he seemed to possess an enhanced intellect."

"Macey."

Her grandfather smiled. "What about her?"

"How was she related to you?"

The smile stretched, making his lips more sinister. "My father was a terrible man, and he abused my mother in every way imaginable.

He fathered many children, but I was the only one who inherited his name."

"And the mental instability that went with it," she said. Celeste wondered which of Dr. Maze's half-siblings had been Macey's grandparent. *How long had he known? Had he invaded her body and tried to kill Macey in the car wreck? Had he sped up the Great War by using her influence over Braeden?*

Dr. Maze continued his thoughts about her father. "Gable worked hard and attempted to make me happy. His ideas spurred new developments, and his empathy.... Well, I don't have to tell you about his compassion."

"It's just another reason he's not like you."

Her grandfather tilted his head. "I'll concede the point, but he is the reason time has slowed down for me."

She rolled her eyes. "Yes, a horrible human being gets more time while good people, like my father, die."

"I have given back to this community." A fire behind his words almost caused her to jump. "Think of all the babies who owe me their lives."

"They owe you nothing."

His eyebrows darted up. "Really? I'm the reason they exist. In fact, I'm the reason you exist."

David continued to follow Movey through winding paths. In his time, the building had been a functional courthouse, and its layout was simple. The design changed, and David couldn't tell if he was in the front or back of the facility.

"How can you tell where we're going?" David asked.

Movey lowered his voice to mirror the tone he expected from David. "I used to work here, and I see one of the attendants in the nursery sometimes."

David wondered how long it had been since Movey had worked at the facility. Had he been one of the attendants who had checked on Celeste when she led David to believe Caroline loved him?

"It's this one," Movey whispered.

The door was windowless, so they'd have to take a chance that no one was inside. Movey put Emma on one arm, and their closeness amazed David. For a moment, he wondered what would happen if he left Caroline and Emma in this time and went back to his own. Sure, he'd have to go to prison, but Emma and Caroline's alternate identity would be safe with Movey. David certainly felt more confident around the self-assured man.

He didn't seem rattled by Emma's growth. Maybe he thought Emma had grown over years in another time period.

David guessed she kept most of her baby features. She had a prominent nose and chin, so it could have given him a clue to her identity. David shook his head. "How many toddlers knocked on Movey's office door? Of course, he'd made the assumption.

By the time David slipped into the room, Movey was placing Emma in the attached bathroom and closing the door. He looked back at David, and the solemness in his features kept David from speaking.

Movey waved his index finger toward a bed where a young woman lay. David had a vague recollection of a similar bed where he had been stationed. The beeping machines told him little, except for a screen that monitored the patient's blood pressure and heart rate, but he scanned them anyway.

Everything registered at zero.

David didn't examine the machines that were light years beyond the equipment he used. He flew over to the patient's bedside to physically assess her.

"She's dead," Movey said, emotion choking him.

"Did you know her?" David asked. He pulled away from the woman, placing a tentative hand on Movey's shoulder.

"Yeah, Celeste and I went to school with her. Celeste caught the bouquet at her union ceremony."

David put his arm around Movey's broad shoulders. It felt uncomfortable to hold a man larger than him, but Movey seemed to appreciate his gesture.

Even though he was used to death, David always struggled to find the right words to express his condolences. Death easily unraveled rational people, and he had been inconsolable after his father passed away.

"What was her name?" David asked.

Movey leaned over the woman and placed a kiss on her ebony forehead. A tear rolled down his nose and landed on her cheek.

"Her name was Timberly."

Celeste knew what her grandfather was going to say before he started explaining the process. As he described genetics and cloning, she reminded herself that he was a manipulator and he wanted her to feel as isolated as possible.

"So, you see," her grandfather said, "your mother was only some harlot who distracted your father long enough to get pregnant. When she was in her fourth gestational month, she hemorrhaged and died before your father could get her to the hospital."

Celeste couldn't help but speak the question that formed on her lips. "How did you save me? Babies that early in their development can't live."

Her grandfather beamed with pride. "Those babies didn't have Dr. Alexander Maze at their disposal. I saw it as an opportunity to test a theory."

Celeste could believe her grandfather wanted to rush to her father's aid for his own benefit, but she was clueless as to why he would have chosen Gable's baby as the recipient of his revolutionary idea. He said he'd only liked the boy because he pleased him. If her father had gone against Dr. Maze's wishes and married her mother, her grandfather should have been ready to cut any ties with him. It was outside his character to help him. She guessed serial killers still had saving graces, like their love of certain family members or pets, so anything was possible with a narcissist.

Dr. Maze had explained the process he'd used to save Celeste, but she had tuned him out as her thoughts overwhelmed her. She only caught his last sentence.

"Then it was only a matter of extracting Linda's DNA from the hair in the hairbrush and adding a growth accelerator."

Celeste closed her eyes and shook her head. Her grandfather misread her frustration.

"Don't worry, you stopped growing at an advanced rate when you went to high school."

She glared at him. So, I'm technically only six or seven years old?"

He laughed. "No. It was nothing that dramatic. Most of your speedy development happened in utero." He paused, moving his hands up and down like he was assessing the weight in them. "Well, in the uterine environment Gable created for you. In truth, you're approximately twenty-one years old."

She tried to keep her face blank, but he carefully monitored her reaction. Celeste tried to remember it was part of his plan and she couldn't help him succeed at whatever he planned to accomplish. After she'd maintained an unreadable expression for almost a minute, Dr. Maze spoke.

"I guess I don't need to spell it out for you, but Emma's burst of development results from residual growth hormones, not from her trip into the past. After all, she traveled to the past, not the future. She should level out faster than you, though." A smug smile pressed his cheeks. "Maybe in her second or third year of primary school."

Celeste wanted to jump across the desk and claw out his eyes. If Harvey hadn't been in her arms, she would have ended Dr. Maze in all time frames.

He studied her, and an idea seemed to come to him. He stroked some keys on his keyboard and turned the monitor to face her. "If you don't believe me, maybe you'll believe Gable."

A video played, and she recognized her father. His dark hair swept over his blue and green eyes and he had to keep moving it out of his face.

It was always too long in the front, she reminisced sadly.

"*As you can see,*" her father said on the screen, "*we've taken the replicated DNA from my mother and housed it in the incubator.*"

He pointed to a watery incubator behind him where a noticeable human had formed. The tube-like structure stretched from the counter to the ceiling and a clear fluid filled it.

"After several failed attempts with the Andromeda and Orion versions, I could finally construct a machine that would act as a placenta. I took the underdeveloped fetus and combined it with—"

Celeste broke out in a sweat. Dr. Maze had told her the truth. That meant only part of her was a biological human and the other part was a synthetic design, making her a child with two mothers. Emma wasn't the only one with three biological parents.

Her father was continuing his scientific log on the screen. *"The result allowed the fetus to mature and receive the hormones needed for growth."* He jerked his thumb back. *"We estimate the fetus at six months' gestation, and the project started last week."*

It hurt to hear her father talk about her like a science project. She tried to remember that he'd lost the most important people in his life and could have been distancing himself from emotion as he inwardly grieved. After all, he'd been a loving parent, and she never felt like he was studying her when he rocked her to sleep or passed a football with her.

The man on the screen rubbed his hands together. Celeste smiled at her father's grin. It had always been a sign he was proud of her.

"Due to my success, Father says I can name the project. As my last connection to the woman I love, it makes me feel the creation is real, even though the result won't be a true baby and only a combination of my lover and me."

He moved to the side to give a clear view of the forming baby sucking her thumb in the tank. Blonde hair coated the fetus, even though Celeste could only remember dark locks falling around her field of vision.

"I'm going to call her Celeste."

Chapter 49

"Is that—" David started, but he couldn't finish.

The woman he'd known as Mindy was dead. He'd spent countless hours with her, and he'd decided to marry her. Now she was gone, and her baby had died with her.

Her questionable involvement with him was difficult to process, but he knew things about Timberly—real things—like her favorite position in bed, her love of ripe apples, and her fear of closing her bedroom door at night. A bubble rose from his throat, and he gasped.

Movey noticed his reaction and put a hand around David's waist. "I guess you knew her, too."

David couldn't even nod to answer him.

Movey offered to retrieve Emma, but David stopped him. It took him a moment to form the words, and when he did, they sounded hoarse.

"Was she killed? Was she killed because she warned Celeste and me?"

Movey sighed. "Timberly is not the first casualty in Dr. Maze's war, and she won't be the last."

"Turn it off," Celeste commanded.

Her mind whirled as she re-evaluated her relationship with her father. She had adored him, and she no longer knew if he had loved her in return or if she was only a science experiment.

Of course, her time with her grandfather always felt measured by her performance, but her father had shown her kindnesses that her grandfather would never understand. It was almost like she and her father had shared a secret or they were on a team that excluded the man they both loved and feared, but maybe it hadn't been confidential. Maybe *she* was a joke, and her father and grandfather had been laughing the whole time.

Was the man she loved her father, or was he more like a brother? Biologically, would he be her nephew or even her son in some sick, twisted curse of genetics?

Her thoughts swam away from the room and focused on her youth. *Her father had told her about the hairbrush and said it was her grandmother's. She'd never connected the silver hairbrush in Mrs. Winsome's writings about Linda to the one her father kept, but why would she?* There were thousands of brushes just like it.

"Why are you telling me now?" Her voice cracked with emotion and her grandfather—or whatever he was—asked her to repeat it.

"I thought you should know what you're up against," he said calmly, folding his hands on the table. "I created you. Do you even know what you're fighting for?"

For a moment, she drew a blank, and her eyes landed on Harvey. "I started out fighting for David and Emma, but now, all I care about is doing what's right."

Dr. Maze was unfazed. "Some people would argue that you're not supposed to be alive—"

"But you created me to hop through time."

"At the time, I didn't know you would be useful."

"But then you saw I could destroy your enemies." She moved Harvey's head into a more comfortable position, resting his head in the crook of her arm.

Dr. Maze looked away, and she followed his eyes to the picture of Eleanor Winsome. "I've grown tired of that."

"Yeah, she's dead."

"I don't have to worry about unrequited love anymore. That's true." He sighed. "But when my enemies walk into my time so willingly..."

Celeste didn't have to ask him what he meant. Her vision narrowed and her chest tightened, weakening her resolve to seem unaffected by anything Dr. Maze said.

David had followed her. She could feel it with every fiber of her being.

He turned the monitor to face him and typed a few keys. When he turned the screen back to her, it did not surprise her to see David in the facility, but her heart stopped when she saw Movey beside him, staring at Timberly's dead body.

"WHAT DID YOU DO TO HER?" she stormed.

Dr. Maze closed his eyes as if he were gathering the strength to speak to someone beneath him. "I did nothing to her. She stepped into a faulty program during an unauthorized mission. There was nothing I could do." He held up his hands in mock defeat.

Celeste wondered how far she could knock him backward if she hit him. "She was pregnant. Don't you value human life?"

He flipped his hand in the air. "I have a feeling there will be plenty more births in this time." He stretched. If their conversation was boring him, he'd end it soon, and with Timberly dead, Celeste didn't know what to expect. "I drew some of Emma's blood and developed a cure for most infertilities. Not to mention the number of elites who would like to have smaller versions of themselves produced through my new cloning process." He winked. "I may have to keep that one a secret, though."

He gestured to his plaques along the wall. "I'll probably get another award."

"You'll never touch my daughter again," Celeste cried, waking Harvey from his peaceful doze. His cries filled the air. "Even if I have to die, I will keep you from my daughter!"

Dr. Maze smirked and let his eyes travel in the direction of the monitor. Celeste glanced at the screen. To her horror, a small, blonde head popped out of the bathroom.

David had brought Emma with him.

Celeste moved faster than she'd thought was possible. She kicked the outdated monitor with her foot, sending it sailing at Dr. Maze. While he was stunned, she ran around the desk and punched and kicked him while holding Harvey in one of her arms.

Dr. Maze fought back. He kicked her legs out from under her. She cradled the baby as she fell, opening her up for strikes. Her face, head, and body received blow after blow before she had enough time to counter his force. She couldn't think of the self-defense lessons she'd learned from the tutors her grandfather had hired. She could only lie there with her bleeding body over the baby.

The baby screamed with a force equal to the punches thrown around him. Celeste tried to keep him from harm, and she wished she'd left him in his crib. She had taken him while thinking she could get him away from Dr. Maze.

She knew he was angry, but the click of the gun pulled her out of the fetal position. For once, Dr. Maze didn't have haughty comments. He was seething with rage.

Celeste was just in time to cover Harvey before the bullet pierced her back.

Chapter 50

Mrs. Winsome put her arm around Celeste as she led her around the Winsomes' home. Celeste leaned into the older woman, surprised by her strength.

"You weren't blonde, were you?" she chuckled. "Your hair's so thick and pretty."

Celeste shook her head, appreciating the freckles on her fair skin for the first time and pulling her dark hair over her shoulders. "Thank you. I got it from my mother... and my grandmother."

Mrs. Winsome nodded. "I knew Linda. She was a good friend of mine." She leaned in confidentially. "And she loved to brush her hair."

Celeste's eyes watered. "I guess I'll get to meet her now."

Mrs. Winsome patted her arm with her wrinkled hand. "Maybe in time."

Celeste sucked in a breath over her tears. "It's about time."

Mrs. Winsome made a sound deep in her chest. "There's something about time you may not know. It's not exactly set." Her brown eyes pierced Celeste. "There are many worlds of different choices with missed chances and new opportunities. The universe is full of them."

There were so many things Celeste wanted to ask Mrs. Winsome, but she decided it didn't matter. *What good was knowledge if she couldn't use it?* In her world and time, she was dead.

Chapter 51

Killing him had been easy.

When David rounded the corner of the house and caught sight of his salt and pepper hair in the moonlight, he had no problem pulling the trigger. Movey had knocked the bodyguard unconscious, and it shocked him when he saw David had murdered Dr. Maze.

"Did he attack you?" he asked David.

David shook his head. "It was almost like someone else shot him. I just knew it was the right thing to do."

"I don't know, man," Movey said between breaths. "I think you should have taken him to the authorities."

They ended their debate by searching for Celeste. Emma waited safely in Movey's car, and the two men went from room to room looking for her.

A baby's cries led them to an upstairs office. Celeste lay on the floor, her green shirt covered in blood.

David pulled her to him. "No, no, no!"

Movey surveyed the baby while trying not to cry. He couldn't look at his first and only love. If he saw her wounds, they would become real to him, and he wasn't ready to accept her death, even though—from the look of the disarray in the room—she chose an honorable one.

David gasped. "She's breathing!"

They hoisted her and ran to the vehicle. They didn't stop to look around the room for evidence against Dr. Maze or admire family paintings. As they walked outside, David registered the absence of a dead body on the lawn.

"I guess you didn't kill him," Movey observed.

David sighed, but his shoulders relaxed a little. "That means I still have work to do."

No matter how hard they'd tried, they couldn't rid themselves of Dr. Maze. He hurt everyone, and he showed no signs of stopping.

He carried a grudge for generations, and he destroyed the lives of anyone from his first group of friends. David believed he was an irredeemable soul. He may not have thought that way before he'd seen Timberly dead and Celeste dying, but it wasn't the first time Celeste—in Hailey's body—had died or been ripped from him.

David told Movey about his observations. The younger man's eyes stayed focused on the darkening night, but David could tell he was considering their next move.

Movey made one communication. As they made Celeste comfortable in the vehicle, he raised his voice higher than David thought was possible for him.

"You said you loved her!" Movey screamed into the phone. "She needs you now, but you're going to bail on her to be with a woman who pales in the shadow of her host's body?"

He must be talking to Zam, David thought, but it didn't give him a lot of hope.

"If you ever cared for Celeste, meet us at the facility," Movey barked.

He grabbed Celeste's hand. "Don't worry, Love. I'll take care of you."

At that moment, everything flew into a hyper-focus for David. He loved Celeste—for that was her real identity. He adored his family, and as he held his dying love in his arms, he knew he needed to fight for her.

She wasn't the cruel-hearted Caroline, who had aborted Lewis's baby and crushed him in a divorce. She was the woman who could eat pizza and french fries almost every night, fixed the townspeople's treasures, and mended something inside him he had never known was broken.

"Celeste," he said. It wasn't the first time he'd said it, but it was the first time he'd given a name—not to a physical body—but to a soul.

Her eyes fluttered, trying to open for him. She hadn't responded to Movey, but she tried to stir to hear him.

"I'm not even a real person," she muttered. "I don't matter."

"That's not true," David told her. "Whatever that piece of—" he paused to restrict his language. "Whatever Dr. Maze told you is wrong."

"I was created to be his living science experiment, and Dr. Maze thought it'd be fun to make his own clone army."

David adopted one of his father's favorite scriptures. "You were fearfully and wonderfully—"

She cut him off. "Your mama spent all that time trying to get me in church, but it didn't matter. I don't have a soul."

No living person should feel that way, David thought as he pressed her closer to him.

David decided he was going to save Celeste if he had to walk through fire and sacrifice every moral fiber in his being. If he could erase the conversation that had destroyed her spirit, he'd do that, too. Celeste and Emma were all that mattered to him, and it was about time he showed it.

David held Celeste in the backseat while Emma rode in the passenger seat. Movey sped down almost familiar streets and balanced a shrieking Harvey in his lap.

David had glimpsed the baby's name on the blanket Movey had grabbed out of a room and wrapped around him. In the absence of any other identification, David assumed it was the child's name.

They drove past the emergency entrance to the facility and parked in the lot beside the building. The facility was quiet, and Emma sat on the pavement and held Harvey while Movey charmed another receptionist.

When he waved them in from an open door, David picked up Celeste and hurried to shoulder the door while Movey went back out to retrieve Emma and Harvey. When he got to the opening, Movey had calmed Harvey.

"How did you get Harvey to stop crying?"

Movey winced. "What an unfortunate name. I've been calling him Morrison. That's what my mom was going to call me, but she named me after my father."

"You should keep calling him that," David said. He pulled the already hanging blanket from the child and dropped it to the floor.

"His name won't matter if Dr. Maze gets his hands on him. He'll turn this little guy into a monster." Despite his assertion, Movey caressed the baby with gentle strokes.

David looked down at Celeste. "She wasn't a monster."

"No," Movey said. "She's the love of my life."

"Mine, too," David admitted. It felt good to say it and understand what it meant.

It was hard to carry Celeste, even though she was a small woman. David worried about aggravating her injury, but she had passed out again from the pain. Her breaths were comforting, but the amount of blood dripping onto him concerned him.

They hurried into a room with no one in sight. Morrison cooed, and Movey laid him on a hospital bed, lifting the railings. "I'm going to send Zam on his part of the mission."

"Mission," David mused. "I like it. It reminds me of the stories my mama used to tell me about..." There was no way he could finish his thought. If he did, it meant he'd be giving credibility to the stories his mother had told him in his youth.

When David stopped speaking, Movey stepped out of the room and left him with Emma and Celeste. David smiled at his daughter.

Emma placed her hand on David's knee. "I miss Ins."

"Me, too." He let out a long breath and rubbed the palms of his hands over the ridges of her fingers.

Celeste lay on the bed, her blonde hair falling over the pillow behind her. He supposed it wasn't her hair, but it belonged to her while her soul occupied Caroline's body.

When had his mind made the switch from disbelief into acceptance? It was hard to say. Maybe he had always felt it, even though he hadn't embraced it until he'd traveled to the future.

He was probably in shock after his mind had been challenged with situations that repeatedly questioned the fabric of time and existence. He knew he wasn't dreaming, and he was glad. From his position, he had a chance to make everything right. It had to be timed perfectly, but if Zam could go through with the plan, they could go back to their lives.

It was all up to Zam.

Zam woke up next to Celeste.

The woman occupying her body had lived in it since her birth, and she was beautiful. She still thought she loved him, and she returned his kiss willingly.

Celeste checked the time. "It's eight o'clock. I know you're gonna miss me, but I have to be at the facility by nine, or Grandfather will let Timberly take my place." She pecked his lips, and he closed his eyes. "You'll have to think about last night while I'm gone, and maybe we can repeat it when I come back."

She laughed at her joke, but she didn't realize she was close to the truth.

Zam felt her warmth leave the bed. She might not roll in the sheets with him, but he'd make no apologies for how often he touched her before they left.

"I can't wait to go to a real museum!" she said as they walked down Main Street. "I may not be able to go to the bigger ones, but I heard there was one with a railroad and—"

"You may not have time for that," he said.

"You're right." She sobered, grabbing his hand. "There's so much my father talked about that I never got to experience."

"Yeah," he agreed. "The war took that away from all of us."

The air was different that morning, and it wasn't because he was visiting from a different time. It was pregnant with possibilities. Celeste could be successful, or they could all go home in defeat. Zam was the only one who knew the outcome.

Zam had seen the primitive sketch of the time machine and was amazed Celeste had reconstructed it to modern standards. The only difference between the original and the new model was that the new model held the traveler's body in place, only allowing their consciousness to jump to another time.

Dr. Maze told Celeste it was his original design. Even before Celeste had jumped the first time, Zam had his doubts. The man's talents had always been in other areas.

The facility buzzed with early morning activity. The high ceilings echoed the laughter and muffled cries of couples in various stages of their fertility journey. Zam couldn't handle the mournful cries and focused on the lively chatter near the receptionist's desk.

A crowd had gathered around Dr. Maze, their faces turned up to him in reverence. When he spoke, no one's eyes strayed, and when he moved, they rushed to ask more questions, hoping to stay in his presence a little longer.

Celeste stood at her grandfather's side, patiently waiting for him to acknowledge her. Mostly, she concealed her resentment, but the clench of her fist betrayed her when he spoke about his accomplishments.

Dr. Maze accepted the credit for his projects while those who helped him remained nameless. Celeste had constructed the time machine, and she would risk her life to prove the worth of the equipment, but he never mentioned her work and sacrifices. Of course, only a select group of people knew about the Predictor and the time travel experiment, but it would have been nice to receive a nod of approval at appropriate moments.

Dr. Maze disentangled himself from the hero worshippers, and Celeste and Zam followed him to a restricted area. Without ceremony, the doctor motioned to the equipment, and Celeste was prepared for the time jump.

Zam helped her onto the bed and watched Timberly and Talon secure the equipment. He moved his focus to Celeste. The moments held more meaning, and he wished Movey had sent him to a few hours before he and Celeste had dragged themselves out of bed. Even without sex, he missed the intimate moments he'd shared with her.

Zam stroked her cheek. "I love you."

Celeste pretended to be distracted by the cacophony of sounds and wires moving around her. It was the same as last time.

If it had been any other doctor, the leader of the experiment would have commemorated the experience with a speech. Dr. Maze only wanted to finish the first part of the experiment and watch his Predictor.

The first time Zam had witnessed the events unfolding around him, he had thought they were rushing to prevent the Great War. Now he knew differently. Dr. Maze had only wanted to punish his perceived enemies and make events unfold in a foreseeable way.

Knowing it was too late to stop her, Zam held Celeste's hand as Dr. Maze counted back and pushed the button. Timberly closed Celeste's eyes, and Zam dropped her hand.

In another time that reflected the current one, after a quick stop at Dr. Maze's office, Zam had celebrated with the small group who were privileged to know about the mission. This time, though, he knew about the ulterior motive for the project.

Zam was the first to leave, making certain to station himself just outside of Dr. Maze's office. It was no different than his actions the first time. He had asked to be placed in David's body, but Dr. Maze had declined his request.

The gun weighed more than the knife that he'd used to stab Mrs. Winsome, but it was easier to conceal. In his pride, Dr. Maze wasn't concerned about scanning his Predictor for threats against his life. He only wanted to know if Celeste was affecting David's family. Zam had known it would be a short window, but he had proposed it as the best chance for success.

When he saw Zam in the hall, Dr. Maze smiled and shook his fist in the air. "Success!"

Zam echoed the sentiment, but his smile wasn't as wide as it was before his beloved fell for David Winsome. "It was brilliant!"

Dr. Maze put a finger to his lips and unlocked his door. Zam fell in behind him.

As soon as the door clicked behind him, Zam fired the gun. The report was louder than he'd expected, but he didn't think he'd be there long enough to suffer the repercussions.

Zam had shot him at an angle, and when the bullet exited the doctor's skull, it released a spray of blood against the opposing wall. Zam couldn't believe all the blood droplets missed him.

Zam didn't look at Dr. Maze after he murdered him. He had seen enough death to last a lifetime, but he was glad he had ended Maze's plans.

"You'll never threaten my great-grandmother again," he spoke to the corpse.

Movey had told Zam he would pull him back after Dr. Maze disappeared in their time. It could take a few minutes, so Zam ran out of the room, dropping the gun behind him.

He settled in the break room, attempting to appear normal. Nurses ran past the door, and one woman shrieked, but he sat at the table, sipping bitter coffee.

Any time now.

Minutes ticked by. In the aftermath, no one looked for him or noticed him. They cried and attempted to resuscitate a man they could not bring back from the afterlife.

He waited.

They'll pull me back, he thought, *and I'll go back to Caroline. She's a poor substitute for Celeste, but at least everyone will believe we're a happy couple. She's a whining, lazy woman, but it's better than being alone.*

Several times, he thought he was dizzy, and Movey was transferring him, but he was wrong. He paced the length of the break room, watching the authorities carry a bag with the murder weapon to their lab. He noticed a drop of blood on his uniform. He rubbed it, but only smeared it across the side of his pants. It was a small stain, but it made Zam feel like it was a flashing beacon signaling the authorities.

All at once, it hit him. They weren't going to pull him back. Somehow, David knew what Zam had done to his mother, and this was his punishment.

Without Dr. Maze, no one could bring Celeste back from her mission. They didn't have the code. They'd put her in a ward for long-term coma patients until her body passed.

He resolved to raise Caroline while she was in Celeste's body. He'd tell her the things Dr. Maze had whispered to her before she'd agreed to marry Zam.

After all, being with another woman in Celeste's body was better than being alone. It had been his plan, anyway, but in his own time frame.

He decided to follow through with his plan, but two detectives met him at the door. "Are you Zam?"

He nodded.

"You'll need to come with us."

The taller detective led him out of the room. "We found a gun, and a witness says she saw you drop it as you left Dr. Maze's office."

He glanced at another detective speaking with Timberly. When their eyes met, he knew the identity of the witness.

David Winsome may have won, for now, but Zam would find a way to destroy him.

<h1 style="text-align:center">Chapter 52</h1>

He stared at Emma, begging her to understand. "I love you, but I can't live my life wondering if I could have done something to stop it." He glanced at Celeste. "And saved her."

The toddler took his hand. It was an empathetic action uncommon for her age, and it gave him peace.

David had enlisted the help of the only person who would understand his reasons. Movey Shelton took Emma from him and held her easily.

When Zam disappeared, assuming his past form as a host, David knew his plan would work. The only drawback was that he had picked a time in the past that could erase his daughter's life.

David scrubbed his face. "If this works, I don't think you'll have to worry about anything, but if it doesn't—"

"I'll take care of her," Movey promised.

They did not know if Zam's mission was a success. Movey might locate Dr. Maze's name in a database, but he lacked tracking skills. They'd have to hope for the best.

David placed the equipment on Celeste, and it whirled to life. Soon, he would be hooked up to a similar machine. He hoped he could make the necessary adjustments.

He took a deep breath. "If I'm wrong, nothing should happen to us."

Emma reached for him, and he hugged her. He thought about the love he'd felt for Celeste. Even though she wouldn't agree, if he died in the transfer, it was still worth the risk.

Either Zam's mission or David's quest would end Alexander Maze's plans.

"If you had a chance to end a terrible person before he harmed the people you loved, would you do it?" He had posed the question to no one in particular, but Movey answered.

"I'd do it and never look back."

David pressed the button and closed his eyes.

She woke with a start.

Even though she'd grown accustomed to Caroline's body months ago, she felt jittery and nauseated. She supposed it was due to the early months of her pregnancy. Her blood sugar was low from her decreased appetite and her hormones were giving her hot flashes and other strange feelings.

A pile of objects littered the floor next to the dresser. She had no clue how she was going to fix Mrs. Bailey's ancient DVD player, but she had to get to it soon. Mrs. Bailey expected it by Sunday.

The shower was running, but it shut off abruptly. Feet pounded across the floor, and the door burst open.

David hadn't bothered to grab a towel before he'd run into the room, and water dripped off him.

"What are you doing?" she said.

He flew onto the bed, embracing her, and covering her with kisses. "Thank God," he said over and over.

She loved the attention, but she forcefully pushed him away. "David, what's going on? Why are you acting like you haven't seen me in ages?"

He stared at her and said the words she'd longed to hear. "I love you, Celeste."

At that moment, she knew. Something had gone wrong in the future, and David had found a way to erase it.

Her thoughts immediately went to her grandfather. "Does he—"

David had been expecting her response. "I took care of it. He's dead. That evil monster is dead."

Her grandfather had always been secretive and unkind, but she cared for him. David's assertion was meant to make her feel validated.

She choked back a sob. "Did he hurt me?"

David's face registered a range of emotions before he spoke. "He did things to all of us that I'm glad you don't remember."

He returned to kissing her, slow and sweet. She interrupted him with another revelation.

"What happened to me?"

He shook his head, unwilling to talk about it.

She pressed her forehead to his. "I deserve to know."

"You died, sweetheart. I could tell you how I brought you back, but—"

She shook her head. "I don't need to know."

She should have felt some sort of emotion, but she drew a blank. Maybe people weren't able to grieve for themselves.

"You came back for me?" she asked.

His mother's voice traveled up the stairs and through his open door. "You may be married, but sexual congress should be conducted behind closed doors."

Ag shushed her mother, but not before Mrs. Winsome spoke more of her mind. Thankfully, her words didn't reach them.

David closed the door and settled into Celeste's embrace. He should have been the one holding her, but since her death, he'd needed the comfort.

She rested her chin on his head. "Is there anything you want to know?"

"No. You've already told me everything." He glanced up at her. "Well, everything I need to know right now."

She shifted uncomfortably. He'd been lying against her growing stomach, and he relieved the pressure."

"I'm glad I can stay," she said. "I don't know what would have happened to the baby if I'd been pulled back."

"The baby would have been fine."

She took a deep breath, and he could imagine all the thoughts tumbling through her mind. He couldn't shake his desire to be closer to her, even though she was trying to process the events as they'd happened or hadn't happened.

Would she remember their daughter? Would she recall her time as Hailey Hall, or their terrible fight to be where they were today?

She moved around him, pressing her lips to him, and he decided it didn't matter. He could relate the important parts and protect her from misery.

He pulled the woman who had crossed time for him to him and realized he'd done the same for her. It was about time they shared each other's love and challenges, and he was ready to jump into the future with the woman he loved.

A man's voice echoes up the stairs, calling them for breakfast.

David drew back, and tears welled in his eyes. "Daddy?"

Celeste cocked her head to the side. "He's here. Did something happen to—?"

David only paused long enough to throw on a pair of boxers before he bounded down the steps. When he saw his father, he crashed into him, almost knocking him over. He was still crying and hugging him when Celeste made her way down the steps.

Obviously, Celeste hadn't been the only one who had died, and when Mrs. Winsome approached them, David grabbed her and covered her in kisses.

"Now you stop that," she admonished. "I don't know where your mouth has been."

"Let the boy love you, Ellie," Bill said. He saw Celeste and opened his free arm up to hold her. "You never know how much time the good Lord is gonna give you, so you've got to soak up every second."

"Where's Ag?" David blubbered.

"I'm here," Ag said from the kitchen. She peeked around cautiously.

"I'm taking you to an art gallery in Knoxville next month," David told her.

"Okay," Ag responded, drawing out the last syllable.

He looked at his dad. "And you and Mama are coming with us. Tell Deacon Baily to take over the service that Sunday, and—"

His father held up a hand. "Now, Davey, I—"

David didn't wait for him to finish. "You just said that you never know how much time you have left." He pulled his parents closer to him, and Celeste was crunched into another hug. "It's important to me."

Bill patted his son's back. "Okay. If it's important to you, it's important to me."

Celeste couldn't be one hundred percent certain, but she thought David had just saved his father's life.

She stood back from the group and took in the scene. Ag walked into the living room, joining the hug, and pulling Celeste back into it.

Celeste may not be able to share who she was with the world, but David knew the truth, and that was good enough for her. She put her hand over the growing life inside her, happy that she could bring a child into a loving family.

She finally had everything she wanted. She was home.

The labor had been difficult, but the delivery was easy. Celeste pushed until a beautiful little girl entered the world.

The angelic creature was passed from one set of hands to the next as her family took in her beauty. No one wanted to let her go, and they pressed Celeste and David for the name they'd kept a secret for nine months.

Finally, Mrs. Winsome could take it no longer. "You better tell me that baby's name before I string you both up by your toenails."

Celeste looked at David. He'd had a name in mind since the baby's conception, never wavering in his assertion that the child was a girl, even though Celeste refused to find out the baby's sex. Celeste was ready for him to share their daughter's name, and she nodded in his direction, allowing him the honor of presenting it to their family.

He held their daughter up, and Ag, Bill, and Mrs. Winsome marveled at her lovely blonde hair, dimpled chin, and eyes that would soon show golden flecks in the irises.

"Emma," he announced proudly. "Her name is Emma."

Can You Help?

If you liked the story, please leave a review on Amazon, Goodreads, BookBub and wherever you purchased the book. Social media recommendations help, too!

Join my newsletter for free books and new release information!

Courtnee's Website (Join at the bottom of the website's page.)

Thank you for your support!

Acknowledgments

When I started writing this series—and this book—my mama was alive. She influenced my love of reading and encouraged my writing journey. Many of Mrs. Winsome's characteristics, from her love of deer to her blunt words, were inspired by my mama. As I stated in my dedication, I wish I had a time machine to tell her how much I miss her. Thank you, Mama.

Tosha, you read my work and were always involved with this story. Thank you for reading it over several times and for managing my website. I love you.

Avalee, one day you will publish a book, and I will read it from cover to cover. Thank you for supporting my work!

Stereling, thank you for being happy for me and paying attention when I talk about my work. You are so encouraging!

Legacee, Journee, Jubilee, Legende, and Rynegade, thank you for getting excited when I show you guys a new cover or tell you about my small successes. You mean the world to me.

Debbie, thank you so much for spreading my stories to other people. You mean so much to me!

Thank you, Sweet 15 Designs, for a beautiful cover. You knew exactly what to do to put the best touch on the book. My mama's favorite flower was a hydrangea, and you placed it perfectly.

I have a big thank you for some of my readers, Linda, Judy, Julie, and Catherine!

Thank you, dear readers. I appreciate you more than you'll ever know!

About the Author

Courtnee Turner Hoyle lives her dreams every day. She's the parent of seven children and loves each of them dearly.

The recent loss of her mama has plagued her thoughts and may have shown up in this book. Her mama was one of her biggest supporters, and Courtnee will miss her.

Courtnee has a few fancy degrees, but none of them reflect her personality or commitment to her family. She might be intelligent, or she could have been gifted at telling her professors whatever they wanted to hear. Whatever the answer, she walked away from formal education with two undergraduate degrees and one master's degree. She should have held out for a PhD. I know. She was a total slacker.

She's content writing, reading, watching her younger children grow, and beaming with pride over the accomplishments of her older progeny. They make her life worth every moment.

If she had a time machine, she'd visit her deceased relatives. Courtnee would record their words and give them extra hugs.

She hopes you never feel like you need a time machine.

Alternate Possibilities

Without diving into physics and subatomic particles, Parallel and multiverse theories suggest there are an infinite number of worlds with a limitless number of possibilities. If that's the case, my story could have ended in many different ways. If you're happy with the conclusion (and/or believe in parsimony), avoid this part of the book. Otherwise, please enjoy these short alternate endings.

Movey Shelton woke up in a different man's body. He tried to run a hand through his hair, but his palm met flesh instead of his long, black locks.

A wallet lay on the seat next to him. He flipped it open, and a man with a stoic expression peered back against a blue background.

Drivers had different forms of acknowledgment in his time, but they were digital. He read the name on the plastic card: Bryan Shelton.

His new limbs were long and powerful, stretching fully as he stepped out of a gasoline-powered truck. Evidence of futuristic tattoos danced across his forearms, and he approved of his host's clothes: a pair of jeans and a Led Zeppelin shirt.

The baby and Emma had transferred with him in their own forms. The baby looked up at Movey with wide eyes but didn't move his head to study his surroundings.

Familiar mountains rolled around the valley, seeming to hold up a cornflower sky. Distant traffic hummed, and a breeze tickled his ears.

He had chosen his host, the day, and the time for a reason, and he located Celeste in under a minute. She stood on the sidewalk in Caroline Fletcher's body next to the entrance to the emergency room. She held her wrist and his heart in her hand.

Her mission and the emotions associated with her host's body overwhelmed her, so she fell into his arms. Somehow, Celeste knew it was him as soon as she saw his tattoos.

"How did you get here?"

Emma had stayed in the truck. Movey had worried about overwhelming Celeste by presenting her with her daughter right away.

He passed the baby to her, and she took him. "In another time I lost you, and I couldn't live without you."

She looked from the hospital's entrance to the man who had once loved her enough for both of them. "But I have to distract David Winsome. It will help prevent the war, and—"

"It won't matter," Movey interrupted. "The warmongers will have their body counts and starving orphans."

Celeste's hands flew to her face, wiping away the tears that coursed down her cheeks. "I thought what I was doing would matter."

Movey put his hand on her shoulder. "It will, but we won't follow your grandfather's plan. We *will* make a difference."

He leaned forward, pressing his lips to hers and reveling in their warmth. "I love you, and I'll do anything to save you."

Celeste broke their contact. "What about Zam?"

She stared into his eyes, and he wished he could lie to her. Instead, he told the truth.

"He's waiting for you, but he only *thinks* he loves you." He put his hands on her arms, bending to meet her at eye level. "Zam is obsessed with you, and I think we both know you don't love him."

It took a long moment before Celeste nodded. "Well, if you're here, something went terribly wrong." She gave the hospital another glance before tearing her eyes away. "I really felt like I was supposed to go into that ER."

She sighed and let Movey put his arm around her shoulders. Looking at the baby, she asked, "What's his name?"

"Morrison," Movey answered. "And we're going to start a *new* future."

Ag tore the parts of the time machine out of the building where they had been hidden and carried them inside. She locked her bedroom door and spent three days piecing the equipment together.

If Caroline was right, her biological mother would have been alive during the Second World War, and Ag was determined to find her. Nothing short of death would stop her.

She had wanted to beat Caroline within an inch of her life when she'd suggested Eleanor Winsome wasn't Ag's mother, but the more she thought about it, the more it made sense. Ag suffered from hypertension, and it had caused her aneurysm. No one in her family had it, but Dot Bailey and her son took blood pressure pills.

Sam was another nagging thought. If she had belonged to Dot Bailey's sister, Sam would have been her first cousin. Surely her mama wouldn't have allowed her romance with Sam to bloom if he was so closely related to her!

The baby Ag had delivered showed no signs of deformities, but not every baby born between cousins had outward abnormalities. *Still, wouldn't her Christian mama think it was an abomination?*

There were rumors that Sam had been adopted to replace a baby Mrs. Bailey had lost to Sudden Infant Death Syndrome. If her mama had believed the rumor, it would explain her indifference to Sam's proposal.

Ag brushed it off until she rummaged through the top part of her mother's closet, looking for a vacuum cleaner attachment. She found the attachment and a blanket with the name "Danielle" sewn into it.

A plan formed in her mind. If her mother's writings held any truths, she'd find her real mother and keep Eleanor Winsom from stealing her from her rightful mother.

She loved her mama. She'd never forget her, but she couldn't let the woman take her away from a loving parent. It wasn't fair, and she couldn't allow her own abduction.

It took much longer than she expected to put together the equipment. She stopped several times, convinced God was directing her away from her course. Maybe the writings were false. Perhaps she couldn't get the machine together because it had never really existed.

Just before she gave up, the program whirled to life. Ag sat in the chair and threw a rolled pair of socks at the keyboard. Each time it missed the button to execute the program, she wondered if she was doing the right thing.

Becky Martin had been killed in her early twenties. *Had Eleanor Winsome saved Ag from an untimely fate?*

Ag decided the next attempt would be her last. If the socks hit their mark, she'd travel through time and accept the consequences. If they missed the button, she'd go into the kitchen and warm a can of soup.

She waded up the socks into a tight ball and focused on the target. She took a deep breath and watched them sail at the button that controlled her destiny.

Dr. Alexander Maze stood over the family as they lay in David's bed. The man still held Celeste's lifeless body.

After Dr. Maze had coerced Caroline into the machine, he had administered a killing compound, eliminating her and pulling Celeste back into her body. Once Celeste's consciousness entered her mind, her light was extinguished, ending her influence over the men who loved her.

When Eleanor's son woke, they would charge David with Caroline's death and blame him for Emma's disappearance. He'd never see the outside of a prison again.

Dr. Maze stared at the clock by David's bedside, matching it with the relic on his wrist. No one wore watches anymore, but he still owned a digital version.

With only seconds before he'd instructed his accomplice to transfer him back, the doctor grabbed Emma, easily taking her from her father's arms. Moments later, he returned to the facility with Emma, barely giving David time to jerk awake. Emma kicked and struggled against the doctor, and he released her when they entered his time frame.

Talon looked at him nervously.

"Thank you for pulling me back. I have just one more thing to do in the past." He adjusted the date and time on the monitors. "As long as I make it back here in four hours, you will not have to worry about your past relatives' lives."

Talon swallowed audibly, glancing at Fanto as he stood in the doorway. "I'll bring you back on time."

Dr. Maze nodded. He was used to people following his directions.

"What do you want me to do with Emma?" Talon asked.

"Take her to the nursery," he commanded.

"And Zam is in your office," Talon reminded him.

A cruel smile spread across the doctor's face. "I don't think he'll be there much longer. I'm going to pay a visit to Laura Silvers."

Talon couldn't disguise a shudder. After Dr. Maze settled into position, Talon sent him back to a period just before the turn of the millennia.

Eleanor Winsome's Tomato Soup Cake

Campbell's Soup Company introduced the cake on a soup label in 1950, but variations of the culinary oddity were recorded as early as the 1920s. Are you brave enough to try it?

INGREDIENTS

- vegan butter

- granulated sugar

- eggs (or egg substitute, like non-dairy yogurt)

- vanilla extract

- condensed tomato soup

- all-purpose flour

- baking soda

- baking powder

- cinnamon

- nutmeg

FROSTING

- cream cheese

- vegan butter

- powdered sugar

- vanilla extract

- soy milk

PROCESS

1. Preheat the oven to 350 degrees, and ready a 9X13 pan.

2. Combine a stick of butter and half a cup of sugar at medium-high speed until creamy.

3. Add a small container of non-dairy yogurt and a teaspoon of vanilla extract.

4. Put in one can of tomato soup and mix until just blended.

5. In another bowl, whisk two cups of flour, a teaspoon of baking powder, a teaspoon of baking soda, half a teaspoon of cinnamon, and half a teaspoon of nutmeg.

6. Add the dry ingredients to your first mixture while mixing at a low speed.

7. Pour the batter into the pan and bake it for twenty-five to thirty minutes.

8. In a bowl, combine one bar of cream cheese and a stick of butter until smooth.

9. Gradually, add a half a cup of powdered sugar, half a teaspoon of vanilla extract, and three tablespoons of almond milk.

10. Spread over cooled cake.

11. Enjoy! (Let me know if you like it!)

Where Will You Go?

Are you thinking about a trip to Disney or Orlando Studios?
Do you want to sail away on a cruise ship?
I can help!
Destination Companies pay me to help you, so you won't pay extra for my travel services.
I can:

- help plan and book your travel, accommodations, and tickets

- order special event tickets

- manage any hiccups

- arrange travel insurance

- make hard-to-get dining reservations

I will:

- send emails with tips and tricks customized to your travel and destination

- monitor deals to grab the best prices for you

- keep my eye on the destination's weather and crowd calendars

* answer questions quickly

Courtnee's Magical Vacations
turnerco6@yahoo.com

References

Holy Bible. New International Version. Zondervan Publishing House, 1984. Psalm 139:13-14.

Tomato Soup Cake. Campbell's soup recipe. cambells.com. https://www.bing.com/images/search?view=detailv2&iss=sbi&FORM=recidp&sbisrc=ImgDropper&q=campbells+kitchen+tomato+soup+cake+recipe&imgurl=https://bing.com/th?id=AMMS_29foadf18177dofe111300d488f4c1db&idpbck=1&sim=4&pageurl=https%3a%2f%2fwww.campbells.com%2fkitchen%2frecipes%2feasy-tomato-soup-spice-cake%2f&idpp=recipe&ajaxhist=0&ajaxserp=0